D1713642

BOOKS BY K. R. DWYER

Chase
Shattered
Dragonfly

DRAGONFLY

DRAGONFLY

K.R. DWYER

Random House New York

Library of Congress Cataloging in Publication Data

———

Dragonfly.
I. Title.
PZ4.K8335Dr [PS3561.O55] 813'.5'4 75–9877
ISBN 0–394–49214–5

Manufactured in the United States of America
2 4 6 8 9 7 5 3
First Edition

To Bill Pronzini and Barry Malzberg—
two-thirds of a friendship that keeps
the telephone company solvent.

ONE

Carpinteria, California

When he woke shortly after three o'clock Wednesday morning, Roger Berlinson thought he heard strange voices in the house. A quick word or two. Then silence. An unnatural silence? He was clutching the sweat-dampened sheets so tightly that his arms ached all the way to his shoulders. He let go of the sodden linens and worked the cramps out of his fingers. Trembling, he reached out with his right hand, pulled open the top drawer of the nightstand, and picked up the loaded pistol that was lying there. In the moon-dappled darkness he performed a blind man's exploration of the gun until he was certain that both of the safeties were switched off. Then he lay perfectly still, listening.

The house was on a low bluff overlooking the Pacific Ocean. In the empty early-morning hours the only sounds at the windows were the voices of nature: the soughing of a southwesterly wind, distant thunder, and the steady rush of the tide. Inside the house there were no voices, no squeaking floorboards, nothing but Berlinson's own heavy breathing.

It's just your imagination, he told himself. Putney is on the midnight-to-eight duty. He's downstairs in the kitchen right now, monitoring the alarm systems. If there was any trouble, he'd take care of it before it got serious. Putney's a damned good man; he doesn't make mistakes. So we're safe. There's absolutely no danger. You've had another nightmare, that's all.

Nevertheless, Berlinson threw back the covers and got out of bed and stepped into his felt-lined slippers. His moist pajamas clung to his back and thighs; chills swept down his spine.

He held the gun at his side. In an instant he could bring it up, swivel, and fire in any direction. He was well trained.

His wife, Anna, stirred in her sleep, but thanks to her nightly sedative, did not wake up. She turned over on her stomach and mumbled into the pillow and sighed.

Quietly, cautiously, Berlinson crossed the room to the open door and eased into the second-floor hall. The corridor was much darker than the bedroom, for it had only one window at the far end. Berlinson had just enough light to see that everything was as it should be: the telephone table was at the head of the stairs; a large vase full of straw flowers stood on the window bench at the end of the hall; and the flimsy curtains billowed in the draft from the air-conditioning vent high on the right-hand wall.

Berlinson walked past the staircase and on down the hall to his son's room. Peter was in bed, lying on his side, facing the door, snoring softly. Under the circumstances, no one but a teenager, with an appetite for sleep as great as his appetite for food and activity, could possibly have slept so soundly, so serenely, without the aid of a drug.

There you are, Berlinson told himself. Everyone's safe. There's no danger here. No one from the agency can possibly know where you are. No one. Except McAlister. Well, what about McAlister? Hell, he's on your side. You can trust him. Can't you? Yes. Implicitly. So there you are.

However, instead of returning straight to bed, he went to the stairs and down to the first floor. The living room was full of dark, lumpish furniture. A grandfather clock ticked in a far corner; its pendulum provided the only movement, the only noise, the only sign of life, either animal or mechanical, in the room. The dining room was also deserted. The many-paned glass doors of the china hutch—and the dishes shelved beyond the glass—gleamed in the eerie orange light. Berlinson went into the kitchen, where the Halloweenish glow, the only light in the house, emanated from several expensive, complicated machines that stood on the Formica-topped breakfast table.

Putney was gone.

"Joe?"

There was no reply.

Berlinson went to look at the monitors—and he found Joseph Putney on the other side of the table. The night guard was sprawled on the floor, on his back, his arms out to his sides as. if he were trying to fly, a bullet hole in the center of his forehead. His eyes glittered demonically in the orange light from the screens.

Now hold on, keep control, keep cool, Berlinson thought as he automatically crouched and turned to see if anyone had moved in behind him.

He was still alone.

Glancing at the four repeater screens of the infrared alarm system which protected the house, Berlinson saw that the machines were functioning and had detected no enemies. All approaches to the house—north, east, south, and west from the beach—were drawn in thermal silhouette on these monitors. No heat-producing source, neither man nor animal nor machine, could move onto the property without immediately registering on the system, setting off a loud alarm, and thereby alerting the entire household.

Yet Putney was dead.

The alarm system had been circumvented. Someone *was* in the house. His cover was blown; the agency had come after him. In the morning Anna would find him just as he had found Putney . . .

No, dammit! You're a match for them. You're as good and as fast as they are: you're one of them, for Christ's sake, a snake from the same nest. You'll get Anna and Petey out of here, and you'll go with them.

He moved along the wall, back toward the dining room, through the archway, past the hutch, into the living room, to the main stairs. He studied the darkness at the top of the staircase. The man—or men—who had killed Putney might be up there now. Probably was. But there was no other way Berlinson could reach his family. He had to risk it. Keeping his back to the wall, alternately glancing at the landing above and at the living room below, expecting to be caught in a crossfire at any moment, he went up step by step, slowly, silently.

Unmolested, he covered sixteen of the twenty risers, then stopped when he saw that there was someone sitting on the top step and leaning against the banister. He almost opened fire, but even in these deep shadows, the other man was somehow familiar. When there was no challenge made, no threat, no movement at all, Berlinson inched forward—and discovered that the man on the steps was Peter, his son. The front of Petey's pajama shirt was soaked with blood; he had been shot in the throat.

No! Dammit, *no!* Berlinson thought, weeping, shuddering, cursing, sick to his stomach. Not my family, damn you. Me, but not my family. That's the rule. That's the way the game's played. Never the family. You crazy sonsofbitches! *No, no, no!*

He stumbled off the steps and ran across the hall, crouching low, the pistol held out in front of him. He fell and rolled through the open bedroom door, came up onto his knees fast, and fired twice into the wall beside the door.

No one was there.

Should have been, dammit. Should have been someone there.

He crawled around behind the bed, using it as a shield. Cautiously, he rose up to see if Anna was all right. In the moonlight the blood on the sheets looked as viscous and black as sludge oil.

At the sight of her, Berlinson lost control of himself. "Come out!" he shouted to the men who must now be in the corridor, listening, waiting to burst in on him. "Show yourselves, you bastards!"

On his right the closet door was flung open.

Berlinson fired at it.

A man cried out and fell full length into the room. His gun clattered against the legs of a chair.

"Roger!"

Berlinson whirled toward the voice which came from the hall door. A silenced pistol hissed three times. Berlinson collapsed onto the bed, clutching at the covers and at Anna. Absurdly, he thought: I can't be dying. My life hasn't flashed before my eyes. I can't be dying if my life hasn't

Washington, D.C.

When the doorbell rang at eleven o'clock that morning, David Canning was studying the leaves of his schefflera plant for signs of the mealybugs he had routed with insecticide a week ago. Seven feet tall and with two hundred leaves, the schefflera was more accurately a tree than a house plant. He had purchased it last month and was already as attached to it as he had once been, as a boy, to a beagle puppy. The tree offered none of the lively companionship that came with owning a pet; however, Canning found great satisfaction in caring for it—watering, misting, sponging, spraying with Malathion—and in watching it respond with continued good health and delicate new shoots.

Satisfied that the mealybugs had not regenerated, he went to the door, expecting to find a salesman on the other side.

Instead, McAlister was standing in the hall. He was wearing a five-hundred-dollar raincoat and was just pulling the hood back from his head. He was alone, and that was unusual; he always traveled with one or two aides and a bodyguard. McAlister glanced at the round magnifying glass in Canning's hand, then up at his face. He smiled. "Sherlock Holmes, I presume."

"I was just examining my tree," Canning said.

"You're a wonderful straight man. Examining your *tree?*"

"Come in and have a look."

McAlister crossed the living room to the schefflera. He moved with grace and consummate self-assurance. He was slender: five ten, a hundred forty pounds. But he was in no way a small man, Canning thought. His intelligence, cunning, and self-possession were more impressive than size and muscle. His oblong face was square-jawed and deeply tanned. Inhumanly blue eyes, an electrifying shade that existed nowhere else beyond the technicolor fantasies on a CinemaScope screen, were accentuated by old-fashioned horn-rimmed glasses. His lips were full but bloodless. He looked like a Boston Brahmin, which he was: at twenty-one he had come into control of a two-million-dollar trust fund. His dark hair was gray at the temples, an attribute he used, as did bankers and politicians, to make himself seem fatherly, experienced, and trustworthy. He *was* experienced and trustworthy; but he was too shrewd and calculating ever to seem fatherly. In spite of his gray hair he appeared ten years younger than his fifty-one. Standing now with his fists balled on his hips, he had the aura of a cocky young man.

"By God, it *is* a tree!"

"I told you," Canning said, joining him in front of the schefflera. He was taller and heavier than McAlister: six one, a hundred seventy pounds. In college he had been on the basketball team. He was lean, almost lanky, with long arms and large hands. He was wearing only jeans and a blue T-shirt, but his clothes were as neat, clean, and well pressed as were McAlister's expensive suit and coat. Everything about Canning was neat, from his full-but-not-long razor-cut hair to his brightly polished loafers.

"What's it doing here?" McAlister asked.

"Growing."

"That's all?"

"That's all I ask of it."

"What were you doing with the magnifying glass?"

"The tree had mealybugs. I took care of them, but they can come back. You have to check every few days for signs of them."

"What are mealybugs?"

Canning knew McAlister wasn't just making small talk. He had a bottomless curiosity, a need to know something about everything; yet his knowledge was not merely anecdotal, for he knew many things well. A lunchtime conversation with him could be fascinat-

ing. The talk might range from primitive art to current developments in the biological sciences, and from there, to pop music to
Beethoven to Chinese cooking to automobile comparisons to
American history. He was a Renaissance man—and he was more
than that.

"Mealybugs are tiny," Canning said. "You need a magnifying
glass to see them. They're covered with white fuzz that makes them
look like cotton fluff. They attach themselves to the undersides of
the leaves, along the leaf veins, and especially in the green sheaths
that protect new shoots. They suck the plant's juices, destroy it."

"Vampires."

"In a way."

"I meet them daily. In fact, I want to talk to you about
mealybugs."

"The human kind."

"That's right." He stripped off his coat and almost dropped it on
a nearby chair. Then he caught himself and handed it to Canning,
who had a neatness fetish well known to anyone who had ever
worked with him. As Canning hung the coat in the carefully
ordered foyer closet, McAlister said, "Would it be possible to fix
some coffee, David?"

"Already done," he said, leading McAlister into the kitchen. "I
made a fresh pot this morning. Cream? Sugar?"

"Cream," McAlister said. "No sugar."

"A breakfast roll?"

"Yes, that would be nice. I didn't have time to eat this morning."

Motioning to the table that stood by the large mullioned
window, Canning said, "Sit down. Everything'll be ready in a few
minutes."

Of the four available chairs McAlister took that one which faced
the living-room archway and which put him in a defensible corner.
He chose not to sit with his back to the window. Instead, the glass
was on his right side, so that he could look through it but probably
could not be seen by anyone in the gardened courtyard outside.

He's a natural-born agent, Canning thought.

But McAlister would never spend a day in the field. He always
started at the top—and did his job as well as he could have done
had he started at the bottom. He had served as Secretary of State
during the previous administration's first term, then moved over to

the White House, where he occupied the chief advisory post during half of the second term. He had quit that position when, in the midst of a White House scandal, the President had asked him to lie to a grand jury. Now, with the opposition party in power, McAlister had another important job, for he was a man whose widely recognized integrity made it possible for him to function under Republicans or Democrats. In February he had been appointed to the directorship of the Central Intelligence Agency, armed with a Presidential mandate to clean up that dangerously autonomous, corrupt organization. The McAlister nomination was approved swiftly by the Senate, one month to the day after the new President was inaugurated. McAlister had been at the agency—cooperating with the Justice Department in exposing crimes that had been committed by agency men—ever since the end of February, seven headline-filled months ago.

Canning had been in this business more than six months. He'd been a CIA operative for twenty years, ever since he was twenty-five. During the cold war he carried out dozens of missions in the Netherlands, West Germany, East Germany, and France. He had gone secretly behind the Iron Curtain on seven separate occasions, usually to bring out an important defector. Then he was transferred Stateside and put in charge of the agency's Asian desk, where the Vietnam mess required the attendance of a man who had gone through years of combat, both hot and cold. After fourteen months in the office, Canning returned to field work and established new CIA primary networks in Thailand, Cambodia, and South Vietnam. He operated easily and well in Asia. His fastidious personal habits, his compulsive neatness, appealed to the middle- and upper-class Asians who were his contacts, for many of them still thought of Westerners as quasi-barbarians who bathed too seldom and carried their linen-wrapped snot in their hip pockets. Likewise, they appreciated Canning's Byzantine mind, which, while it was complex and rich and full of classic oriental cunning, was ordered like a vast file cabinet. Asia was, he felt, the perfect place for him to spend the next decade and a half in the completion of a solid, even admirable career.

However, in spite of his success, the agency took him off his Asian assignment when he was beginning his fifth year there. Back home he was attached to the Secret Service at the White House, where he acted as a special consultant for Presidential trips overseas. He helped to define the necessary security precautions in those countries that he knew all too well.

McAlister chaired these Secret Service strategy conferences, and it was here that Canning and he had met and become friends of a sort. They had kept in touch even after McAlister resigned from the White House staff—and now they were working together again. And again McAlister was the boss, even though his own experience in the espionage circus was far less impressive than Canning's background there. But then, McAlister would be boss wherever he worked; he was born to it. Canning could no more resent that than he could resent the fact that grass was green instead of purple. Besides, the director of the agency had to deal daily with politicians, a chore of which Canning wanted no part.

"Smells good," McAlister said, stirring cream into his steaming coffee.

Canning had set the table as if he were serving a full meal, everything properly arranged, every item squared off from the nearest other item: placemats, paper napkins, silverware, cups and saucers, a platter of rolls, a butter dish, butter knives, a cream pitcher, sugar bowl, and sugar spoon. He poured his own coffee and set the percolator on a wrought-iron coaster. "The raisin-filled buns are pretty good." He buttered a roll, took a few bites, washed it down with coffee, and waited to hear why McAlister had come to see him.

"I was afraid you might have gone away for your vacation and I'd have trouble locating you," McAlister said.

"I've traveled enough over the last twenty-five years."

McAlister buttered another piece of roll and said, "I was sorry to hear about you and Irene."

Canning nodded.

"Divorce or separation?"

"Separation. For now. Later on—probably a divorce."

"I'm sorry."

Canning said nothing.

"I hope it was amicable."

"It was."

"How long have you been married?"

"Twenty-seven years."

"Traumatic after all that time."

"Not if there's no love involved on either side."

McAlister's blue eyes looked through him as if they were X-ray devices. "I tried to reach you at your house in Falls Church, but Irene sent me here. How long has it been?"

"We split eight weeks ago. I've been renting this apartment since the middle of August."

"The children?"

"Mike's twenty-six. Terri's twenty. So, no custody fight."

"And there's no animosity between you and them?"

"They aren't taking sides." Canning put down his half-eaten roll and wiped his fingers on his napkin. "Let's stop the psychoanalysis. You need me. You want to know if I'm emotionally stable enough to handle a new job. I am. The separation's for the best. And a new assignment, something more interesting than this White House post, would be a tonic."

McAlister studied him for a moment. "All right." He leaned forward, his arms on the table, and folded his hands around his coffee cup as if to warm his fingers. "You must know some of the things that I've uncovered since I came to the agency."

"I read the papers."

"Has any of it shocked you?"

"No. Anyone with a trace of common sense has known for years that the agency's a haven for crackpots. There's a lot of work the agency *has* to do. Most of it's dirty, ugly, and dangerous. But necessary. It isn't easy to find normal, sensible, decent men to do it."

"But you're normal, sensible, and decent."

"I like to think so. I wouldn't get involved in some of these crazy schemes you've unearthed lately. But there are agents who *want* to get involved, adolescents playing out the cheapest masturbatory fantasies. But they aren't just in the agency. They're everywhere these days." A fierce, prolonged gust of wind drove rain against the window. The droplets burst and streamed like tears. Or like colorless blood, a psychic intimation of blood to come, Canning thought. "These lunatics got into the agency because they had the proper politics. Back when I joined up, loyalty mattered more than philosophy. But for the last fifteen years, until you came along, applicants who were solid middle-of-the-road independents, like me, were rejected out of hand. A moderate is the same as a leftist to these nuts. Hell, I know men who think *Nixon* was a Communist dupe. We've been employing neo-Nazis for years. So the newspaper stories don't shock or even surprise me. I just hope the agency can survive the housecleaning."

"It will. Because, as you said, we need it."

"I suppose," Canning said.

"Did you know any of the agents who have been indicted?"

"I've heard some of the names. I never worked with them."

"Well," McAlister said, "what you've read in the newspapers isn't half as shocking as what you'll *never* read there." He drank the last of his coffee. "I've always believed in the public's right to know . . ."

"But?"

Smiling ruefully, McAlister said, "But since I've learned what the agency's been doing, I've tempered that opinion somewhat. If the worst were made public during our lifetime, the country would be shaken to its roots, blasted apart. The Kennedy assassinations . . . The most hideous crimes . . . They'd riot in the streets." He wasn't smiling any longer. "It wasn't the agency alone. There are other threads. Powerful politicians. Mafiosi. Some of the richest, most socially prominent men in the country. If the people knew how *far* off the rails this nation went for more than a decade, we'd be ripe for a demagogue of the worst kind."

For the first time since he'd opened the front door and seen McAlister in the hall, Canning realized that the man had changed. At a glance he looked healthy, even robust. But he'd lost ten pounds. His face was more deeply lined than when he'd first assumed the directorship. Behind the aura of youthful energy, he was weary and drawn. His eyes, as blue and clear as they'd ever been, were filled with the sorrow of a man who has come home to find his wife happily gangbanging a group of strange men. In McAlister's case the wife was not a woman but a country.

"It's one of these other horrors, something besides the assassinations, that's brought you here." Canning poured more coffee.

"You don't seem surprised by what I've told you."

"Of course I'm not surprised. Anyone who reads the Warren Report has to be a fool to believe it."

"I guess I was a fool for years," McAlister said. "But now I need a first-rate agent I can trust. A dozen good men are available. But you're the only one I'm even half sure isn't a Committeeman."

Frowning, Canning said, "A what?"

"We've discovered that within the CIA there's another organization, illegal and illicit, a tightly knit cell of men who call themselves The Committee. True Believers, fanatical anti-Communists."

"Masturbating adolescents."

"Yes, but they're dangerous. They have connections with extreme right-wing, paramilitary groups like the Minutemen. They're friendly with certain Mafiosi, and they're not short of patrons among men in New York banking and Texas oil. The Committee had a part in assassinations, other things . . . They answer to no one in government."

"Then why haven't you broken them?"

"We don't know who they are," McAlister said. "We have two names. Two of the men already under indictment. But there are at least twenty or twenty-five others. Hard-core operatives. They'll serve their time rather than do any plea bargaining. They'll never testify against the others. So we're still working on it. I'm setting up a staff of investigators—men who've had no contact whatsoever with the agency, men I know I can trust."

Canning understood that when McAlister spoke of investigators, he meant lawyers, men who approached this kind of problem in terms of subpoenas, grand juries, indictments, prosecutions, and eventual convictions. But for the most part Canning was a field op, a man who liked to take direct action the instant he saw what the trouble was; he was not a paper shuffler. Although he respected the mass of laws upon which civilization was built, he was trained to solve problems quickly by circumventing all authorities and legal channels. He knew McAlister was fully aware of this. Nevertheless, he said, "And you want me on this staff?"

"Perhaps later." Which meant never. "Right now I need you for something more urgent." He sipped his coffee: a dramatic pause. "This is so important and secret that no one must know you've been brought into it. That's why I came to see you instead of sending for you. And that's why I came alone. I was especially careful not to be followed."

That was Canning's cue to ask what this was all about. Instead of that, he said, "What makes you think *I'm* trustworthy?"

"You're too much of a realist to be a brown shirt. I know you."

"And *you* are too much of a realist to choose a man for an important assignment because you happen to like him. So what's the rest of the story?"

Leaning back in his chair, McAlister said, "Did you ever wonder why you were taken off the top job in the Asian bureau?"

"I shouldn't have been."

"Agreed."

"You know why I was?"

McAlister nodded. "I've read the entire agency file on you. It contains a number of unsigned memos from field ops stationed in South Vietnam, Cambodia, and Thailand during your tenure there. They complain that you put them under too much restraint."

Canning said, "Too damned many of them were ready to settle any problem with a gun or knife." He sighed softly. "They didn't even like to stop and think if there might be a better, easier way." He ran one hand over his face. "You mean that's all it took for the director to pull me out of Asia? Unsigned memos?"

"Well, there was also Duncan, Tyler, and Bixby."

They were three men who had served under Canning. Karl Duncan and Mason Tyler, who had once operated in Thailand, had tortured to death an American expatriate whom they "suspected" of being involved in illegal arms sales to guerilla leaders. Derek Bixby did his dirty work in Cambodia. He tortured the wife and eleven-year-old daughter of a Cambodian merchant, in front of the merchant's eyes, until he had obtained a hidden set of papers that were en route from Hanoi to a guerilla general who was a close friend of the merchant. Once the documents were in his hands, Bixby murdered the man, wife, and child. In both cases neither torture nor murder was warranted. Infuriated, Canning had seen to it that Duncan, Tyler, and Bixby were not only taken out of Asia but were also dismissed from the agency when they returned Stateside.

"They were animals," Canning said.

"You did the right thing. But Duncan, Tyler, and Bixby had friends in high places. Those friends engineered your withdrawal from Asia and saw you were given a harmless domestic assignment at the White House."

Sharp lines of anger webbed Canning's skin at eyes and mouth.

"Furthermore," McAlister said, "Duncan, Tyler, and Bixby are all quite close to the two men we *know* are Committeemen. We've reason to believe that Duncan, Tyler, and Bixby are working in a civilian capacity with The Committee and are being paid with misappropriated agency funds. No proof—yet. Anyway, it seems unlikely that *you* have ever been one of them. Otherwise, why would you have fired those three?" He leaned forward again. "As I said, I'm *half* sure of you. There's a chance I'll be stabbed in the back. But the odds of that happening are lower with you than with anyone else I know."

Canning rose, took his cup and saucer to the sink and rinsed them thoroughly. He came back and stood at the window, watching the rain that slanted icily across the courtyard and pooled on the bricks. "What is this urgent assignment you have for me?"

Taking a pipe from one jacket pocket and a pouch of tobacco from another, McAlister said, "During the last six months we've been building a new file from dribs and drabs of information—a name here, a rendezvous point there, a dozen rumors; you know how it works in this business—concerning a very special project the Committeemen have going for them."

Canning got a ten-inch circular white-glass ashtray from a cupboard and put it in front of McAlister.

"Five days ago an agent named Berlinson came to me and said he was a Committeeman. He was about to be indicted for his role in several domestic operations that were aimed at destroying the political careers of three potential liberal Presidential candidates. He didn't want to stand trial because he knew he would end up in jail. So he and I reached an agreement. He was quite willing to talk. But as it happens, lower-echelon agents of The Committee know only one or two others in the organization. Berlinson couldn't give me a complete roster. He couldn't tell me who stands at the head of the group. That was quite a disappointment."

"I can imagine."

"But it wasn't a total loss," McAlister said as he tamped the tobacco in the bowl of his pipe. "Berlinson *was* able to give me a general outline of this special project I'd been hearing about. It centers on an as yet unknown Chinese citizen who has been made, quite literally, into a walking bomb casing for a chemical-biological weapon that could kill tens of thousands of his people. The Committeemen have a code name for him—Dragonfly."

Canning sat down at the table again. "These reactionaries—these *idiots* intend to wage their own private war against China?"

"Something like that." McAlister struck a match, held the flame to the tobacco, and got his pipe fired up. He carefully put the burnt match in the center of the ashtray.

"Berlinson has no idea who the carrier is?"

"All he knew was that Dragonfly is a Chinese citizen who was in the United States or Canada sometime between New Year's Day and February fifteenth of this year. That doesn't really narrow it down much. Canada has had friendly relations with China considerably longer than we have; she does a great deal of business with them. At any given moment there are at least two hundred Chinese citizens in Canada: government representatives, officials of various Chinese industries, and artists who are involved in cultural exchange programs. In the United States, of course, there's the Chinese delegation to the United Nations. And at one time or another during the forty-six days in question, we also played host to a contingent of trade negotiators, a touring group of forty officials from the Central Office of Publications who were here to study American publishing processes and printing methods, and finally, a symphony orchestra from Peking."

"How many suspects are there in both the U.S. and Canada?" Canning asked.

"Five hundred and nine."

"And I take it that Dragonfly, whoever he is, doesn't know anything about what's been done to him."

"That's right. He's an innocent."

"But how could he be? How was it done?"

"It's a long story."

"I'll listen."

McAlister poured himself another cup of coffee.

While he picked up crumbs from his placemat and put them, one at a time, in the center of his paper napkin, Canning listened to McAlister's story and took the facts from it and placed them, one at a time, in the neatly ordered file drawers of his mind. No matter with whom he was talking, no matter where or when, Canning was a good listener. He interupted only to ask essential questions and to keep the conversation from digressing.

With McAlister, of course, there were no digressions. He recited the facts with so few hesitations and with such economy of words that he might have been retelling a short story that he had committed to memory.

It began with Dr. Olin Eugene Wilson—product of a strict and extremely religious family, witness at the McCarthy Hearings, where he testified against alleged Communists in the Pentagon, John Bircher, and self-styled fascist—who believed implicitly in Shockley's theories of Negro inferiority and the supremacy of the White Race.

Although he had not conceived the specific operation that was now known as the Dragonfly project, Dr. Wilson was the one man without whom the scheme could never have been realized. For thirty years Wilson had worked for the Department of Defense. He was a research biochemist, one of the most brilliant men in his field. The greater part of his important work had been done at Fort Detrick, in Maryland, where he supervised the development of half a dozen chemical and/or biological weapons that could topple an enemy government within seventy-two hours of the declaration of war. In 1969, when President Nixon announced that the United States would no longer engage in research for offensive biological warfare, Wilson was so infuriated that he presented his resignation to the chief of staff at Detrick. Certain highly placed civilian and military officials quickly assured Wilson that the President's speech had been more of a public-relations gimmick than a genuine commitment. Yes, Detrick's labs would be converted into facilities for cancer research. Yes, only weapons projects labeled "defensive" would be developed from this day forward. However . . .

Fort Detrick had already become too much of a target for crusading journalists and peace demonstrators; therefore, it was time to move the CBW program into more modern and less well publicized quarters. As to whether or not the doctor would now be limited to defensive-weapons research . . . Well, they had a qualification of the President's statement which satisfied Wilson. They explained that once the United States was attacked with a chemical and/or biological weapon, it would have to strike back immediately; and then those weapons which might have been labeled offensive when used for a first strike became defensive the moment they were used for retaliatory purposes. Thus educated in semantics, Wilson returned to work, happy and relatively secure. Within days of the President's speech, Olin Wilson launched a program to study the feasibility of encapsulating anthrax, plague virus, and other disease strains and implanting them within the human body to create a walking biological time bomb that could be triggered either ten minutes from now, ten years from now, or at any moment in between.

"Naturally," Canning said, "Wilson was successful. The agency heard about it. And the Committeemen made Wilson an offer to come over to them."

"Which he did."

Canning frowned. "And Army security, Pentagon security, the security forces at the lab—none of them tumbled to the fact that he was farming out his data?"

"None of them."

In late 1972, loudly professing his disenchantment with the current U.S.–Soviet détente, Olin Wilson resigned from his position with the Department of Defense. By that time his absolute disgust with Nixonian foreign policy was widely known. He was one of a group of five hundred prominent scientists, teachers, doctors, lawyers, businessmen, and other professionals who sponsored a series of anti-Communist advertisements in *The New York Times*. For the Sons of Truth, an up-and-coming right-wing organization similar to the John Birch Society, Wilson wrote a pamphlet entitled *Communism, Richard Nixon, and the End of the American Dream.* When he quit his job he said he was leaving because of his disillusionment with government policies and because of his despair over new national defense guidelines. He retired on a comfortable pension and on the income he received for speaking before any organization that would have him. For six months he jetted all over the country, addressing as many as five and six groups a week at a fee of seven hundred dollars plus expenses. Gradually, he was called to fewer and fewer podiums, until he began to spend most of his time at home in Alexandria, where he puttered in his garden and wrote angry letters to newspapers and magazines that supported or even gave voice to a liberal cause. A year after he resigned from government service, Wilson was leading such an uneventful life that any government security force that might have been watching him certainly must have decided to pack up and go away and leave him to his retirement. *That* was when Dr. Wilson went to work for The Committee.

"You mean they have a laboratory all their own?" Canning asked incredulously.

"That's correct."

"But the sophisticated machinery, the maintenance . . . It would cost millions!"

After he had taken time to relight his pipe, McAlister said, "Nearly all its life the agency has not been held accountable to anyone for how it spends its funds. Not to the Congress. Not to the President. No one. Furthermore, it receives considerably more money from the federal budget than is readily apparent. Attached to the largest appropriations bills like Defense and Government Operations, there are dozens of smaller appropriations—five million here, two million there—for programs which are seldom if ever scrutinized. Some of these programs don't even exist. Their appropriations are funneled directly to the agency. Once the agency has the money, it disburses it to a couple of hundred companies all over the world, firms that are nothing more than CIA fronts. No one man within the agency ever knows where all the money goes. So . . . It would be quite simple for these Committeemen to siphon off a couple of million a year for their own, private purposes. I'm sure that's what they've done—and are *still* doing."

"But a laboratory devoted to chemical-biological warfare research is going to employ hundreds of people."

"As recently as a week ago," McAlister told him, "I'd have said the same thing. But since I learned about Dragonfly, I've been doing my homework. For Olin Wilson's purposes, a laboratory can be rather small. It can be staffed by as few as twelve specialists who are willing to be their own assistants. This kind of work is nowhere near as complicated as, say, searching for a cure for cancer. Any virus or bacterium can be cultured for pennies. For a few dollars you can grow enough plague virus to kill nine-tenths of the Russian population. Then you hit the remaining tenth with anthrax. Or worse. It's the delivery systems that pose the real problems, but even that kind of experimentation isn't prohibitively expensive. Biological warfare is *cheap*, David. That's why most all of the major world powers deal in it. It costs substantially less than the money needed to build more and more and more nuclear missiles."

In the courtyard below, a young couple, sheltering under a newspaper, ran for an apartment door. Their laughter drifted up through the rain.

Cherry-scented tobacco smoke hung in the humid air in Canning's kitchen.

"If the lab employs only a dozen men," Canning said, "there'd be no trouble keeping it a secret."

"And if one of the wealthy businessmen who sympathize with the Committeemen happens to be the owner, director, or president of a chemical company, he could help create a plausible front for Wilson's work."

"There ought to be records of some sort at this lab, something that would identify Dragonfly," Canning said. "They'll be in code, but codes are made to be broken."

"But we don't know where the lab is."

"Berlinson couldn't tell you?"

"He'd heard of it. He'd been associated with Wilson. But he had never been to the lab."

"And you haven't put a tail on Wilson?"

McAlister laid his pipe in the ashtray and smiled grimly. "Can't do that, I'm afraid. He's dead."

"I see."

"He was electrocuted while making his breakfast toast."

"Quaint."

"Seems there was a nasty short in the toaster's wiring. Brand-new toaster, too."

"The Underwriters' Laboratories would be surprised to hear about that," Canning said.

"I daresay."

"When did this happen?"

"The day after Roger Berlinson came to my home and offered to tell me what he knew about The Committee, exactly sixteen hours after I first heard Olin Wilson's name."

"How coincidental."

"It's for Ripley."

"And convenient."

"Of course, Berlinson couldn't give me the names of any of the other scientists who are working at this lab. But from that moment on, I never talked with him in my own home or in my car or anywhere else that might be electronically monitored."

"What more *did* Berlinson tell you?"

Early in 1971, while he was still employed by the Department of Defense, Dr. Wilson, with the aid of a hundred researchers, made several important breakthroughs in his work. He really did not strike out into any new territory, but he refined substances, processes, and techniques that were already in use, refined them in the sense that an electric light bulb is merely a refinement of a wax candle, which, of course, it is, although it is much more than that. First of all he developed a petro-plastic spansule that was airtight, one hundred percent resistant to osmosis, neutral to body tissues, free of surface condensation, not even fractionally biodegradable— yet which was quite rubbery, unbreakable, and resilient. Second, he discovered a way to store deadly microorganisms within this spansule—a way to store them without the organisms losing more than five percent of their fertility, virility, and toxicity, *no matter how long they were sealed up*. Next, he worked out a procedure for implanting one of these spansules inside a human body in such a way that the carrier could not sense it, X-rays could not expose it, and only the most unlikely of accidents could open it before it was meant to be opened. Finally, he went outside of his specialty and applied other disciplines—surgery, psychology, pharmacology, espionage—to the problem until he perfected a way of turning any man into an unwitting, undetectable biological time bomb.

"Which is Dragonfly," McAlister said.

"And now you're going to tell me how it actually works."

"It's achingly simple."

"I believe it," Canning said. "Just from what you've told me so far, I think I can figure it out myself."

"So *you* tell *me*."

"First, there's one thing I need to get straight."

McAlister waited.

"The Dragonfly project was never meant to decimate the Chinese population, was it?"

"No." McAlister picked up his pipe. "According to Berlinson, Dragonfly is carrying a severely mutated virus, something manufactured in the laboratory and essentially artificial in nature. It won't respond to any known drug; however, it was designed to have a poor rate of reproduction and a short life span. Seventy-two hours after the spansule is broken, the microorganisms in it and ninety percent of their progeny will be dead. In ninety-six hours, none of the microbes will exist. The threat is limited to four days. There isn't time for it to spread throughout China."

"Wilson never intended to kill tens of millions."

"Just tens of thousands. The stuff's apparently so toxic that a hundred to a hundred and fifty thousand people will die in four days. But that will be the extent of it. Although I must say that this apparent concern for human life is not the product of any moral sensibility. It's a matter of logistics. If you kill millions of your enemy in a few days, you have an impossible logistics problem when you take over their country: how to get rid of the corpses."

McAlister's eyes suddenly seemed to have become a bit more gray than blue.

Shaking his head in disgust, Canning said, "If the kill target is so low, then the intent is to destroy the political and military elite—all of the highest officers of the Party, their possible successors, and their families. In the turmoil and confusion, a relative handful of men could take control of Peking, the strategic ports, and all of China's nuclear weapons."

"And it looks as if the Committeemen have more than a handful of men at their disposal," McAlister said. "We think they've made a deal with the Nationalist Chinese. For over a month there have been reports of frantic military preparations on Formosa. In the oh-so-glorious memory of Chiang Kai-shek, they evidently intend to reconquer the homeland."

"Jesus!" The implications became more staggering by the moment. In twenty years of day-to-day contact with the world of high-power espionage, Canning had never heard, had never *conceived,* of the agency's getting involved in an operation as crazy as this one. Blackmail of domestic and foreign politicians, yes. The overthrow of a small South American or African nation, yes. Political assassination at home and abroad, yes. But he had never imagined that any element within the agency, no matter how fascistic and fanatical, would try to upset the delicate balance of world power all on its own hook. "But even if the operation were a success and the Nationalists reoccupied the mainland—"

"We'd be on the brink of World War Three," McAlister finished for him. "The Russians would figure that if we used that sort of weapon against China, we'd use it against them too. They'd be very tense. And rightfully so. The first time that Moscow suffered an epidemic of ordinary influenza, the first time a high Party official got a bad cold, they'd think they were under attack. They'd strike back at us with biological *and* nuclear weapons. No doubt about it." Beneath his Palm Beach tan, his pallor deepened. "We *have* to stop Dragonfly."

Canning went to the bar in the living room and came back with a bottle of Scotch and two glasses. He got four ice cubes from the refrigerator, popped them into the glasses, and poured two or three shots into each glass.

Picking up his Scotch, McAlister said, "I'm really not that much of a drinking man."

"Neither am I."

They both drank.

Canning sat down again.

The rain continued to snap against the windows. Lightning cracked across the black sky and threw flickering shadows onto the top of the kitchen table.

When he had nearly finished his Scotch, McAlister said, "You said you thought you knew how Dragonfly, the Chinese carrier, had been chosen and set up."

Clearing his throat on the first few words, Canning said, "If only the Party elite is to be killed, then Dragonfly has to be someone who has contact with a number of men at the top of the Chinese government. He has to be someone who would spread the plague in the right circles."

"That really doesn't narrow it down too much. Fully half the Chinese who visit the U.S. and Canada are high Party officials themselves."

Canning said, "I'm not trying to pinpoint a suspect. I'm just trying to see if I can reconstruct the way Wilson set it up." He folded his hands on the table in front of him. He never gestured when he talked. Outwardly, except for the cleaning and polishing and lint-picking, he was not a nervous man. "To start with, Wilson needed a carrier. For the purpose of this discussion, let's say he

picked someone from that group of trade negotiators you mentioned a while ago."

"There were a couple of hundred more likely targets available,"
McAlister said. "It would have been easier to get to someone in the
symphony orchestra, for example. At least ten of the musicians
were from families that wield political power in Peking. But for the
moment, let's say that it *was* someone from the trade negotiators."

"We ought to have a name for him," Canning said. "How about
Charlie Chan?" He wasn't trying to be funny; it was the first name
that came to mind.

"All right. How would Wilson get to Charlie Chan?"

Canning thought about it for a moment. Then: "These groups
are always chaperoned by people from the State Department. Their
itineraries are known. Most nights they eat dinner in a restaurant
rather than at a catered banquet or in someone's private home.
Since the itinerary would usually be made out days before the
Chinese arrived, the agency could easily learn the names of the
restaurants well ahead of time. Members of The Committee, with
all the right credentials for agency men, would approach the owner
of one of these restaurants, feed him some solemn bullshit about
national security, and get his permission to put a couple of
operatives in the kitchen. Better yet, a Committeeman would be the
waiter who serves Charlie Chan."

McAlister didn't object to the scenario.

Staring at the rain that trickled down the window, Canning laid
out Wilson's plan as quickly and neatly as he would have peeled
and sectioned an orange. In a perverse way he was enjoying
himself. This was what he had been born to do. After all those
stifling years at the White House, he was back in action and glad of
it. "In his coffee or dessert Charlie Chan receives a fairly powerful
but slow-acting sedative. Around nine-thirty, half an hour after he
consumes it, Charlie pleads exhaustion and returns to his hotel
room even if something else has been arranged for the rest of the
night. By ten-thirty he's sleeping soundly. Three or four agents
enter his room, pack him in a crate or shipping trunk, and take him
out of the hotel. By midnight he's lying unconscious on an
operating table in Wilson's lab."

Reaming out the bowl of his pipe with a small gold-plated blade,

McAlister said, "So far I believe you've got it right. I can't be sure. Berlinson wasn't in the lab. He wasn't one of the agents who took Charlie out of the hotel in a shipping trunk. But he was a friend of Wilson's. He pieced together bits of information that he picked up from the good doctor. So far you sound like you're his echo. Go on."

Canning closed his eyes and could see the laboratory where it had happened: cool fluorescent light that sharpened the edges of cabinets and cupboards, tables and machines; white tile walls and a tile floor; a yellow-skinned man lying nude on a cushioned operating table; half a dozen men dressed in hospital greens; murmured conversation rich with tension and excitement; the stench of antiseptic cleaning compounds and the sharp tang of alcohol like a knife slicing the air . . . "Wilson makes a half-inch incision in Charlie. Where it won't show. In an armpit. Or in the fold of the buttocks. Or maybe high on the inside of a thigh. Then he inserts the spansule."

"Only the spansule?"

Canning, his eyes still closed, could see it: a blue-white capsule no more than half an inch in length, a quarter of an inch in diameter. "Yes. Nothing else."

"Won't there be a mechanism to puncture the spansule and free the microorganisms when the time comes for that?"

"You said this entire thing was of a material that won't show up on an X-ray?"

"That's correct."

"Then there can't be any metal to it. And any mechanism that was meant to puncture the spansule on, say, the receival of a certain radio signal, would have metal in it. So there's just the spansule, the capsule, that little cylinder of plastic."

Finished with his pipe, McAlister put it in a jacket pocket and looked for something else to do with his hands. "Continue," he said.

"The spansule fits less than an inch below the skin. When it's in place, Wilson sews up the incision—using sutures that'll dissolve by the time the healing's complete, a week at most—and places an ordinary Band-Aid over it." He paused to think, and while he thought he used one finger to draw a Band-Aid in the finely beaded moisture that had filmed the inside of several kitchen windowpanes. "Then I suppose Charlie would be given a second drug to wake him up—but he'd be put into an hypnotic trance before he really knew where he was or what was happening to him. Wilson would have to spend the rest of the night clearing Charlie's memory and implanting a series of directives in his deep subconscious mind. Like . . . telling him that he will not see or feel the incision when he wakes up in the morning. And he'd have to be told when and how he's to break open the spansule."

"All this would be done just with hypnosis?"

"Since 1963 or thereabouts, we've had drugs that condition the mind for hypnotic suggestion," Canning said. "I used them when I was in Asia. The Committeemen would have used them on Charlie Chan. With the drugs it's not just hypnotic suggestion, it's sophisticated brainwashing."

"You're still echoing Berlinson. But how do you think they'd eventually trigger Charlie?"

"You sound as if you don't know."

"I don't. Berlinson made a good guess. I've talked with some of the experts in the field, and I have a fair idea. But I don't *know*."

"It would have to be a verbal trigger. A key phrase," Canning said. "When he hears it, Dragonfly will . . . detonate himself. Or maybe all he has to do is read the phrase in a letter."

"No good," McAlister said. "The letter, I mean. You forget that China is a totalitarian society. All mail going into China is opened and read. And most of it is destroyed no matter how harmless it might be."

"Then whoever triggers Dragonfly will be inside China already, and he'll do it either in person or on the telephone."

"We feel it'll be in person."

"One of our agents," Canning said.

"Yes."

"How many do we have in China?"

"Three. Any one of them could be a Committeeman."

"Or all of them."

Reluctantly, McAlister agreed.

Increasingly excited about the assignment, Canning got up and began to pace. "Let's go back to the laboratory and pick up where we left off. Through a drug-induced hypnosis, Charlie has been programmed with all necessary directives. Next, he is told to fall asleep and not to wake up until his hotel-room telephone rings in the morning. Before dawn, he is returned to his room. He wakes up a few hours later, knowing nothing and feeling nothing about last night. Sooner or later he goes back to China. He lives precisely as he would have done had Wilson chosen someone else. Then one day a man walks up to him on the street, says the key phrase, and walks away. Per his program, Charlie goes home, where he has privacy of a sort. He breaks the capsule. Then he goes about his business as if it's just another day. *He still remembers nothing*—not the man on the street who triggered him, not Wilson, not the microorganisms that are breeding within him, *nothing!* In twenty-four hours he'll infect two or three hundred government people, who will pass the plague on to hundreds more, thousands more, before the virus dies out."

McAlister rose, picked up the ashtray and carried it to the wastecan, where he emptied it. "The spansule won't show up in an X-ray. The petro-plastic lets the rays pass through. There are no metal parts. We've been through this before. There are no inorganic materials other than the petro-plastic. There's nothing implanted with it to puncture it on a given signal. So how does Mr. Chan break it and infect himself once he's been triggered?"

Canning smiled. "Easy. Deep in his subconscious mind he'll know exactly where the spansule has been sewn into him. He'll feel for it and find it in a few seconds; it's less than an inch beneath the skin. He'll take a pin or a needle and prick himself, stab down far enough to pierce the wall of the spansule. Repeatedly."

Leaning against the counter, McAlister said, "You're good."

"Every man's good at something." He went back to the table and sat down.

"But there's something that hasn't occurred to you," McAlister said softly.

He met the blue eyes. He frowned. Then he scowled. "I must be rustier than I thought. They set this thing up back in January or February. It's now September twenty-ninth. Charlie Chan went home a long time ago. So what is The Committee waiting for?"

McAlister shrugged.

"Is it possible Charlie *did* realize what was done to him and turned himself in to the authorities the moment he was back in Peking?"

"It's possible."

"Or maybe he was triggered—and it didn't work."

"Maybe. But we can't risk it. Now that the Committeemen know I'm on to them, they aren't going to wait much longer. If Charlie is still a viable weapon, he'll be used within the next few days."

"Which brings us to the last question," Canning said.

"That is?"

"What do you want me to do about it?"

3

Stafford, Virginia

The driver, Roy Dodson, shifted his gaze from the busy superhighway to the nine-inch screen of the electronic scanner that was mounted on the console between the halves of the front seat. A blip of green light, winking like a star, had been at the center of the screen but was now moving rapidly toward the right-hand edge. Every time the light pulsed, the monitor produced a beeping signal. When the light first began to move to the right, the tone of the signal had changed; and it was this new sound that had caused the driver to take a look at the screen. "He's on an exit ramp," Dodson said.

They were heading south on rain-washed Interstate 95, more than thirty miles from Washington and forty miles from the point at which they had begun to follow Robert McAlister. Traffic was moderately heavy. Hundreds of big trucks were working down toward Richmond and Norfolk. McAlister's white Mercedes was one mile ahead of them, as it had been ever since they'd begun to tail it. They couldn't see it at this distance, of course. But thanks to the electronic gear, there was no need for them to keep the other car in sight.

"Close in on him," the passenger said. He was a heavy-set man with a dour face and a hard, no-nonsense voice.

Dodson depressed the accelerator, swung the Thunderbird into the passing lane, and swept around a chemical tank truck.

The light was nearly to the edge of the screen.

"Faster," said the fat man.

Dodson jammed the accelerator all the way to the floor. The speedometer needle rose from sixty to seventy to eighty and hovered just below the ninety mark. Wind screamed along the car's streamlined flanks, and raindrops like gelatinous bullets snapped against the windshield. They passed another truck, two cars, and a motor home. The Thunderbird began to shimmy and float on the film of rain that covered the pavement. Dodson pulled out of the passing lane, then left the highway altogether, braking just as they shot into the exit ramp. The single lane curved farther to the right; the blip of green light eased back toward the center of the screen—then continued away to the left. At the foot of the ramp, not even pausing for the stop sign, Dodson turned left on the secondary road and stepped on the accelerator again. The green signal returned to the center of the monitor: the Mercedes was now directly in front of them, still out of sight beyond a low hill.

"Slow down," the fat man said.

Dodson did as he was told. Malloy, the fat man's previous aide, had been a twenty-eight-year-old veteran of the CIA's West German office, and Malloy had not always done as he was told. Poor Malloy had not been able to understand why the fat man, who had never worked for the agency, should be in charge of the extremely important and extremely secret Committee. Malloy *could* see why there was a need to cooperate with wealthy and powerful civilians who were in sympathy with their goals. But having a civilian in charge of the operations was more than Malloy could stand. To become the top man's aide, he had been required to resign from the agency himself, so that no government investigation of the CIA would ever zero in on him and then move from him to his boss and to the core of the apple. Before he became the fat man's aide, Malloy had not known who was in charge, but he had thought that it was a man high in the agency or at least a former agency executive. When he learned the truth he was sullen, brusque, and rude to the very man who had brought him into the center circle of the organization. Eventually, the fat man saw that

Malloy's dissatisfaction with his boss might metamorphose into total disaffection with The Committee's program itself; therefore, Malloy was killed in an accident when his car apparently skidded on a perfectly dry roadbed and collided with a telephone pole outside of Alexandria, Virginia. Roy Dodson knew precisely what had happened to his predecessor and why; his boss had told him all about it the first day that Dodson had come to work. No matter what he might think of the fat man, Dodson did as he was told, always had and always would.

Just before they reached the crest of the hill, the green blip moved sharply to the right on the monitor. Then it disappeared past the edge, although the dark screen continued to produce a faint *beep-beep-beep.*

Topping the hill they saw a large truck stop—twenty gasoline pumps on five widely spaced concrete islands, a service garage, three automatic truck-washing bays, a truckers' motel, and restaurant—on the right side of the road. The huge parking lot contained sixty or seventy tractor-trailer rigs.

"No Mercedes," Dodson said.

"He might have driven behind the buildings or in among all those trucks."

They drove through the nearest entrance and past the fueling stations where a dozen pump jockeys in bright yellow hooded rain slickers were tending to half a dozen trucks. Following the chain-link fence that encircled the property, they went around to the rear of the restaurant and the small, rather shabby motel. The *beep-beep-beep,* in counterpoint to the thumping windshield wipers, grew somewhat louder, and the light returned to the edge of the monitor—but there was no Mercedes here. On the south side of the complex, they cruised slowly down an aisle between the two rows of parked trucks—dull gray tailgates on both sides—which loomed like parading elephants. The signal was getting stronger by the second; the light edged back into the center of the screen. The beeping became so loud that it hurt their ears. Halfway down the aisle Dodson stopped the car and said, "We're almost on top of it."

There was nothing around them except trucks.

Barely able to control his anger, the fat man said, "Which one is it?"

Putting the car in gear and letting it drift forward, Dodson studied the monitor on the console. Then he slipped the car into reverse and let it roll backward while he watched the green blip. At last he stopped again and pointed at a tractor-trailer that had SEATRAIN painted on the rear door. "McAlister must have found the gimmick on his Mercedes and switched it to this truck. We've been following a decoy."

Suddenly, without warning, the fat man raised his arms and leaned slightly forward and slammed both heavy fists into the top of the padded dashboard. Inside the closed car the blow reverberated like a note from a bass drum: and then a whole rhythm, a series of solid thumps. The fat man had gone berserk. His arms were like windmill blades. He hammered, hammered, cursed, hammered, growled wordlessly, his voice like an animal's snarl, and hammered some more. His face was an apoplectic red, and hundreds of beads of sweat popped out on his brow. His eyes bulged as if they were being pushed out of him by some incredible inner pressure. The blood vessels at his temples stood up like ropes. He pounded the dashboard again and again, harder and harder . . . Beneath the padding the thin sheet metal began to bend. The fat man had tremendous strength in his thick arms. The dash sagged under the furious blows. Then, as suddenly as he had begun, he quit. He leaned back in his seat, breathing heavily, and stared out at the gray rain and the gray trucks and the wet black macadam.

Stunned, Dodson said, "Sir?"

"Get us the hell out of here."

Dodson hesitated.

"*Now,* damn you!"

Most of the way back to Washington, the fat man said nothing. He wasn't embarrassed, and he wasn't angry with Dodson. He was angry with himself. He'd had these rages before. Quite a few times, in fact. This was the first time, however, that anyone had seen him lose control. Always before, when he had felt that overpowering need to smash something with his fists, he had been able to wait until he was alone. Or with some whore. Over the last several days he had been under unbearable pressure. He never knew what that damned McAlister might do next. Keeping one step ahead of the bastard had been horribly difficult. And now he seemed to be one step behind. So this time he hadn't been able to go off by himself and work off his frustrations unobserved. He'd exploded, much to his own surprise, in front of Dodson. It was frightening. He simply could not let go like that when anyone was around, not again, not even for an instant.

As they entered the Washington suburbs, the fat man said, "Well, we know he's got someone he trusts to send to Peking."

Dodson glanced nervously at his boss. "We do?"

"Yes. We can deduce that much from his switching the transmitter to the truck. If he hadn't been rendezvousing with an agent, he'd have let us waste time and manpower following him."

"That makes sense, I guess."

"I'll find out who his man is. Before the day's over. One way or another, I'll find out."

"Yes, sir."

"It's just that if we could have learned his name now, this morning, we'd have more time to—eliminate him."

Dodson licked his lips. Hesitantly, he said, "If we can't find out who he's sending to China—what then?"

"Then, somehow we've got to activate Dragonfly immediately."

The rain had let up. Dodson put the windshield wipers on the lowest speed. "I've never been told what Dragonfly is."

"I know," the fat man said.

Washington, D.C.

When McAlister first arrived at the G Street apartment, David Canning was like a patch of barren earth: gray soil, ashes, broken twigs, cinders, and pebbles. The gray soil was his current uneventful career at the White House. The ashes were of his marriage. And the rest of it was the detritus of a day-to-day existence which held little excitement and no meaning. When he realized that McAlister had a new job for him, it was as if a green shoot had appeared in the barren earth. And now, a short while later, as McAlister began to explain the nature of the assignment, the shoot soared up and opened with leaves and budded and blossomed. Canning suddenly felt *alive* for the first time in years.

"We've already alerted Peking," McAlister said. He came back to the kitchen table and sat down across from Canning. "General Lin Shen Yang, head of their Internal Security Force, has ordered a thorough physical examination for every one of the five hundred and nine Chinese citizens who visited North America during January and February. We've told them that's the wrong approach. No physical examination is going to unmask Dragonfly. If it were that easy to defuse the operation, Olin Wilson wouldn't have bothered with it."

"Have you given General Lin the names of the three agents we have in China?" Canning asked.

"Good Lord, no!" His blue eyes were big and round, like a pair of robin eggs. "Whether or not they're Committeemen, we can't let our men be grilled by Chinese intelligence experts. They'd find out who Dragonfly is—but they'd also learn everything worth knowing about our operations within their borders. No matter how tough an agent is, he can be broken if the interrogator uses a combination of extreme torture and drugs."

"Of course."

"Our entire Chinese network would be blown to pieces."

Canning nodded agreement. "And any Chinese citizens who have been cooperating with our agents would be rounded up and imprisoned. 'Reeducated' to better serve the People's Republic."

"Exactly. And we'd probably suffer damage to our primary networks in most of Asia. Furthermore, if one of these three men is a Committeeman, and if he knows about some of these other things I've alluded to . . . Well, just imagine what the Chinese could do with that sort of information."

Rubbing one hand over his long and bony jaw, fingering the vague dimple in his chin, Canning thought for a moment and then said, "So you have to send a man to Peking to help General Lin find the Committeeman and, through him, Dragonfly."

"Yes."

"And I'm the man."

"As I've said, you're the only one I can trust."

"The Chinese are expecting me?"

"They're expecting someone. Right now, I'm the only one who knows it'll be you. They won't get your name until they absolutely have to have it. The longer I can play this close to my vest, the longer it will take The Committee to find out just how much I know and what I'm going to do about it."

"What happens when I get to Peking? How close to the vest do *I* play it?"

McAlister took his pipe out of his pocket again. He didn't fill and light it this time. He just kept turning it over and over in his hands. "You'll know the names of the three agents we have in China, but you won't reveal them all at once to General Lin. Instead, you'll provide him with one name at a time."

"So he'll still need me."

"Yes."

"After I've given him a name?"

"You will accompany him when he takes the operative into custody. You will see that he brings that man directly to the United States consulate. There, with General Lin participating only as an observer, you will question our operative, using a sophisticated polygraph which is already security-sealed and on a plane en route to our consul in Peking. If the agent is not a Committeeman, if the polygraph shows that he knows nothing whatsoever about Dragonfly, then you will see that he is held under armed guard within the diplomatic compound until he can be flown back to Washington. Under no circumstances must the Chinese get their hands on him. Then you will move on to the next agent on the list. In each case, even when you discover the Committeeman, you will not permit Lin to be alone with our man, and you will see that the agent is whisked out of China on the first available flight of any United States government aircraft. If the first agent you interrogate happens to be the Committeeman, the trigger man for Dragonfly, you will not reveal any more names to General Lin, of course."

File drawers opened and dozens of phantom secretaries moved busily back and forth across the ethereal office in Canning's mind. "The Chinese are going to go along with this? They aren't going to seize the opportunity to discover which of their own people have been passing information to us?"

"They have no choice but to handle it our way."

"I'll be on their turf."

"Yes, but we could always just leave them to find Dragonfly on their own—which they simply cannot do."

"That's a bluff."

"It is," McAlister admitted.

"And they'll know it's a bluff."

McAlister shook his head no. "Regardless of what the newspapers may print about it, the great détente between the United States and the People's Republic of China is quite fragile. Oh, sure, most of the Chinese people want peace. They really aren't all that imperialistic. They want open trade with us. But the great majority of the Party leaders don't trust us. Not the least bit. God knows, they have good reason. But with most government officials, the distrust has grown into paranoia. They wouldn't find it hard to believe that we'd let Dragonfly strike, because they're certain that we'd like to split their country between ourselves and the Russians."

"They actually think we're *all* wild-eyed reactionaries?"

"They *suspect* that we are. And for most of them, suspicion is as good as proof. If he believes you're capable of committing the most despicable acts against China, General Lin won't push you too far. He'll believe your threats if you have to make them."

"But don't threaten him lightly?"

"Yes. Diplomacy is always best."

Canning's eyes were a crystalline shade of gray. Ordinarily they contained a sharp cold edge that most men could not meet directly. At the moment, however, his eyes were like pools of molten metal: warm, glistening, mercurial. "When do I leave?"

"Four o'clock this afternoon."

"Straight to Peking?"

"No. You'll catch a domestic flight to Los Angeles." McAlister took a folder of airplane tickets from an inner jacket pocket and laid it on the table. "From L.A. you'll take another flight to Tokyo. There's only a one-hour layover in Los Angeles. It's an exhausting trip. But tomorrow night you'll rest up in Tokyo. Friday morning you'll board a jet belonging to a French corporation, and that'll take you secretly to Peking."

Canning shook his head as if he were having trouble with his hearing. "I don't understand. Why not a government plane direct to Peking?"

"For one thing, I'd have to go through the usual channels to get you a seat. Or the President could go through them for me, with no need to explain anything to anyone. But either way, The Committee would learn about it. And if they knew . . . Well, I'm not so sure you would ever get to Peking."

"I can handle myself," Canning said, not boasting at all, just stating a fact.

"I know you can. But can you handle a bomb explosion aboard your airplane while it's over the middle of the ocean, hundreds of miles from land? Remember Berlinson?"

"Your informer?"

Jagged lightning, like a dynamite blast in a bus-terminal locker, slammed across the purplish sky. The stroboscopic effect pierced the window and filled the kitchen with leaping shadows and knife-blade light. The crack of thunder followed an instant later—and there was an electric power failure. The refrigerator stopped humming and rattling. The fluorescent tubes above the kitchen counter blinked out.

The meager, penumbral light of the early-afternoon storm sky, further filtered by the misted window, left them dressed in shadows.

"Do you have any candles?" McAlister asked.

"Let's give them a few minutes to fix it. You were explaining why you think these Committeemen would go to any lengths to kill me. It has something to do with Berlinson . . ."

McAlister sighed. "Once he had whetted my appetite by telling me a bit about Dragonfly, I promised Roger Berlinson three things in return for the rest of his information: exemption from criminal prosecution for anything he did as a CIA operative; a rather large cash payment; and last of all, a new name and a whole new life for him and his family. So . . . After he told me what he knew, I went to Ryder, the new FBI director, and I asked him for the use of an FBI safe house. I told him I needed it for a man whose name and circumstances I could not divulge. I explained that Ryder himself was the only man in the Bureau who could know the safe house was harboring someone *I* wanted to protect. Ryder was great: no questions, complete cooperation. The Berlinsons were spirited out of Washington and, by devious route, ended up in Carpinteria, California. So far as the FBI agents knew, Berlinson was a Mafia figure who had ratted on his bosses. Meanwhile, I went to various non-agency sources to obtain new birth certificates, passports, credit cards, and other documents for Roger, his wife, and his son. But I was wasting my time."

"They killed Berlinson."

His voice leaden, McAlister said, "The house in Carpinteria was protected by an infrared alarm system. It seemed as safe as a Swiss bank. What I didn't know, what the FBI didn't know, was that the Army has recently perfected a 'thermal isolation' suit that is one hundred percent effective in containing heat. It can be used by commandos to slip past infrared equipment. Two of these suits were stolen from an Army-CIA experimental lab in MacLean, Virginia." He stopped for a moment as thunder rattled the windowpanes. It was convenient thunder, Canning thought, for

McAlister needed to compose himself and clear his phlegm-filled throat. Then: "You can spend only twenty minutes inside the suit, because your body heat builds and builds in there until it can roast you alive. But twenty minutes is sufficient. We believe two men, wearing these suits, entered the Carpinteria house through a living-room window. Inside, they quietly stripped down to their street clothes before they broiled in their own juices. Then they went out to the kitchen and murdered the FBI agent who was monitoring the infrared repeater screens. When he was out of the way, they went upstairs and shot Berlinson, his wife, and his son."

The only sounds were those of the storm. The heavy dark air could not hold the words McAlister had spoken, but it did retain the anguish with which they'd been freighted.

Canning said, "Families are never hit."

"We're dealing with fanatics."

"But what did they have to gain by killing the wife and son?"

"They probably wanted to set an example for anyone else who might be thinking of informing on The Committee."

Recalling Duncan, Tyler, and Bixby, Canning decided that such a thing was not only possible but likely. "Lunatics!"

"The point is, if they would do a thing like this, then they wouldn't hesitate to blow up a government aircraft, passengers and crew, just to get you. We *must* keep your involvement a secret until you're safely inside China. If they kill you, I've got no one else I can send. I'll have to go myself. And they'll kill me."

"But why don't they just trigger Dragonfly? Why don't they get it over with before we can stop them?"

"That's the one thing that doesn't make sense," McAlister said. "I just don't know the answer."

It was a paranoid nightmare.

Yet Canning believed every word of it.

Orange-red numerals suddenly glowed in the shadows. McAlister checked his electronic read-out watch and said, "We don't have much time left."

"If we're taking all these precautions," Canning said, "then I assume I'll be traveling under another identity."

Reaching into an inside pocket of his suit coat, McAlister produced a passport, birth certificate, and other identification. He passed the lot to Canning, who didn't bother to try to examine it in the poor light. "Your name's Theodore Otley. You're a diplomatic courier for the State Department."

Canning was surprised. "Wouldn't it be better for me to go as an ordinary citizen? Less conspicuous that way."

"Probably," McAlister agreed. "But an ordinary citizen has to pass through anti-hijacking X-ray machines and later through customs. He can't carry a gun. A diplomatic courier, however, is exempt from all inspections. And this is one time you don't want to be without a gun."

Like a blind man reading Braille, Canning paged through the passport. "Where did you get this stuff? Any chance The Committee will learn about old Ted Otley?"

"In the last few months I've learned a few things. I know that only three intelligence agencies in the world have kept the CIA from planting a double agent. The Israelis run a tight outfit. So do the French. The British are the best, most efficient, most impenetrable intelligence specialists anywhere, period. I went to my opposite in Britain's SIS, what used to be called M.I.6. I asked for and was granted a favor: one full set of papers in the Otley name. There is no way The Committee can crack it."

Canning knew that was true. "Theodore Otley it is."

"When you get to Tokyo you will check into the Imperial Hotel, where reservations have been made."

"The Imperial?" Canning asked, amazed. "Since when does a lowly op rate that kind of luxury?"

"Since never. That's why you're getting it. In other Tokyo hotels—the Grand Palace, Takanawa Prince, Fairmont, just about anywhere—you might run into an agent who knows you. There's not much chance of that if you stay at the Imperial."

"What about the French jet? How do I connect with it?"

"That will be taken care of by your assistant."

Canning blinked. "Assistant?"

"You don't speak Chinese. You'll need an interpreter."

"General Lin speaks no English?"

"He does. But you don't want to be completely cut out of a conversation when he uses Chinese with his subordinates."

"I don't like it," Canning said sourly.

"The interpreter isn't an agency rep. I'm not tying you to a possible Committeeman."

"A tenderfoot is just as bad."

"Hardly. Once you're inside China, there won't be any guns or knives or rough stuff. A tenderfoot can handle it."

"Who is he?"

"This is strictly a need-to-know operation, and you don't need to know the name. I'm especially concerned that no harm should come to the interpreter. They can't torture a name from you if you haven't got it."

Resigned to it, Canning said, "How do I contact him?"

McAlister smiled, obviously amused. "He'll contact you."

"What's so funny?"

"You'll find out."

"What I *don't* need is surprises."

"This one's pleasant. And remember: 'need-to-know.' "

The electric power came back into service. The refrigerator rumbled to life, and the living-room lights popped on like flash bulbs. Canning got up, went to the kitchen counter, worked the light switch until the fluorescent tubes fired up. He and McAlister squinted at each other for a few seconds.

McAlister stood up and stretched. If he had been all lion when he had come through the front door, Canning thought, he was now at least ten percent tired old house cat. "That's everything. You have any questions?"

"Are you going to be working on the case from this end?"

"I've built up a rather large, youngish, go-getting legal staff since I took over at the agency. I'm going to turn those lawyers into detectives."

"You could get them killed."

"Not if I send them out in teams of two and three, and not if there's an armed United States marshal with each team."

"You can swing that?"

Adjusting his cuffs, McAlister said, "The President has promised me anything I need."

"Where will you start?"

"We'll try to find Wilson's laboratory. If we can get our hands on the files or on a scientist who worked with Wilson, we ought to be able to learn Dragonfly's identity." He led the way into the living room and waited while Canning got his raincoat from the foyer closet. "There's another angle we'll cover. Berlinson managed to kill one of the men sent to get him. The corpse wasn't in the house in Carpinteria, but our forensic experts swear there was a fifth killing. There was a great deal of blood near the bedroom closet, and it doesn't match types with any of the Berlinsons or with the FBI agent who was killed in the kitchen. So . . . Somewhere there's a dead CIA operative, a dead Committeeman. I'm going to try to pin down the whereabouts of every agent who is supposed to be in Mexico or North America, any agent who might have slipped into Carpinteria, California. If one of them isn't where he's supposed to be, if his absence is unexplained, if I can't get a line on him one way or another, then we can be pretty certain that he's the one Berlinson killed. We'll find out which agency employees were most friendly with him. They'll probably be Committeemen. With luck, we might get hold of one of these fanatics before he knows what's happening."

Canning held the hooded raincoat, waited until the other man had his arms in the sleeves, let go of the collar, and said, "Then what?"

McAlister turned around to face him. Buttoning his coat, he said, "We interrogate him."

"Oh?"

"We learn who runs The Committee."

"If he knows."

"Or we see if he can tell us where Wilson had his lab. Or who Dragonfly is."

"If he knows."

"He'll know *something*."

Putting one hand on the doorknob but making no effort to turn it, Canning said, "Like you said earlier, these are all tough boys, hard cases. They won't break unless you hit them with a combination of extreme torture and drugs."

"That's right."

"You aren't the kind of man who could use those techniques."

McAlister frowned. "Maybe I could."

"I hope you don't have to. But I hope you *can* if it comes to that."

"I can. If it gets down to the wire."

"If it gets down to the wire," Canning said, "it's already too late."

5

The White House

At one-twenty that afternoon McAlister entrusted his Mercedes to a federal security officer and hurried toward a side entrance of the White House. The enormous old building, streaming with rain, looked like a piece of elegantly sculptured alabaster. All over the spacious grounds, the trees of many nations shared a common autumn: the leaves had begun to turn a hundred different shades of red and gold. McAlister was not aware of this beauty. His mind was on the Dragonfly crisis. He went straight to the door, exchanged hellos with the guard, and stepped into a small marbled foyer, where he left puddles of rain on the polished floor.

Beau Jackson, the sixty-year-old tuxedoed black man who was on duty at the cloakroom, gave McAlister a toothy smile. Jackson was an anachronism that never failed to intrigue McAlister. His look and his manner seemed pre-Lincolnian. "Nasty out there, Mr. McAlister?"

"Wet enough to drown ducks, Mr. Jackson."

The black man laughed as he took McAlister's coat. Hanging it up, he said, "You just hold on a minute, and I'll wipe the rain off your attaché case."

"Oh, I'll get it," McAlister said, putting the briefcase on a small mahogany stand and reaching for the display handkerchief that was folded to a perfect double point in the breast pocket of his suit jacket.

"No, no!" Jackson said urgently. "You mustn't mess up your nice hanky, Mr. McAlister."

"Really, I—"

"Why, you have it folded so nice . . ." He tilted his graying head to admire the handkerchief. "Look at them folds. Would you look at them folds? Sharp enough to cut bread."

McAlister smiled and shook his head. "Okay. I'll use the bathroom." He went into the visitors' lavatory, splashed cold water on his face, combed his hair, and straightened his tie. When he returned to the cloakroom, he found Jackson folding the dustcloth he had used to wipe off the attaché case. "Thank you, Mr. Jackson."

"You're welcome, I'm sure."

He picked up the case. "How's that son of yours getting along? The one who was trying to buy a McDonald's franchise."

Jackson smiled. "He got the store all right. He's deep in debt, but he's working sixteen hours a day and selling hamburgers faster than they can kill the cows to make them."

McAlister laughed. "Good for him."

"Have a nice visit with the boss," Jackson said.

"That's up to him."

Five minutes later, passed along by the appointments secretary, McAlister stood outside the door to the Oval Office. He hesitated, trying to relax, trying to get a smile on his face.

On his left, three feet away, the ever-present warrant officer sat on a chair in the hallway. On his lap lay a black metal case, The Bag, the file of war codes that the President needed if he were to start—or finish—a nuclear war. Thirtyish, clean-cut and lean, the warrant officer was reading a paperback suspense novel. It had a colorful cover: two people running from an unseen enemy. Above the title was a line of copy: "Unarmed in the desert—with hired killers on their trail." Without looking up, thoroughly hooked, the Bag Man turned a page. McAlister wondered how a man who might one day help to cause mega-deaths could possibly be enthralled by a fiction in which only two lives hung in the balance.

He knocked on the door, opened it, and went in to see the President.

The Oval Office was quintessentially American. It was clearly a room where business was transacted and not merely a place set aside for ceremonial purposes. The furniture was expensive, often antique, but also sturdy and functional. A United States flag hung from a brass stand at the right and behind the chief executive's desk, as if everyone had to be reminded this was not Lithuania or Argentina. Every corner and glossy surface was squeaky clean. The room held a vaguely medicinal odor composed of furniture polish, carpet shampoo, and chemically purified, dehumidified air. The ubiquitous blue-and-silver Great Seal of the President of the United States officialized the carpet, the desk, the penholder that stood on the desk, the pens in the holder, the stationery, the stapler, the blotter, each of the many telephones, the sterling-silver pitcher full of ice water, and a dozen other things. Only American chiefs of staff, McAlister thought, could wield so much power and yet cling to such simple-minded status symbols as these.

The focal point of the office was, of course, the President. He was a tall, broad-shouldered man who managed to look austere and approachable, sophisticated and of simple tastes, fatherly and quite sensual all at the same time. In spite of his London-tailored suit and hand-stitched Italian shoes, he had the rugged, rangy image of a cowboy actor. His hair was thick, salt-and-pepper, artfully mussed; and his eyebrows were dark and bushy. And he had the best collection of vintage 1960, white-white, porcelain-capped, steel-pin, jaw-sunk, permanently implanted, artificial teeth extant.

"Good to see you, Bob," he said, coming out from behind his desk, his right hand extended, his teeth gleaming.

"Good afternoon, Mr. President," McAlister said as they shook hands. The elaborate, long-time-no-see greeting made McAlister ill-at-ease, for he'd spent an hour with the President just last evening.

"Nasty out there, Bob?"

"Wet enough to drown ducks, Mr. President," McAlister said, listening to the other man laugh, remembering Beau Jackson, wondering if there was actually all that much difference between a cloakroom attendant and a chief of state.

The only other person present was Andrew Rice, the President's number-one man. To his credit, he didn't laugh at the duck joke;

and his handshake was softer than the President's; and he had imperfect teeth. McAlister didn't particularly like the man, but he respected him. Which was exactly how he felt about the President, too.

"You look as exhausted as I feel," Rice said.

"When this is over," McAlister said, "I'm for the Caribbean."

As Rice groaned and shifted and tried to get comfortable in his chair, McAlister wondered what David Canning, compulsively neat as he was, would think of the senior advisor. Rice's gray suit looked as if it had been put through a series of endurance tests by the idealists at the Consumers Union. His white shirt was yellow-gray, his collar frayed. His striped tie was stained, and the knot had been tied haphazardly. Standing five ten, weighing two-eighty, he was easily a hundred pounds too heavy. The chair creaked under him, and just the effort of getting settled down had made him breathe like a runner.

Of course, Rice's *mind* was quick, spare, and ordered. He was one of the country's sharpest liberal thinkers. He had been twenty-six when Harvard University Press published his first book, *Balancing the Budget in a Welfare State*, and he had been electrifying political and economic circles ever since.

"I received your brief report of this morning's tragedy in Carpinteria," the President said. "I called Bill Ryder at the Bureau to find out how in hell his security was breached. He didn't know."

"We made a mistake putting Ryder at the FBI," Rice said.

The President allowed as how his senior advisor might be right.

"Berlinson, Carpinteria . . . all of that's become moot," McAlister said. "Mr. President, have you had any new communications with Peking?"

"Thanks to a satellite relay, I had a twenty-minute talk with the Chairman a short while ago." The President put a finger in one ear and searched for wax. "The Chairman isn't happy." He took the finger out of his ear and studied it: no wax. He tried the other ear. "He half believes that the entire Dragonfly hysteria is a trick of some sort. They've examined about half of the five hundred and nine suspects, and they haven't found anything yet."

"Nor will they," McAlister said.

"The Chairman explained to me that if a plague should strike

Peking, he will have no choice but to target all of China's nuclear missiles on our West Coast." The President found no wax in the second ear.

"Their ballistics system is antiquated," Rice said. "Their nuclear capabilities don't amount to much." He dismissed the Chinese with one quick wave of his pudgy hand.

"True enough," the President said. Dissatisfied with the results of the first exploration, he began to make another search of his ears, beginning again with the left one. "Our anti-missile system can stop anything they throw at us. They don't have a saturation system like Russia does. We'll intercept two or three hundred miles from shore. But the fallout won't leave either Los Angeles or San Francisco very damned healthy."

Rice turned to McAlister. "The Chairman wants to know the name of the agent you're sending over to General Lin."

"They want time to run their own background check on him," the President said, giving up on his waxless ears and drumming his fingers on the desk. "They haven't said as much. But that's what I'd want to do if the roles were reversed."

"The only problem is that The Committee may be able to monitor all communications between us and the Chinese," McAlister said softly, worriedly.

"Not likely," Rice said.

"It would go out on the red phone," the President said. "That line can't be tapped."

"Any line can be tapped," McAlister said.

The President's jaw set like rough-formed concrete. "The red phone is secure."

"I'm not questioning your word, Mr. President," McAlister said. "But even if the red phone *is* safe, we can get my man killed by giving his name to the Chinese too early in the game. The Committee will have sources in China's counterintelligence establishment. Once the Chinese have the name and start running a background check, The Committee will know who I'm sending. They'll have my man hit before he's safe in Peking."

"For God's sake!" Rice said, huffing with frustration. "Look, we're dealing with dangerous, crackpot reactionaries who have gotten deep into the CIA, perhaps deep into the FBI as well. For fifteen years now they've corrupted the democratic process. I think we all agree on that. We all understand what a grave matter this is. But these Committeemen aren't omniscient! They aren't lurking *everywhere!*"

"I'd prefer to act as if they were," McAlister said, shifting uncomfortably in his chair.

The President continued to drum his fingers on the desk, using his left hand to counterpoint the rhythm he had developed with his right. He looked at McAlister from under his bushy eyebrows and said, "I think Andy's right about this."

"Caution is admirable," Rice said. "But we've got to guard against paranoia."

The President nodded.

Wondering if he had gotten into a position where he would once again have to defy a President or resign his office, McAlister said, "I don't want to transmit my man's name to the Chinese any sooner than twelve hours before he's due in Peking. That's cutting it close enough so that The Committee won't have time to organize a hit."

"Twelve hours," the President said.

"The Chairman won't like that," Rice said. His small, deep-set eyes and his pursed lips admonished McAlister.

"Whether or not he likes it, that's the way I want it."

Rice's face was gradually mottling: red, pink, and chalk-white. He was like a malfunctioning boiler swelling up with steam. A rivet would pop any second now.

In a surprisingly quiet voice the President said, "From the way you're talking, Bob, I assume that you've found a man you think you can trust."

"That's right, sir."

Taking his cue from the President, Rice controlled his anger. "An agency man?"

McAlister told them how his morning had gone thus far: a visit to the British Embassy to pick up the set of forged papers that the SIS had prepared for him, a thorough search of his Mercedes until he located the transmitter he had known would be there, a quick switch of the transmitter to the tractor-trailer that had stopped for a red light, a meeting with the agent who would be sent to China . . .

While McAlister talked, the President used a thumbnail to pick incessantly at his artificial teeth. He made a continual *click-click-click* noise. Occasionally he found a bit of tartar, which he carefully inspected. In public McAlister had never seen the man pick his teeth or bore at his ears or clean his fingernails or crack his knuckles or pick his nose. And even in the Oval Office he didn't begin worrying at himself unless he was under pressure to make a policy decision. Now, wound tight by the Dragonfly crisis, he was rapidly going through his entire repertoire: he stopped picking his teeth, and he began to crack his knuckles one at a time.

When McAlister finished talking, the President said, "You've neglected to mention the agent's name." He smiled.

Crack!: a knuckle.

"Before I tell you," McAlister said, "I feel strongly that I should receive your assurance that you won't pass it along to the Chairman any sooner than I want it to be passed."

Rice started to say something, decided that silence was at least valuable if not golden, and glowered at the President's hands just as another knuckle cracked.

The President got up and went to the Georgian window behind his desk. He stared at the traffic that moved through the rain down on Pennsylvania Avenue. He obviously knew, as did McAlister, that the name did not really matter. Getting the name was important not for practical reasons; it was merely a matter of face now. "What would you do if I refused to give you that assurance? Would you tell me his name—or defy me?"

"Mr. President," McAlister said, "I would do neither."

"Neither?"

"I would resign, sir."

Not turning from the window, the fingers of both hands tangled behind his back and writhing like trysting worms, the President said, "That's out of the question. This has to be resolved quickly, and you're the only man I know who can handle it. You have my assurance."

"Your promise, sir?"

"Yes, Bob. The Chairman will get the name twelve hours before your man gets to Peking. My promise. Don't push it any further."

Doggedly, McAlister said, "One step further, sir."

The President said nothing.

McAlister said, "I wouldn't want to talk any more about this if I thought we were being recorded. The tape might get into the hands of a Committeeman."

Turning to face them, grinning humorlessly, the President said, "Do you think any President since Nixon would be foolish enough to record his own conversations?"

McAlister nodded. "My man's name is David Canning."

"He's on assignment here at the White House," Rice said.

"Why Canning?" the President asked.

McAlister told him why. He also explained that Canning would travel as Theodore Otley and would leave Washington in two hours, on a four o'clock flight to Los Angeles. "I'm sending him by a series of civilian airlines, from Los Angeles to Tokyo and finally to Peking."

"That seems a waste of time," Rice said, shaking his head disapprovingly. "Why not lay on a direct government flight—"

"Which might easily be set up to explode over the ocean," the President said.

"Exactly," McAlister said. "The Committee would *have* to know about it. They'd either put a bomb aboard here or at a fuel stop on the way."

Reluctantly, grudgingly, Rice said, "I suppose you're right. We've been behaving like chronic paranoids, but they've left us no other way *to* behave."

The President said, "You'll be trying to break the Dragonfly project from this end?"

"Yes, sir," McAlister said.

"Have you been doing any thinking about why Dragonfly hasn't already been triggered?"

"That's the question that kept me up most of last night," McAlister said. "I can't find an answer I like."

Looking at his watch, the President said, "Anything else, then? Anything more you need, Bob?"

"In fact, there is, sir," McAlister said as he got to his feet.

"Name it."

"I'd like twelve federal marshals put under my control, four men each in three eight-hour shifts. I'll need them for the protection of my investigative staff."

Glancing at Rice, the President said, "See to that, Andy."

Rice struggled out of his chair, which squeaked with relief. "They will be in your office tomorrow morning at eight-thirty," he said. "You can brief them then and divide them whatever way you want."

"Thank you."

"And now *I* have a request," the President said.

McAlister said, "Sir?"

"From now on, don't go anywhere without your bodyguard."

"I don't plan to, sir."

"It'll get worse. They'll get desperate the closer we get to Dragonfly."

"I know," McAlister said.

"My God," Rice said, "What are we coming to when the highest officers of the land can't trust their own subordinates? These reactionary bastards have nearly driven us into a police state!"

No one had anything to say about that.

When McAlister left the Oval Office, the warrant officer looked up to see if the President might be at the open door with news of the world's end. Then he went on with his reading.

McAlister felt a bit weak behind the knees and in the pit of his stomach. He had known four Presidents and had been appointed to office by two of them. He had seen that they were all flawed, sometimes tragically so. They were all, in whole or part, vain and foolish, misinformed and sometimes even crooked. Yet he had not lost his respect for the office—perhaps because it was the keystone of that system of laws and justice which he so admired—and he stood in awe of any halfway decent man who held it. His intellect and emotions had reached a compromise on this subject, and he experienced no need to analyze his feelings. This was simply how he was, and he had grown accustomed to the weakness in his knees and stomach after every conference in the Oval Office.

Don't you know you're from a fine Boston family with a forty-foot genealogical chart? he asked himself. A *Boston* family. There is no better. Didn't you listen to your mother? She told you at least a million times. And your father. Didn't anything he said get through to you? You're Bostonian, *old* Bostonian! You're from the stock that patronized the *Atlantic Monthly*, and your father was a member of the Porcellian Club at Harvard! Don't you know that no one's better than you?

He laughed softly.

He still felt a bit weak.

When McAlister entered the back corridor, the guard at the end saw him coming and said, "Leaving now, Mr. McAlister?"

"As soon as I get my coat."

The guard pulled on his rain slicker and went out to see that the Mercedes was brought around.

Beau Jackson was not in the cloakroom.

McAlister put down his attaché case and went to the open-front wall-length closet. As he put on his coat he noticed a thick black-and-gold hardbound book lying on the hat shelf. With the curiosity of a book lover, he picked it up and looked at the title: *The Complete Kafka—The Stories, Annotated and Analyzed.* On the flyleaf there was a three-inch-square bookplate:

From the Library of
B.W. JACKSON

Beau Jackson came out of the lavatory into the cloakroom. He stopped and stared at the book in McAlister's hands, and said, "Somebody left that here last week. It yours, Mr. McAlister?"

"Belongs to a B.W. Jackson. Know him?"

The black man smiled. "Surprise you?"

"Not really. I've always figured you can't be what you seem to be." He put the book back on the hat shelf.

Carrying McAlister's attaché case, Jackson walked him across the cloakroom, into the hall. "Then I guess I belong here."

McAlister pulled up his hood, buttoned his coat collar. "Oh?"

Handing him the case, Jackson said, "Around here a lot of people just aren't what they seem to be."

Grinning, McAlister said, "You mean that you're disappointed with the way the boss has been running things? You're sorry you voted for him?"

"I *did* vote for him," Jackson said. "And for once in my life I figure maybe I pulled the right lever." His broad, dark face was sober, almost glum. "Compared to that Sidney Greenstreet of his, the boss is as real and genuine and unphony as they come."

"Sidney Greenstreet?" McAlister said, perplexed.

At the end of the hall, the guard came back inside and said, "Car's ready, Mr. McAlister."

"Who's Sidney Greenstreet?" McAlister asked the black man.

Beau Jackson shook his head. "If you aren't a fan of the old movies, then it can't mean anything to you. Just goes right over your head."

For a long moment McAlister stared into the other man's watery chocolate-brown eyes. Then he said, "You're an original, Mr. Jackson." He went down the last stretch of the hallway toward the door that the guard was holding open for him.

"Mr. McAlister," the black man called after him.

He looked back.

"You're sure enough the only one I ever met here who is just exactly what he seems to be."

McAlister couldn't think of anything to say. He nodded stupidly, embarrassed by the compliment, and he went outside into the rain and wind that lashed the capital.

The Executive Office Building

Crossing the small reception lounge at two-twenty that afternoon, Andrew Rice told his secretary, "Officially, I'm not back yet. I don't want to talk to anyone. I don't want to see anyone. I'm not feeling very well." And before she had a chance to tell him who had telephoned during the morning, he hurried past her desk and went into his private office and slammed the door behind him.

The office was a reflection of Rice himself: the furniture was large, bulky, heavy; the chairs were overstuffed; there was a slight but pervading sloppiness about the place. The wall shelves overflowed with books that had been jammed into them every which way. The desk was six feet by four feet, held three telephones, and was littered with dozens of letters and memoranda and government reports. Three rumpled easy chairs, all of them wide enough and deep enough to comfortably accommodate Rice himself—therefore, so large that they dwarfed many other men—were arranged in a semicircle around a water-stained oak-and-chrome coffee table.

Roy Dodson was sitting in the easy chair nearest the windows. Because he was six four and weighed two-twenty, the chair did not dwarf him. He was holding a cup of coffee in one hand and a recent issue of a news magazine in the other. When Rice came in,

Dodson leaned forward and put both the coffee and the magazine on the low oak table.

Rice said, "We have to move fast."

Dodson got up.

Not bothering to take off his raincoat, scarf, or hat, Rice went around behind the desk and collapsed into a king-size, caster-equipped, posturematic chair. He pulled several paper tissues from a chrome dispenser on the desk; he wiped his face, which was greasy with perspiration. "McAlister's man is David Canning."

"He's had a desk job for years."

"Obviously, McAlister doesn't think the man's gone to seed, desk job or no desk job," the fat man said. "Get out of here. Get to a public phone." He picked up a pen, scribbled on the back of a used envelope, and handed the envelope to Dodson. "That's the number of a phone in the agency's main file room. It'll be answered by a Miss Rockwalt. She's one of ours. She'll find Canning's home address for you."

"Then?"

"You take two men out to his house. Look it over. Find a way to hit him."

"Make it look like an accident?"

"There's no time for that approach," Rice said irritably. "He's leaving Washington on a four o'clock flight to Los Angeles."

"Which airline? Which airport?" Dodson asked. "It might be a lot easier to hit him in an airport parking lot or restroom than in his own home."

"Well, I don't *know* which airline or which goddamned airport," the fat man said. "McAlister didn't say. If I'd insisted on knowing, I'd have had to explain why I was so damned curious."

Dodson nodded. "One problem."

"What's that?"

"The only other men I know in our group are Maxwood and Hillary. Maxwood's in Texas on an assignment. Hillary's here in the city, but I don't know where. How do I reach him? Who do I get for backup?"

The fat man thought for a moment. Hillary and an agent named Hobartson were on security duty at Wilson's laboratory. They could be spared for this. "I'll get to Hillary and his partner. They'll meet you downstairs in the lobby at a quarter of three—twenty minutes from now." He shook his head. "I just don't see how you're going to have time to hit Canning before he leaves for the airport."

"Maybe we won't have to set him up at home. If we can get there in time to follow him, we can still do the job at the airport."

"Get moving."

"Yes, sir." Dodson took his coat from a hook on the back of the door, and he went out, closing the door behind him.

Rice's three telephones were three different colors: one black, one blue, and one white. The white phone was a private top-security line that did not pass through the building's switchboard. He lifted the white receiver and dialed the unlisted number of the laboratory.

The man on the other end did not identify himself or the place from which he was speaking. "Hello?"

"Hillary?"

"Yes."

"This is the Spokesman." That was the name Rice used with agents of The Committee, for nine out of ten of his men did not know who he was.

"Sir?"

"You and your partner leave that place and go to the first-floor main lobby of the Executive Office Building. At two forty-five you'll meet Dodson there. He has a job he'll explain to you."

"Yes, sir."

"You haven't much time. Don't be late."

"We're leaving now."

Rice put down the receiver, opened a desk drawer, and put his right hand into a bag full of chocolate-covered marshmallow cookies. He ate one of them, licked his fingers, and flicked an intercom switch.

"Yes, Mr. Rice?"

"Miss Priestly, I need a list of all U.S. marshals assigned to the Washington area. Do we have a thing like that on file?"

"No, sir."

"Then get hold of Fredericks over at the Justice Department. Ask him to have such a list hand-delivered to me within the half-hour. Tell him it's connected with a matter of national security."

"Yes, sir."

Finally, he took off his scarf and hat, stood up and wrestled loose of his coat. He didn't bother to hang up anything; he tossed the garments onto the nearest easy chair.

Now what?

He answered himself: Just wait. Just relax.

The pessimistic half of his mind told him: Impossible. It isn't just the Dragonfly project that's at stake. If this bastard McAlister breaks us on this one, he's going to destroy us altogether.

The optimistic Rice told the pessimistic Rice: He won't touch you. He *can't* touch you. You have all the advantages.

But I can lose everything I've built these last seventeen years . . .

Don't be a fool. You'll lose nothing. If he gets too close to you—or if anyone *else* gets too close to you—you can have him killed. You're more ruthless than any of them. That counts for something.

This brief, internal pep talk didn't help Rice at all. He still felt a deep pressure in his chest. He was still tense.

He sat down at his desk again, reached into the open drawer, picked up a second cookie and ate it in one bite. A few crumbs fell onto the front of his shirt. Before he had fully swallowed the second cookie, he popped a third one into his mouth. Then a fourth. A fifth and sixth . . . The very process of masticating, salivating, and swallowing affected him as a tranquilizer might have done. The combination of chocolate and marshmallow seemed to act like an emetic on the time stream of his mind, causing him to flush out the present and the future until only the past remained to tantalize him . . .

Perhaps the single most important hour of Rice's existence came at eleven o'clock at night, two days before Christmas, in the middle of his twenty-fourth year—although he was not at that time aware of the irresistible forces of change that were already working relentlessly within and upon his life.

At that time he was living in Boston, doing graduate work at Harvard, studying economics and political systems during the day and writing feverishly about politics and social theory at night. Once a month he took the train down to New York City, where he met J. Prescott Hennings, the young editor and publisher of two periodicals that were devoted to the dissemination of every facet of ultra-conservative American thought. Scott Hennings, at least in Rice's opinion, was proof that the American Dream could still come true. Hennings had inherited a twenty-million-dollar real estate fortune which he had built into a *fifty*-million-dollar empire by his thirtieth birthday. Now he let his businesses run themselves while he dedicated himself to the preservation of the capitalistic system in a world where Communists squirmed on all sides like worms in the walls of an old mansion. Each of his magazines had a circulation of just twenty thousand and a combined readership of a hundred thousand, and every issue lost money. Hennings hardly cared, for he could lose money every day for the remainder of his life, even if he died an octogenarian, and nonetheless leave a fortune behind him. Once a month Rice personally submitted an article to Hennings, with whom he had become close friends. Routinely, Hennings read it the same day, paid two or three hundred dollars for it, and published it forthwith.

None of Rice's Harvard acquaintances had ever read one of these articles or seen a copy of Hennings' magazines. That was of little consequence to Rice. He made rent money writing them—and he was reaching thousands of readers who were already enough in agreement with him to give his theories the careful consideration he could not have received in liberal circles. Indeed, at Harvard he was not well known. He merely used the university's library and other educational facilities much as a man might use a whore—or a whore use a man; he ignored the propaganda and took only the knowledge, and he tried not to be tainted by the extreme left-wing attitudes which lay, in his opinion, like an oppressive blanket of smog over the entire campus. Twice a year he was invited to a party at Hennings' penthouse apartment on Park Avenue, where he could socialize without having to mute or conceal his political views. At these affairs, which he treasured more than he did the money Hennings paid him, he met conservative congressmen, millionaire businessmen, generals and admirals, a few movie stars—and once even George Lincoln Rockwell, head of the National Socialist Party in the United States, had been there in a swastika-emblazoned uniform which, to Rice, was not at all anachronistic here in the 1960s. This was rare air for Rice. This was

Mount Olympus, and he had somehow been allowed to mingle with the gods. Rice did not care, therefore, that the Harvard elite had never read or even heard of his monthly essays.

At eleven o'clock at night, two days before Christmas, in his twenty-fourth year, Rice completed a book-length manuscript, an inspired—if unbalanced and unfair—attack on Lyndon Johnson's War on Poverty. Exhausted but unable to sleep, he stayed up all night rereading, correcting words and phrases, agonizing over sentence structure for more dark hours than he'd ever spent agonizing over the condition of his immortal soul.

The next morning he slept on the train to New York. He delivered the script to Hennings, hoping it could be serialized in one of his magazines and that Hennings could place it with a publisher who specialized in conservative political theory. Although he hadn't known Rice was writing a book, Hennings promised to read it in a few days.

On Christmas Eve, 1964, Rice was alone in New York. He spent the evening in his hotel room, eating candy bars and pretending to watch television and trying not to think of his book. He had a nightmare in which Hennings rejected the book, called it a piece of unpublishable trash, and tried—with the help of four men in storm troopers' uniforms—to use the three hundred typewritten pages as a suppository which, though applied to Rice's anal canal, would cure him of his mental hemorrhoids. He woke up with loose bowels and ran for the bathroom.

Hennings didn't call Christmas Day, and Rice told himself this was to be expected. Scott had two children. He wouldn't give up his holiday to read the script. Yet Rice cursed him and ate more candy.

That evening the pressure became unbearable. He went walking in Times Square, where happy crowds lined up at theaters and street-corner Santas endured the final hours of their reincarnations. Oblivious of the cold wind and snow flurries, he kept his mind on that commodity which he had left his room to find: a professional piece of ass.

He found one: a pretty young brunette on Forty-second Street. He weighed only two-thirty in those days, and she wasn't much put off by him as some prostitutes eventually came to be. They set a price. He said he had no hotel room, but she knew a place where a key cost six dollars and there was no register to sign.

In the room he sat and watched her undress. She stripped without ceremony or style. Her breasts were large, belly flat, legs long and lovely. She was firm, unmarked. She seemed sweet and wholesome except for the plastic sheen of her eyes and the hard twist of her mouth.

When he began to take off his clothes, she stretched out on her back in the center of the bed, closed her eyes. Nude, he got onto the bed and straddled her chest as if he wanted her to use her mouth on him. She opened her eyes in time to see that he was about to strike her. She screamed—just as his fist chopped her chin, split her lip, broke a couple of her teeth, and knocked her unconscious. Breathing heavily, muttering, giggling, he pummeled her face, breasts, and stomach. He used his fists and open hands and fingernails. His climax was spontaneous and intense. Then, whimpering, he washed the blood off his hands and chest. He dressed and left the room and walked out of the hotel into the wind and snow.

That night he slept well.

The telephone woke him at nine o'clock. It wasn't Hennings, as he expected it to be. The voice was cool, businesslike, and yet feminine. She identified herself as Evelyn Flessing, personal secretary to Mr. A.W. West of Southampton, Long Island. She said, "Mr. West would like very much to have you to dinner this evening—if you are free, of course."

Although he had never met him, Rice didn't have to ask who A.W. West was. West's grandfather, Edward Wallace West, had been in the oil business in the early days of the Texas fields but was driven out of that racket by John D. Rockefeller's hired thugs. Salvaging only a few million dollars from his oil interests, Edward hired his own thugs, cops, judges and congressmen. Then he bought a railroad. He had learned ruthlessness from Rockefeller, and he proceeded to make tens of millions of dollars out of his many trains, resorting to violence when there was no legitimate way to destroy a competitor. Later, Edward's son, Lawrence Wallace West, moved the family money out of railroads and into aircraft design, production, and sales. During the Second World

War he quadrupled the West fortune. When the Korean War began, Alfred Wallace West, grandson of Edward, was in charge of the wealth, and he expanded the West holdings in war-related industries. He also invested in Las Vegas hotels and casinos when he foresaw that the desert town would become the richest resort in the United States. Booming gambling revenues, munitions sales, and profits from a dozen other industries swelled the West fortune past the billion-dollar mark in 1962. And now the name A.W. West was synonymous with the kind of superwealth unknown before the twentieth century; it was as common and revered a name in banking circles as were Rockefeller, Getty, Hughes, Rothschild, and a handful of others.

Evelyn Flessing said, "Mr. Rice?"

He knew this was not a hoax. Hennings was the only one who knew where he was staying—and Hennings was utterly without humor. "Why would A.W. West want to have dinner with me?"

"You've written a book that interests him a great deal."

"I see."

"Then you'll join him for dinner?"

"Yes. Certainly. I would be delighted."

"Mr. West's limousine will be at your hotel at five-thirty."

After the woman hung up, Rice tried to call Hennings, but Scott was unavailable. He had left a message: "Have a pleasant dinner in Southampton."

What in the hell was going on?

What did it *mean*?

Had Hennings read the book? Apparently.

Had he passed it on to West? Obviously.

Had a busy man like A.W. West taken the time to read the script, virtually overnight? So it seemed.

Why?

The next eight hours passed slowly. He paced around the room, switched on the television, switched it off, paced, switched the set on again . . . He ate two lunches in the hotel coffee shop, came back to his room, paced. He snacked on peanuts and would have devoured time if it had been edible.

At five-thirty, when the Phantom IV Rolls-Royce arrived, Rice was waiting for it. He identified himself to the chauffeur who came around the car to greet him, and he allowed the rear passenger door to be opened and closed for him. He was conscious of people looking at him as no one had ever looked at him before, and he felt giddy.

Behind the wheel once more, the chauffeur put down the electrically operated glass partition between the driver's and the passenger's compartments. He showed Rice the small bar—ice, glasses, mixers, four whiskies—that was hidden in the back of the front seat by a sliding chrome panel. To the left of the bar another panel concealed a small television. "If you wish to speak to me," the chauffeur said, "push the silver intercom button. I can hear you, sir, only when the button is depressed."

"Fine," Rice said, numbed.

Leaving Manhattan, they crawled with the rush-hour traffic. Once on the superhighway, however, they *moved,* doing nearly twice the posted speed limit. They passed four police cruisers, but were not stopped. At seven-thirty they entered the oak-framed drive that led up a gentle slope to the West mansion.

The house loomed like an ultra-expensive Swiss hotel or clinic. Warm yellow light spilled from fifty windows and painted the snow-skinned lawn. Inside, a doorman took Rice's coat, and a butler showed him to the study where A.W. West was waiting for him.

West *looked* like a billionaire. He didn't appear to be some sort of gangster, as Onassis did, and he didn't look like a high school principal, as David Rockefeller did; nor did he have that prim, asexual, acidic manner that made Getty seem like a Calvinist fire-and-brimstone preacher. West was tall, silver-haired, slim. He had dark eyes and a deep tan. His smile was broad and genuine. He was obviously a man who enjoyed life, enjoyed spending money every bit as much as he liked making it.

In the great man's company Rice felt awkward and insignificant. But before long they were chatting animatedly, as if they were old friends. At eight-thirty they went into the main dining room, where two maids and a butler served dinner. It was the best meal Rice had ever eaten, although later he could not recall what most of the dishes had been. He remembered only the conversation: they discussed his book, and West praised it chapter by chapter; they discussed politics, and West agreed with him entirely. A.W. West's approval was to Rice what a voice from a burning bush might have been to a religious man. He no longer felt awkward and insignificant, and he did not overeat.

After dinner they went to the library to have brandy and cigars. When he had lit the cigars and poured brandy, West said, "You haven't asked why Scott sent me your book, why I read it, or why you're here."

"I thought you'd get around to that in your own time."

"And so I have."

Rice, growing tense again, tasted his brandy and waited.

"It's often said that I'm one of the six or seven most powerful men in the country. Do you believe that?"

"I suppose I do."

"Most people think I can buy and do whatever I want. But even a billionaire's power is finite—unless he's willing to risk everything."

Rice said, "I don't understand what you're getting at."

"I'll give you an example." West put his cigar in an ashtray and folded his hands on his stomach. His feet were propped on a green-velvet-covered footstool. "In 1960 I was determined John Kennedy would never sit in the White House. He was soft on Communism, an admirer of Roosevelt's socialism, and a fool who refused to see Communists in the black equal-rights crusades." West's face was red beneath his tan. "In order to stop Kennedy, I channeled three million dollars into various political organizations. I wasn't alone. Friends of mine did nearly as much. Kennedy won just the same. Then we had the Bay of Pigs, the Berlin Wall, missiles in Cuba, the Nuclear Test Ban Treaty, race riots . . . Anyway, it was clear that Kennedy was destroying this country. And it was also clear that even a man of my power and wealth couldn't keep the Irish bastard from serving a second term. So I had him killed."

Rice couldn't believe what he had just heard. Gaping, he waited for West to smile, waited for him to say it was a joke.

West didn't smile. "I wasn't the only one involved. I can't take all the credit. Hennings was part of it. And two other men."

Rice shook his head and repeated the litany which the American people had been taught by television, radio, and newspapers: "Lee Harvey Oswald was a psychotic, a loner, one man with one gun."

"Oswald *wasn't* very stable," West agreed. "But he wasn't even slightly psychotic. He was a sometimes CIA agent, a scapegoat. He never pulled the trigger."

"But the Warren Commission—"

"Wanted to reassure the public, and quickly. Those men *wanted* to believe in Oswald. Investigators often prove what they want to prove. They're blinded by their own precepts."

Andrew Rice quivered inside. He felt weak, faint, almost giddy. He *wanted* to believe West, for if one could assassinate a President and get away with it, the future of the United States was not, would never be again, in the hands of men who were in sympathy with the worldwide Communist movement. If men of great wealth, those who had the most to lose in a Communist takeover, were willing to assume this sort of indirect leadership of the country, leadership through assassination and whatever else was necessary, then democracy and capitalism were safe for an eternity! But it was too good to be true, too easy . . . He said, "It's difficult to believe so many people could be misled."

"Americans are sheep," West said. "They believe what they're told. They don't read. Most of them are interested only in sports, work, families, screwing each other's wives . . . In the vernacular— 'They don't know from nothing.' And they don't want to know from nothing. They're happy with ignorance." He saw that Rice wanted to believe but was having trouble accepting it. "Look, there are enough clues in the Warren Report to convince any reasonable man that Oswald was either part of a conspiracy or a scapegoat. Yet *you* never bothered to study the report and piece together the facts. If *you* accepted the commission's verdict, why shouldn't the average man accept it. You're a *genius,* or near it, and *you* never doubted."

"What clues?" Rice asked.

Leaning forward in his chair so that they were in something of a huddle over the footstools between them, West began to count them off: "One, the autopsy notes were burned. Do you think that's the usual procedure in a murder case?"

"I guess it isn't."

West smiled. "Two. Oswald was given a paraffin test to see if his cheeks held nitrate deposits—which they would have had to hold if he'd recently fired a rifle. The test was negative. In any ordinary case, in any ordinary court, this would probably have cleared him of murder. Three. The first medical report from Parkland Hospital, later confirmed by autopsy, said the President was shot in the temple. The report still stands. Yet the commission decided that Oswald shot the President in the back of the neck. One bullet?"

Rice said nothing. He was sweating.

Caught up in his argument, smiling, West said, "Four. Julia Ann Mercer, resident of Dallas, observed Jack Ruby debark from a truck and climb that grassy knoll carrying what appeared to be a rifle wrapped in newspapers. Subsequent to the assassination, she tried to report Ruby to the FBI. We had men in the FBI, and she was ignored. The next day, as you know, Ruby murdered Oswald. Five. The Zapruder film shows that the fatal shot slammed the President backward and to his left. The laws of physics insist that the bullet came from in front and to the right of him. The grassy knoll. Yet we're told he was shot from behind. Six. A Dallas businessman named Warren Reynolds saw the man who shot Officer Tippit and chased him for approximately one block. He informed the FBI that the man who had shot Tippit was not Oswald. Two days later Reynolds was shot in the head by an unknown assailant. He survived. FBI men visited him in the hospital, and when he could talk again he had decided that it was Oswald who had shot Tippit. Domingo Benavides was only a few yards from Tippit when Tippit was shot. Benavides described the assailant as a man who did not even vaguely resemble Oswald. He was not asked to testify before the commission. Acquilla Clemons, another police witness, saw Tippit's killer and gave a description matching that supplied independently by Benavides. She was not called to testify before the commission. Mr. Frank Wright, whose wife called the ambulance for Tippit, was adamant that Oswald was not Tippit's killer. He was not called before the Warren Commission. A waitress, whose vantage point for the Tippit killing was not nearly so good as that of Benavides or the others, became the state's star witness. Even she could not identify Oswald, according to testimony in the commission report—yet in the summary the commission says she *did* positively identify Oswald." He was still smiling. "Did you bother to read the report and locate this kind of material? There are hundreds of things like it."

Rice licked his lips. His throat was dry. He was so excited he could barely speak. "No. I didn't look. I never looked."

"And if you still doubt me," West said smugly, "one more thing. Lee Harvey Oswald's Marine records, and testimony of friends he made in the Marines, show that he was an abysmal marksman barely able to pass his requirements. Yet the commission wants us to believe that he fired at a moving target, aiming through an opening in a tree's foliage, a situation that allowed him eight-tenths of a second to aim and fire. And he was using a mail-order rifle." He laughed. "The commission asked three Master riflemen to re-create the assassination, just to show that it could be done as the commission said it had been done. The Masters used the Mannlicher-Carcano rifle Oswald had used, but only after the telescopic sight was remounted."

Rice blinked. "Remounted?"

"The sight wasn't aligned with the barrel and, therefore, whatever one saw through the telescope was not what the barrel was pointing at. We made a mistake planting the Mannlicher-Carcano. We should have made certain the gun at least *could* have been used for the job even if it wasn't. But it worked out well enough."

"The Master riflemen," Rice reminded him.

"Oh, yes. After the telescopic sight had been remounted, the three Masters tried their hands at a re-creation. They were placed on a platform half as high as the sixth-floor window from which Lee Oswald supposedly fired the shot. Their target was not moving, while Oswald's target had been moving. They were allowed all the time they wanted to line up a shot—not eight-tenths of a second, as Oswald supposedly had. Their target was more than twice as large as the President's head had been. You know what? None of them could kill the target—or even come close to killing it." He sighed and leaned back in his chair, picked up his cigar. "There was no need to make a perfect job of it. The files of evidence—which the public has been told again and again contain nothing that hasn't already been told—were sealed in the National Archives and will not be made public until the year 2039. This is for reasons of national security, we're told. And even then, even when they're told that worthless evidence must be kept secret for seventy-five years, the sheep suspect nothing."

Rice finished his brandy in one swallow.

"Do you believe me now?" West asked.

"Yes."

West let smoke out through his nostrils. "I have convinced my associates that we must not waste the contacts and the expertise that we developed while planning and executing the Kennedy assassination. We must organize, establish an underground apparatus—what I like to call The Committee. We must solidify our gains and protect them. And we must look for a new, profitable—operation. Operations. We must use The Committee as if it were a stock-investment plan."

"Other assassinations?" Rice said weakly.

"If it comes to that, yes. But there are other tools. If we can gain even partial control of the FBI and CIA, we ought to be able to engineer events that will keep the Communist sympathizers out of office in the first place. We can use federal officers to harass them. We can put federal taps on their telephones. We can shadow them every minute of the day. If a candidate has a mistress—or some other dark secret—we'll find it and use it to make him drop out of the race even before the primary elections are over."

"And where do I come in?"

Finishing his brandy, West said, "We need someone to run the day-to-day affairs of The Committee. Someone who is dedicated to this country, someone who hates, as we do, the Communist conspiracy. We need a man who is intelligent, as brilliant a man as we can find. He must be willing to take big risks. He must be ruthless. And he must be a man who has no public identity, because we want to build him an identity as one of the foremost liberal thinkers of his day."

"Liberal?" Rice said, perplexed.

"Camouflage," West said. "He'll be a double agent, so to speak."

"But I've written this book—"

"As yet unpublished."

"You mean—destroy it?"

"Do you mind?"

"I guess not. But the articles in Scott's magazines—"

"For all practical purposes, no one reads them. And certainly, no one remembers who wrote them. Scott will burn all unsold issues that contain your articles. Most people who subscribe to the magazines probably throw their copies away. And even if someone runs across one of the essays after you've been established as a liberal theorist, you can blush and say it was the work of a younger and less sensible Andy Rice. Easy."

"May I have more brandy?"

"Help yourself."

They were silent for a few minutes.

Then Rice said, "I'm interested."

"I knew you would be."

"But you risked so much! You told me all of this without being sure I'd want to get involved. You told me *you* set up Kennedy's assassination and—"

"No risk," West said. "If you'd been appalled, if you hadn't wanted to be a part of The Committee, we'd have killed you."

Rice shivered. "I see."

West poured himself another brandy. "Well! Shall we get down to specifics?"

His heart hammering, Andrew Rice nodded, sipped his brandy, and listened to A.W. West reshape his life.

"Mr. Rice?"

Startled, Rice bit his fingers as they were shoving a chocolate-covered marshmallow cookie into his mouth. He grunted with pain. He looked up, but there was no one else in his office.

"Mr. Rice?"

Miss Priestly.

The intercom.

He pushed the button. "What is it?"

"The list just arrived, sir."

"List?"

"The list of federal marshals you asked me to get from the Justice Department, Mr. Rice."

"Oh, yes. Bring it in, please."

She brought it in, and after she had gone he picked up the white telephone and dialed Miss Rockwalt in the CIA file room out in Virginia. He said, "This is the Spokesman."

"Yes, sir."

"I've got a list of names for you. Pencil handy?"

"Go ahead."

"They're all federal marshals assigned to the Washington area." He read off eighty names. "I want an address for each man. I want to know if he lives alone or with someone. I want his age, physical description, everything that you can get. You can call me at the usual number. I'll be here until seven o'clock this evening."

"It may take longer than that, sir," Miss Rockwalt said.

"Then I'll wait here until you've called."

"No later than nine."

"Every minute counts, Miss Rockwalt."

He hung up.

He ate another cookie.

He looked at his watch.

Was David Canning dead by now?

Washington to Honolulu

After McAlister had gone, David Canning spread dropcloths around the schefflera, mixed up a quart of Malathion solution, protected his eyes with ski goggles, and sprayed the tree to prevent a recurrence of the mealybugs. One pint of solution remained, and he poured that into the potting soil to kill any insect eggs that might be there.

While the insecticide dripped slowly from the sharp tips of the schefflera leaves, Canning sat at the kitchen table and wrote a note to the cleaning woman who came in twice a week. If he had to be gone more than seven or eight days, she would have to know how to mist and water the plant. He didn't want to come home and find it yellowed, spotted, and wilted.

In a strange way he felt responsible for the tree. His was more than the sense of responsibility that a man should have for *any* living thing. This was specific. It was personal. Indeed, there was something almost paternal about it; Mike had observed as much when he had come to visit his father two weeks after Canning had moved into the apartment.

"You act as if it's a child," Mike had said, amused.

"There's more to plants than most people realize. I swear that sometimes the damned tree seems—aware, conscious. In its own way."

"You've been reading books. Talk to your plants. Play some classical music for them. That kind of thing."

"I know it sounds crazy—"

"I'm not criticizing. I'm just surprised. I didn't know they taught you reverence for life in the CIA."

"Please, Mike."

"Sorry. I'll keep my opinions to myself."

"I never had to accept the prevailing philosophy of the agency in order to work there."

"Sure."

"I mean it."

"Sure. Okay. Can we talk about something else?"

The way Canning saw it, he had bought the tree and brought it here, and he was the one trying to make it flourish inside of four walls and under a roof where it had never been meant to grow. He had a duty to make every effort to keep it in good health, in return for the beauty that it added to his world and the peace of mind it gave him. He had an unspoken covenant with the tree, and his promise was his self-respect.

Or was he kidding himself? Was his caring for the tree merely an attempt, unconsciously motivated, to atone in some small way for having been a failure as a husband and father? Was he trying to make up for having destroyed his marriage and for having ruined his own children? Was he desperately trying to convince himself that he was not a cold, burnt-out, emotionless son of a bitch?

Don't be so hard on yourself, he thought.

Was it your fault, he asked himself, that Irene became a frigid, nagging bitch? To make her want him again, he paid her every imaginable form of tribute: praise, respect, love, romance, patience, tenderness, gifts and gifts and more gifts. He was a good lover; his own satisfaction mattered less to him than did hers. But because they did not enjoy a natural and mutual lust, because he always had to finesse her into bed with carefully thought-out game plans, his love soon became cynical, his respect feigned, and his praise as hollow as the chambers of the heart.

But to pretend that sex was their only failure was not fair to Irene. They had drifted apart both in and out of the bedroom—and they had become strangers to their children, as well. Yet, as his father had taught him, and as he had learned from the examples provided by his father's friends, he had given his family all of the important things: a good home in a fine neighborhood, a swimming pool in the backyard, a nice school for the kids, allowances for the kids and money for their clarinet lessons and ballet school and baseball camp, the security of a substantial bank account, new cars, membership in a country club, an expensive vacation every year . . . If he had provided all of this and yet the four of them were strangers who merely boarded under one roof, then he had not fully understood his father and had gone wrong somewhere, somehow.

But what was the answer? Could it be explained by the usual pop sociology and pop psychology? Had he provided all the material comforts and then failed to give them love? Had he not managed to communicate to Irene and the children the things he felt in his heart? Had he and Irene been trapped by conventional man-woman roles that stifled their relationship? Had he been a male chauvinist pig without wanting to be, without knowing that he was? Had he walked along the generation gap, his kids on one side and he on the other, without understanding that it was a vast canyon and not just a gully? Running missions for the agency, he had been away from home for one and two months at a time, six months out of twelve. Mike and Terri were adults by the time he received the White House assignment. Should he have been with them more time than he had been when they were young, to serve as an example and as a source of authority? Should he have been home every night to comfort Irene, to share the triumphs and defeats and irritations of daily life? Had his prolonged absences—and perhaps even the sometimes ugly nature of his job—been the cause of the alienation within his family? And if that were true, then wasn't he responsible, after all, for the withering of Irene's desire?

He felt very much alone.

He was adrift. Moving aimlessly toward an unknown future. He had no one. No one. And nothing. Nothing at all.

Except Dragonfly.

He finished the note to the cleaning woman, left it in the center of the kitchen table, switched off the fluorescent lights, and went into the living room. He took up the dropcloths, folded them, and put them away. He called a taxi service and asked to have a cab waiting out front at three-fifteen. Then he went into the bedroom and packed two suitcases.

After he had changed out of his jeans into a pale-brown suit, yellow shirt, brown tie, and leather shoulder holster, he took his gun out of the top drawer of his bureau. It was a nickel-finished Colt Government Model .45 Automatic with an eight-and-a-half-inch overall length and a five-inch barrel. Weighing only thirty-nine ounces, it was perfect for use with a shoulder holster. The sights were fixed, of square Partridge design, and glareproof. Slanted ramp-style, the forward sight caught the light and yet allowed for an easy draw. Canning's holster, which snapped open from sideways pressure and "sprung" the pistol into his hand, thus accommodating a barrel lengthened by a silencer, made the draw even easier. The Colt's magazine held seven standard .45 Auto cartridges, not the most powerful ammunition made, but sufficient. More men in the counterintelligence services of all nations had been killed with this handgun than with any other weapon. Canning had killed nine of them himself: two Russians, two Poles, two Chinese, and three East Germans.

He often wondered why he was able to kill with such complete professional detachment, but he had never found the answer. And in his darkest moments, he thought that a murderer who suffered no remorse should expect to raise a family as alienated as his own.

Struggling to avoid that sort of despair, he took the precision-machined silencer from the bureau drawer and screwed it onto the Colt's barrel. The silencer was five inches long and filled with a new, resilient wadding material that made it one hundred percent effective for at least thirty rounds.

He looked at his watch: three o'clock.

Time to get moving.

He pressed the pistol into his holster and distributed three spare magazines, all fully loaded, in his pockets. He reached for the gun, touched the stock, and smiled as the weapon popped into his right hand. He brought it out, flicked off the safety, studied it for a few seconds, and returned it to the holster.

Once again, he was a field op.

He felt considerably younger than he had when he'd gotten up this morning.

He turned out the lamp and carried his suitcases into the living room, where he suddenly remembered that he hadn't locked the kitchen door. His apartment had two entrances: one off the third-floor landing that was common to two other apartments, and a private entrance from the courtyard by way of a set of switchback stairs. He had used the private entrance this morning when he'd gone out for a quart of milk, before the rain had begun. He put the suitcases down and went to lock up.

Turning the knob on the kitchen door, intending to open it and latch the outer storm door, Canning saw two men enter the courtyard through the archway in the alley wall. The kitchen door was centered with four panes of glass; therefore, he could look through the stoop railing and straight down into the courtyard. He let go of the knob. He knew these men—not who they were but what they did. They were both tall, solidly built, dressed in dark suits and raincoats and matching rumpled rainhats. They paused inside the arch and looked around the courtyard to see if they were being observed.

Twisting the lock shut, Canning stepped quickly away from the door before they could look up and see him.

Lightning shredded the purple-black sky, and a frenetic luminescence pulsed throughout the dark kitchen. The ensuing thunder was like a shotgun blast in the face.

Canning hurried to the living-room windows and cautiously parted the heavy rust-colored velvet drapes that had come with the apartment. Sheets of rain washed the street, made the pavement glisten, boiled and foamed in the gutters, and drummed on the roofs of parked cars. Across the street a blue Ford LTD was at the curb, its parking lights glowing, the windshield wipers beating steadily. From this distance, veiled by the rain, the driver was only a black and nearly formless mass behind the wheel. He was looking out of his side window, looking directly at the apartment house: his face was a pale blur between his dark raincoat and his rainhat. Canning looked up and down the street, but he saw no one else.

By now the two men in the courtyard would have started up the steps toward the kitchen entrance.

He left the windows and went to the front door. He took the Colt .45 from its holster, carefully opened the door, and stepped onto the landing. It smelled faintly of the lemon-oil polish that the superintendent used on the oak banisters. Leaning against the railing, Canning looked down to the bottom of the stairwell and saw that it was deserted. He had expected that much, for they wouldn't want to make a hit in a public corridor if there was a chance they could take him in the privacy of his own apartment.

Listening to an inner clock that was ticking like the timer on a bomb, he went back into the living room, closed the door and locked it. He reached for the wall switch and turned out the overhead light—and now the entire apartment was cast in darkness.

He listened.

Nothing.

Yet.

He holstered the pistol and picked up the suitcases. He carried them into the bedroom and shoved them into a closet. Leaving the closet open, he walked back to the doorway and stood half in the bedroom and half in the living room. He drew the Colt once more and stood very still, listening.

Nothing.

He waited.

Something. Or was it? Yes, there it was again. A rasping sound. Not loud. Like a plastic credit card or some more sophisticated tool working between a doorjamb and a lock. It stopped. Silence. Ten seconds. Fifteen. Were they inside? No, too quiet. Twenty . . . And then more rasping, very soft and distant . . . They were good, but they weren't good enough. A fairly loud *click!* Silence again. Half a minute of dead air: just the rain hissing on the roof, hissing like background static when the radio dial moves off a channel. Then a creak. The kitchen door opening . . .

Canning went to the bedroom closet, stepped inside, and quietly slid the door shut in front of him. He held the Colt at his side, aimed at the door, gut level.

He didn't want to kill anyone, not even one of these fanatical bastards who called themselves Committeemen. He hoped they'd take one look through the apartment and decide he wasn't there. They hadn't come to get anything but him; therefore, if they thought he was gone, they would have no reason to search through drawers, cupboards, and closets. No reason. No reason whatsoever. If they knew enough to come after him, they also knew he was scheduled to leave Washington within the hour. They couldn't know which airport or airline he was using, for if they had known, they would have made the hit at the terminal or would have planted a bomb aboard his flight. Just as McAlister had said. So they must have come here out of desperation. Because they had tumbled to his identity so late in the game, this was their only chance to nail him. They would half expect him to be gone. When they found the rooms dark and deserted, they'd shrug and walk out and—

The closet door slid open.

Shit! Canning thought.

He fired two silenced shots.

The Committeeman grunted softly, one word, a name: *"Damon!"* He must have been calling his partner. But he spoke so softly that even Canning could barely hear him. Then he doubled over, clutching at his stomach, and began to fall into the closet.

Moving quickly, stealthily, Canning caught the dead man and eased him to the floor. He let go of the corpse, stepped over it, and went out into the bedroom.

The other agent wasn't there.

Canning listened and heard nothing.

He went into the living room and, when he saw that the front door was standing wide open just twenty-five feet away, faded into the shadows by the bookcases. He hesitated for a moment and was about to move toward the door—then held his breath as the second agent came back in from the landing. The man—Damon?—closed and locked the door.

"Freeze," Canning said.

Because he already had his gun drawn, Damon evidently decided that he could regain the advantage. His decision was made with the rapid thought and fluid reaction that identified a first-rate agent. He turned and got off three silenced shots in a smooth ballet-style movement.

But he was shooting blind. The bullets were all high and wide of their mark. They ripped—with dull reports—into the spines of the hardbound books which lined the wall shelves.

Also at a disadvantage because of the extremely poor light, Canning fired twice, even as the other man was finishing his turn and getting off his third shot.

Damon cried out, fell to his right, and rolled clumsily behind the sofa. He was hit, probably high in the left arm or in that shoulder.

Canning went down on one knee. He heard Damon curse. Softly. But with pain. Then: deep breathing, a scuffling noise . . .

"I don't want to have to kill you," Canning said.

Damon rose up and fired again.

It was close—but not nearly close enough.

Canning held the Colt out in front of him and moved silently through the shadows. He crouched behind an easy chair and braced the barrel of the pistol along the chair's padded arm. He watched the sofa.

Overhead, thunder cracked and the rain battered the roof with greater fervor.

Ten seconds passed.

Ten more.

A minute.

Suddenly the agent scuttled out from behind the sofa and waddled toward the gray light that spilled in from the kitchen. At the doorway he was perfectly silhouetted.

Canning shot him.

Damon's right leg buckled under him, and he collapsed onto the kitchen floor, failing to choke back a scream.

Cautiously but swiftly, Canning got up from behind the easy chair and went after him.

Damon rolled onto his back and fired through the living-room doorway.

As he reached the kitchen Canning saw the gun coming up at him, and he threw himself to the left. When he heard the *whoosh!* of the silencer an instant later, he pitched himself back to the right and fired twice, at point-blank range, straight down into the man who lay before him.

When he finally let out his breath, Canning sounded like a bellows.

Lightning flashed again, revealing the bloodied body and the open, sightless eyes.

Canning took the magazine out of the Colt and replaced it with a fresh one. He slipped the pistol back into its holster.

"Dad, have you ever killed anyone?"

"What kind of question is that?"

"Well, you work for the CIA."

"Not everyone at the agency wears a cloak and carries a dagger, Mike. Most of us just sit at desks and page through foreign technical journals, looking for bits and pieces of data, clues that someone else can work into a puzzle."

"You're not a desk man."

"I'm not?"

"You aren't the type."

"Well, it isn't easy to—"

"Have you ever killed anyone?"

"Suppose I have."

"Suppose."

"And I'm not saying I have."

"Just suppose."

"Do you think it would have been in self-defense—or do you think your father's a hired assassin?"

"Oh, it would be in self-defense."

"Well, thanks."

"Technically."

"Technically?"

"Well, Dad, if you'd chosen to work for someone besides the CIA, if you were a civilian, then foreign undercover agents wouldn't have any reason to kill you. Right? If you were a lawyer or a teacher, your job wouldn't require you to kill anyone in self-defense. So even if you did kill only in self-defense—well, you chose the job that made it necessary . . . So you must have enjoyed it."

"You think I could enjoy *killing a man?"*

"That's what I'm asking."

"Jesus!"

"I'm not saying it was a conscious enjoyment. It's more subtle than that."

"I've never enjoyed it!"

"Then you admit to murder?"

"No such thing."

"Wrong term, I guess. You admit to killing."

"We agreed this was a purely theoretical discussion."

"Sure."

"Mike, you try to see everything as black and white. The agency isn't like that. Neither is life. There are shades of gray, shadows. I

*don't see any point discussing this with you. You don't seem mature
enough to think about those grays and shadows."*

"Sure. You're right."

"Don't be so damned smug. You only think you've won."

*"Gee, Dad, I didn't know this was a contest. I didn't know I could
win or lose."*

"Sure."

Canning stepped over the corpse, went to the kitchen door, and
looked down at the courtyard. The two potted cherry trees shivered
in the wind. So far as he could see, no other men were waiting out
there.

He locked the door, reached for the light switch, thought better
of that, got a flashlight from a drawer by the sink, and went to
search the dead men. Being careful not to get blood on his clothes,
Canning first attended to the agent who was sprawled on the
kitchen floor. He found a wallet full of papers and credit cards in
the name of Damon Hillary. There was also a thin plastic case
which was full of business cards for Intermountain Incorporated.
Intermountain was an agency front. He went into the bedroom and
dragged the other man out of the closet. This one, he discovered,
was named Louis Hobartson and was also an employee of
Intermountain.

In the bathroom he washed the blood off his hands. He used a
wad of tissues to wipe smears of blood from the wallets, flushed the
tissues down the commode. He checked himself in the mirror to be
certain that his suit hadn't been soiled.

He looked at his watch: three-fifteen.

In the bedroom again, he neatly laid back the covers on the bed,
lifted the mattress, and slipped both wallets far back on top of the
box springs. He dropped the mattress, pulled the bedclothes in
place, and smoothed out the wrinkles. Now, if the Committeemen
retrieved their men before he had time to tell McAlister to come
after them, Hillary and Hobartson would not disappear without a
trace.

He took his suitcases out of the closet and carried them back into
the living room.

He took his raincoat from the front closet and struggled into it
on his way to the living-room windows. Parting the velvet drapes
half an inch, he saw that the LTD was still parked across the street,

the driver still looking this way. Canning glanced at his wristwatch: three-eighteen. When he looked at the street again, a taxi was just angling in beside the curb downstairs. The cabbie gave three long signals with the horn.

Canning left the apartment, locked up, carried his bags downstairs. At the foyer door he hesitated, then opened it, pushed through, and hurried to the cab. Without getting out in the rain, the cabbie had thrown open the rear door. It was a high-roof, British-style taxi; therefore, Canning didn't have to lift his suitcases in ahead of him. He stepped in, cases in hand, and sat down, wondering if the man in the LTD would be crazy enough to try to shoot him right out here on the street.

Reaching over the front seat, the cabbie pulled the door shut for him. "The dispatcher said National Airport."

"That's right. I have a four o'clock flight."

"You cut it close."

"Nice tip if we make it."

"Oh, there's no chance we'll miss."

As they pulled away from the curb, Canning saw the LTD fall in behind them.

That's all right, he thought. The bastard can't drive and shoot at the same time.

To make a successful hit in a public place like an air terminal, you had to have at least two men: one to do the shooting and one to either cause a distraction or drive the getaway car. This man in the LTD could do nothing but follow him, see which flight he boarded, and report back to the boss.

Canning realized, however, that The Committee would probably soon learn the Otley identity and his entire itinerary. Within an hour after he left Washington, agents in California—perhaps the same ones who had murdered the Berlinsons—would be outlining a plan to kill him when he changed planes in Los Angeles.

At four-ten the jet lifted off, and by four-twenty it was above the storm. From his window seat Canning watched the city, the countryside, and then the clouds fall away from him.

"Suppose you'd been a German during the Second World War, someone who had the opportunity to get close to Hitler with a gun. Would you have shot him?"

"Gee, Dad, I thought you didn't want to talk about this sort of thing any more."

"Would you have shot Hitler?"

"This is stupid. Hitler was dead before I was born."

"Would you have shot him?"

"Would you have shot Genghis Khan?"

"You have two possible answers, Mike. Say yes, and you'd be admitting that given the right conditions, you could kill a man. Say no, and you'd be implying that you have no duty to protect the lives of innocent people whom you might have saved."

"I don't get your point."

"Of course you do."

"Tell me anyway."

"The right thing would have been to kill Hitler and save the millions of people who died because of him. Yet, in shooting him, you'd still be a murderer. In other words, a moral act is often a compromise between the ideal and the practical."

Mike said nothing.

"It seems to me that morality and expediency are two sides of the same coin, a very thick coin that more often than not lands with both faces showing."

"Do you feel very moral when you kill?"

"We're not talking about me or—"

"Oh, this is still 'theoretical,' is it?"

"Mike—"

"Hitler was one of a kind, Dad. A man as dangerous and crazy as he was, a man who needs killing as badly as he needed it, comes along once in a century. You're trying to take a unique case like Hitler and generalize from it."

"But he wasn't unique. The world's full of Hitlers—but few of them ever make it to the top."

"Thanks to men like you, I suppose."

"Perhaps."

"Do you feel heroic when you kill one of your little Hitlers?"

"No."

"I'll bet you do."

"I'm . . . surprised. Shocked. I'm just beginning to see how much you . . . hate me."

*"I don't hate you, Dad. I just don't feel much of anything at all
where you're concerned, not anything, not one way or the other."*

An hour into the flight, Canning gave his forged State Department credentials to a stewardess and requested that she pass them
along to the pilot. "I'd like to speak with him when he has a few
minutes to spare."

Five minutes later the stewardess returned. "He'll see you now,
Mr. Otley."

Canning followed her up front to the serving galley. The
galley—now that the flight attendants were dispensing before-
dinner drinks from a bar cart in the aisle—was reasonably quiet.

The pilot was a tall, paunchy, balding man who said his name
was Giffords. He returned Canning's papers, and they shook
hands. "What can I do for you, Mr. Otley?"

"If I read the departures board correctly back at National, this
flight goes all the way to Honolulu."

"That's right," Giffords said. "We let off a few passengers in
L.A., take on a few others, and refuel."

"How long is the layover?"

"One hour."

"Are you booked solid for Honolulu?"

"We're usually overbooked. And there's a waiting list for the
cancellations. We hardly ever have an empty seat on the Hawaiian
run."

"I'd like you to *make* an empty seat for me."

"You want to bump someone?"

"If that's the only way, yes."

"Why is this so urgent?"

"I'm sorry, Captain Giffords, but I can't say. This is highly
classified State Department business."

"That's not good enough."

Canning thought for a moment. Then: "I'm carrying an extremely important message to a man in China. It can't be delivered
by phone, mail, or telegram. It can't go in the scheduled weekly
diplomatic pouch. I didn't use a government plane because it was
easier to keep the mission a secret if I flew on civil airlines.
Somehow the wrong people learned I was the messenger, and they
want to stop me at any cost. An attempt was made on my life just

before I left Washington. It failed only because they didn't have time to set it up properly. But if I change planes in L.A., as planned—"

"They *will* have had time to set it up there, and they'll nail you," Giffords said.

"Exactly."

"This is pretty wild stuff for me," Giffords said.

"Believe me, I don't find it routine either."

"Okay. You'll have a seat to Hawaii."

"Two other things."

Giffords grimaced. "I was afraid of that."

"First of all, I have two suitcases in the baggage compartment. They're tagged for Los Angeles."

"I'll instruct the baggage handlers to retag them and put them aboard again."

"No. I want to get off for them and bring them back to the check-in counter myself."

"Why?"

"I've got to try to mislead the men who're waiting for me. If they know I'm continuing on to Hawaii, they'll just set up something in Honolulu."

Giffords nodded. "Okay. What's the other thing?"

"When we land, get in touch with the airport security office and tell them there's a damned good chance that the next Pan Am flight to Tokyo will have a bomb aboard."

Giffords stiffened. "Are you serious?"

"That's the flight I'm supposed to take out of L.A."

"And these people, whoever wants to stop you, would kill a planeload of innocent people? Just to get you?"

"Without hesitation."

Watching Canning closely, Giffords frowned. He wiped one hand across his face. But he failed to wipe the frown away. "Let me see your papers again."

Canning gave him the State Department documents.

After he had looked those over, Giffords said, "You have a passport, Mr. Otley?"

Canning gave him that.

Once he'd paged slowly through the passport, Giffords handed it back and said, "I'll do what you want."

"Thank you, Captain."

"I hope you realize how far out my neck is stuck."

"You won't get it chopped off," Canning said. "I've been straight with you."

"Good luck, Mr. Otley."

"If I have to rely on luck, I'm dead."

He was the last one off the plane. He took his time strolling the length of the debarkation corridor, and he found his suitcases waiting for him when he reached the baggage carrousel.

Picking up his two pieces of luggage, he turned and looked at the busy crowd ebbing and flowing through the terminal. He paid particularly close attention to everyone in the vicinity of the Pan Am facilities, but he couldn't spot the men who *had* to be watching him—which meant they were damned good.

He turned his back on the Pan Am check-in counter and walked across the terminal toward the main entrance. He walked slowly at first, hoping he could get at least halfway to the doors before he alarmed the Committeemen who were surely watching him. Gradually he picked up speed and covered the last half of the lobby at a brisk walk. He glanced back and saw two obviously distraught men hurrying through the crowd, well behind him. Smiling, he went through the main doors.

Outside, he got into the first taxi in line.

"Where to?" the driver asked. He was a young, mustachioed man with a broad scar on his chin and a broad smile above it.

Canning opened his wallet, which was thickened by five thousand dollars in U.S. currency and Japanese yen. This was the operational fund that McAlister had included in the packet that contained the Otley identification. Canning handed the driver a fifty-dollar bill and said, "There's a hundred more for you if you'll help me."

"I'm no killer."

"You don't have to be."

"Then you name it," he said, folding the bill and thrusting it into his shirt pocket.

"Get moving first."

The driver put the cab in gear and pulled away from the terminal.

Looking through the rear window, Canning saw the two agents hail the next taxi in line.

"We being followed?" the cabbie asked.

"Yes."

"Cops?"

"Does it matter?"

"For one-fifty in cash? I guess it doesn't." He smiled at Canning in the rear-view mirror. "Want me to lose them?"

"No. I want them to follow us. Just keep them from getting too close."

"That cab behind us?"

"That's right." Canning looked back at it again. "Give them all the breaks. It isn't easy to run a tail at night."

"Got you."

"But don't be *too* obvious."

The cabbie said, "Trust me. Where we going?"

"Do you know the Quality Inn on West Century Boulevard?" Canning asked.

"It's a little over a mile from here."

"That's the one."

"Sure. I've taken people there."

"First, I want you to drop me in front of the lobby."

"And then?"

Crisply, succinctly, with his characteristic orderliness, Canning told him the rest of it.

"One of the oldest tricks in the book," the cabbie said, showing his broad white teeth in the mirror.

"You sound like an expert."

"I watch the old movies."

Canning grinned. "Think it'll work?"

"Sure. What you got going for you here's the simplicity of it. These guys won't be looking for anything that uncomplicated."

"No trouble on your end?"

"Easiest money I ever made," the cabbie said.

The other taxi stayed between a hundred and a hundred-fifty yards behind them, nearly far enough back to blend in with the other sets of headlights. Canning had no trouble keeping it in sight because one of its headlamps was dimmer than the other and flickered continuously. Just as, he thought, something about the tail end of this car individualized it and helped the Committeemen to keep it in sight.

"Here we are," the driver said.

"You remember everything?"

"What's to remember?"

Before the screech of the brakes had died away, while the car was still rocking back and forth on its springs, Canning opened the door and got out. He grabbed both suitcases, kicked the door shut, and started toward the lobby entrance. Out of the corner of his eye, he saw the flickering headlight of the other cab, which was now rushing across the motel parking lot.

The super-cooled lobby air snapped whiplike against his sweat-slicked face and sent shivers through him. At the back of his mind, just for a fraction of a second, there was a vivid picture of the dead man lying in blood on his kitchen floor. But the dead man was not Damon Hillary: he was David Canning, himself. He was standing over his corpse, looking down at his own dead body. He had shot himself. One David Canning had killed the other David Canning.

What the hell did that mean?

Forcing himself to walk slowly, he went past the front desk and on across the lobby. He entered a carpeted side corridor and kept going. He moved faster now.

None of the desk clerks called after him. He might have checked in earlier and left his bags in the car until he had eaten dinner. Or perhaps his wife had registered during the afternoon, and he was joining her. Or joining his mistress. Or his girl friend. Whatever the case, because he was tall and handsome and well dressed, he aroused no suspicion.

At the end of the corridor, he climbed a set of stairs, the two suitcases banging against his legs. He stopped at the top to catch his breath, and he looked down to the bottom of the stairwell.

It was silent, empty.

The two agents were either at the front desk or searching frantically through other parts of the motel maze in the hope of finding out which room he had entered.

He had to *move.*

In the second-floor corridor, with closed and numbered doors on both sides, Canning turned left and went to the intersection at the end of that wing. He turned right into another carpeted hall, and it was also silent, deserted. At the next set of stairs, he went back down to the first level, although he was now in a different wing from the motel lobby. He crossed a small concrete foyer that contained a rattling ice machine and two humming, clinking, syncopated soda vendors. Pushing open the outer door, he went into the parking lot at the rear of the motel.

The taxi was waiting there, lights on, engine running, and back door open wide.

Canning threw his suitcases inside, climbed in, closed the door, and laid down on the back seat.

"*Hot-diggity-damn!* So far so good," the driver said with sheer delight.

Massaging his strained, aching arms, Canning said, "Back to the airport. Better move it."

"Sure enough."

After three or four minutes had passed, the cabbie said, "There's no one behind us."

"You're sure?"

"Positive. I've been circling around through these back streets all alone. If anyone was following me, he'd be as obvious as a pimple on Raquel Welch's ass."

Canning sat up. He straightened his suit coat and shirt collar, adjusted the knot in his tie, and shot his cuffs to what he considered the proper one-half inch beyond his coat sleeves. Then he took a hundred dollars from his wallet and gave it to the driver. "You do very good work."

"I told you so. I watch the old movies."

Smiling, Canning said, "Good thing I didn't get a cabdriver who was an opera buff."

"He'd have told you to give yourself up and sing."

Canning winced.

"Well, a pun is *supposed* to be bad."

"It was."

"If you're ever in town again and need to make a fast getaway," the driver said, "don't forget me. Name's Harry Tollins."

"I'll recommend you to all my friends, Harry."

They got back to the airport in plenty of time for Canning to check in at the airline counter and pay for his ticket to Hawaii.

There were even ten minutes for him to take a cup of coffee in the line's VIP lounge before he had to board the plane.

Forty-five minutes after the jet lifted off from Los Angeles International, a stewardess came back the aisle and stopped in front of Canning. "Mr. Otley?"

"Yes?"

She held out a folded sheet of beige stationery. "From Captain Giffords, sir."

"Thank you."

He watched her as she walked back up the aisle; she had long, slim, exceedingly lovely legs. Abruptly, his trousers became too tight in the crotch. He suddenly realized how long it had been since he'd made love to Irene—and how much longer than that since he'd had a fully satisfactory sex life. Forcing himself to look away from her, clearing his throat, he opened the note and read the neatly hand-lettered four-line message:

> Suitcase bomb found in baggage
> compartment of Pan Am's flight
> to Tokyo.
> Safely removed and defused.

He folded the paper and put it in his pocket.

The next time the stewardess came by, he asked her for a Scotch on the rocks. He felt that he could risk at least one small celebration.

When McAlister came on the line from Washington, Canning identified himself and said, "Do you trust your home phone?"

"Not really," McAlister said.

"Then you'd better give me a number where I can reach you, a nice safe phone they'd never think of tapping."

McAlister thought for a moment, then gave Canning another Washington number.

"Will you go there and wait for my call?"

"Yes. But I'll need a while to get there," McAlister said.

Although it was only midnight in Honolulu, it was five hours later than that in Washington. McAlister had probably been asleep when the telephone rang.

Canning said, "An hour?"

"Half that."

"Fine."

Canning hung up and leaned back against the headboard of the hotel bed. He closed his eyes and looked through the stack of file cards in his mind, checking to see if he had remembered everything that he must tell McAlister. Like a dark flood tide, sleep swept up at him. The printing on the imaginary file cards blurred, and the cards themselves began to dissolve into blackness . . .

He quickly opened his eyes, shook his head in an attempt to clear it, got up, went into the bathroom, and splashed cold water in his face. The eyes that looked back at him from the mirror were bloodshot and ringed with loose, dark skin.

Back in the bedroom, he stood at the window and watched the big searchlights at Honolulu Airport, which was less than a mile away. At twelve-thirty he returned to his bed, sat down, picked up the telephone, and placed a call to the number that McAlister had given him half an hour ago.

"David?" McAlister said.

"Yes. Where are you?"

"At my sister-in-law's house," McAlister said. "I don't come here more than once a month. There's no reason for anyone to have a tap on her phone."

"Were you followed?"

"I was, but I shook them."

"You're certain of that?"

"Absolutely. Where are you?"

"Honolulu."

"That's not on the schedule."

"You're telling me?"

"What's happened?"

"My cover's blown."

"It *can't* be!"

Canning explained about the two agents who had come to kill him back in Washington. "You'd better send some men around to take care of the corpses. And if The Committee has already moved them, don't worry. I stripped the bodies of all identification and put everything between the mattress and box springs on my bed. You'll have some nice leads to work on."

"Excellent. I'll have a detail at your place within an hour."

"My cleaning lady comes tomorrow, Friday. She's very neat—and observant. You'll have to see there isn't a trace of blood left behind. Locate every bullet and patch up the holes they made. I used six shots. Four of them are in the dead men. The other two should be in the wall near the front door. The man in the kitchen fired five times. All of the slugs should be in the living room, and I know that three of them are lodged in the bookshelves."

"But how could they tumble to you so *soon?*"

"Maybe you were followed to my apartment."

"I made sure I wasn't."

"You're playing with professionals."

"Look, I found a miniature transmitter attached to the bumper of my Mercedes. I got rid of it before I started for your place. I saw no one following me. I parked four blocks away and walked to your building—and I'm *damned* sure no one tailed me on foot!"

Canning was impressed with McAlister's thoroughness. "Who else knew about me?"

"The President."

"That's all?"

"Andrew Rice was in the Oval Office when I told the President," McAlister said. "Do you think either of them would spread the word?"

"You know both of them better than I do."

McAlister was silent a moment. Then he sighed and said, "One of them might have told a second-level aide."

"And the aide might have told his assistant."

"And the assistant might have told his secretary."

"And somewhere along the line it got to someone who's bent."

"Christ!" McAlister said.

"Spilled milk."

"How does all of this put you in Hawaii?"

Canning outlined the games that he and the taxi driver had played in Los Angeles.

"Then they still think you're in one of the rooms in this Holiday Inn?" McAlister asked.

"Quality Inn. I suppose that's just what they think."

"How many rooms does this motel have?"

"Maybe—three hundred."

"Too many for them to go knocking on doors."

"Exactly."

"So . . . They'll put the motel under surveillance and wait for you to come out." The director laughed softly.

Canning said, "Don't underestimate them. They won't wait there forever. Before long they're going to figure I conned them."

"But they won't know you're in Honolulu."

"No. But they'll pick me up again when I get to Tokyo. There's no question about that. They have to know about my Otley identity by this time."

"You're right, of course," McAlister said resignedly. His pipe-stem rattled against his teeth. Then: "When are you leaving Honolulu?"

Picking up the airline-ticket folder that was lying on the nightstand, next to the telephone, Canning said, "There's a flight to Tokyo leaving here at noon, just about eleven hours from now."

"And when they get on your tail in Tokyo?"

"That's not your worry," Canning said. "It's mine. And I can handle them. But there are three things you're going to have to handle yourself."

"Name them."

"You've got to get hold of my backup man, the interpreter who's waiting for me in Tokyo. Tell him how things have changed and give him my new estimated time of arrival."

"No problem."

"Tell him that he and I are going to have to double up in his room, since any room rented to Otley or Canning is bound to be hit by a Committeeman during the night."

After a brief hesitation, McAlister said, "You're right."

"Number two. We're scheduled to go to Peking aboard that French corporate jet. Will it wait an extra day, now that I'm one day behind schedule?"

"The French are extremely cooperative, especially this company," McAlister said. "I don't foresee any trouble there."

"Make sure they give the plane a thorough search. There might be a bomb aboard it."

"They'll search it. But that probably won't be necessary. I didn't mention the French connection to the President. If there's been a leak to The Committee from someone on the White House staff, it can't have included anything about the French jet." His teeth rattled on his pipestem again. "You said there were three things you wanted me to do."

"Number three: I've got to know who my backup man is. Now that The Committee knows I'm your man, I've got to be sure they don't ring in an imposter when I get to Tokyo."

"The interpreter's name is Tanaka," McAlister said.

"Any identifying marks?"

"Scar toward the left corner of the upper lip. I believe I heard that it was caused by a sliver of broken glass. Perhaps a cut in a bottle fight."

"Anything besides the scar?"

"Mole on the left cheek. Long, thick black hair. Kind of a high-pitched voice, soft-spoken. But don't let that fool you. Physically, mentally, and emotionally, Tanaka's stronger than you would think."

"From the tone of your voice, I gather that you still think Tanaka's going to surprise me."

"Oh, yes."

"How?"

"David, I've told you all that I'm going to tell you. You know enough about Tanaka to keep from falling for some Committeeman trying to pass himself off as your contact. But you don't yet know so much that you'd be a danger to Tanaka if they got their hands on you. Let's keep it that way, okay? Let's keep it on that need-to-know basis."

Reluctantly, Canning said, "All right."

"Good."

"Do you think Tanaka's cover has been blown as thoroughly as mine?" Canning asked.

"Until I told you the name a minute ago, I was the only man who knew Tanaka was involved."

"You didn't tell the President?"

"He didn't ask."

Canning smiled and shook his head. The brief glow of anger he had felt toward the director faded away. "The next worst moment is going to be at the airport in Tokyo. They're bound to be watching for me."

"Do you want me to have the Tokyo police—"

"The last thing we need is a shoot-out," Canning said. "I'll take care of myself at the airport. But once I get out of there, how do I make contact with Tanaka?"

"Go to the Imperial Hotel and check into the room that's been reserved for you in Otley's name. Tanaka will call you there. Don't worry. Even if the other side knows you're staying at the Imperial, they aren't going to try to hit you in the first few minutes after you arrive. They saw what panic bought them when they tried to get to you in Washington. This time they'll be careful, slow, thorough. By the time they're ready to come after you, you'll be hidden away with Tanaka."

Canning thought about it for a moment, stood up, rubbed the back of his neck, and said, "You're probably right."

"You'll be in Peking late Saturday."

And the job wrapped up by Monday morning at the latest, Canning thought hopefully.

"Anything more?" McAlister asked.

"No. That's all."

"Cable me from Peking."

"I will. Upon arrival."

"Goodnight, David."

"Goodnight."

Ten minutes later, having been awake for nearly twenty-four hours, Canning was in bed, curled fetally, fast asleep.

Capitol Heights, Maryland

"This is the house."

"Number checks."

Lights were on downstairs.

The driver pulled to the curb, parked behind a yellow Corvette, and switched off the engine. "How do we operate?"

"As if we're on a case."

"Seems best," said the man in the back seat.

"Neighbors are close here. Can't be much noise."

"There won't be if we use our credentials to get inside," said the man in the back seat.

The driver doused the lights. "Let's go."

At seven-thirty Wednesday evening, Washington time—when David Canning was still high over the Midwest in an airliner on his way to Los Angeles—three men got out of a Ford LTD on a quiet residential street in Capitol Heights, just outside the Washington city limits. In the new autumn darkness, with a light rain drizzling down their raincoats, they went up the walk to the front door of a small, tidy two-story Colonial saltbox-style house. The tallest of the three rang the bell.

In the house a stereo set was playing theme music from a current hit motion picture.

Half a minute passed.

The tall man rang the bell again.

"It's chilly out here," said the man who wore eyeglasses. "I'm sure as hell going to catch pneumonia."

"We'll visit you in the hospital," said the tall one.

"And when I get chilly," said the man in the eyeglasses, "I always have to go to the bathroom."

"Shut the fuck up," said the smallest of the three. He had a thin, nasty voice.

"Well, that's not unusual, is it? Cold air makes lots of people want to go take a piss."

"You're a real hypochondriac. You know that? First it's pneumonia. Then it's bladder problems," said the smallest man.

The tall man said, "Will you two cool it?"

A moment later the porch light came on, blinding them for a second or two, and the door opened.

A tall, beefy, rather good-looking man in his late thirties scrutinized them through the storm-door screen. He had a broad, reddish face with a granite-block chin, sharp mouth, Roman nose, and quick dark eyes under bushy eyebrows. He kept his eyes as narrow as paper cuts while he studied the three of them. "What is it?"

"Are you Carl Altmüller?"

"Yes. Who're you?"

"CIA," the tall man said.

"What do you want here?" Altmüller asked, surprised.

The tall man held his agency credentials up to the screen where Altmüller could see them. "We'd like ten minutes of your time to ask you a few questions."

"About what?"

"A case we're on."

"What case?"

The tall man sighed. "Could we come in and discuss it, please? It's damned chilly out here."

"Amen," said the agent who wore eyeglasses.

Unlocking the storm door and pushing it open for them, Altmüller said, "I don't know any damned thing that could possibly interest the CIA. Now that's a fact."

Stepping inside and following Altmüller down a narrow pine-floored entrance hall, the tall man said, "Well, sir, quite often people know things of which they aren't aware. It's quite likely that something you might find inconsequential, something you saw and which meant nothing to you at the time, will be the exact clue that we've been searching for all along."

In the comfortably furnished living room, an attractive blonde was sitting on one end of the couch. She was wearing a tight blue sweater and a short white skirt; her legs were long and well tanned. She took a sip from an icy drink and smiled at them.

"This is my fiancée," Altmüller said. "Connie Eaton."

"Good evening, Miss Eaton," the tall man said. "I'm sorry to interrupt."

She glanced at Altmüller and then back at the agent. "Oh, that's all right, Mr.—"

"Buell," the tall man said. "Ken Buell."

"Now what's this about?" Altmüller asked, offering them neither chairs nor drinks.

Smiling at the woman, Buell said, "Would you mind going out to the kitchen for a few minutes?"

"Not at all." She stood up and quickly pressed her skirt with her one free hand.

Turning to the agent beside him, Buell said, "Keep Miss Eaton company for a few minutes." When Altmüller started to speak, Buell turned to him and said, "What I've come here to see you about is a top-secret matter. Miss Eaton must not listen in on us. And you must not discuss this with her when we've gone."

Altmüller frowned and said, "I don't understand this."

The woman squeezed his arm and said, "It'll be all right, Carl." She smiled at the agent who wore eyeglasses and said, "The kitchen is this way, Mr.—"

He did not pick up on the cue as Buell had done. Instead, he said, "*God,* it's nice to be in a warm house! The heater isn't working in our car, and I feel like an ice cube." He followed her across the dining room and into the kitchen. He closed the kitchen door behind them.

"Would you just have a seat on the couch, Mr. Altmüller?" Buell asked.

As Altmüller perched on the edge of the couch, the third agent put down the attaché case which he had been carrying and opened it on the coffee table. He took from it a bottle of rubbing alcohol, a cotton pad, a small vial of yellowish serum, and a hypodermic syringe wrapped in a sterilized plastic envelope.

Altmüller's eyes widened. "What's this?"

With that reassuring manner common to the best and worst medical doctors, Buell said, "Mr. Altmüller, you really have nothing at all to worry about. I'm certain you can understand that in a matter like this, with the national security hanging by a thread, extraordinary measures are required."

"What are you talking about? What the fuck are you talking about? What could I have to do with the national security?"

"In time, Mr. Altmüller. I'll explain in time."

Altmüller stood up. "Explain now."

"In a situation like this, when the future of our country is in doubt, we can take no chances," Buell said. "We must—"

"You're talking nonsense," Altmüller said. "I'm not a spy. I'm a nobody. There's nothing I know that—"

"With so much at stake," Buell said, raising his voice slightly, "we must be absolutely sure that you're telling the truth."

"What is that stuff?" Altmüller asked, nodding at the vial. "Is it hyoscine? Amytal? Pentothal?"

"Oh, no," Buell said. "In the agency we are able to take advantage of all the newest discoveries, the latest drugs. This is much more effective than Pentothal."

The third agent broke open the plastic envelope and took out the syringe. He soaked the cotton pad in alcohol and wiped off the membrane that capped the vial. He popped the needle through the membrane and drew yellow fluid into the syringe.

"You need a warrant," Altmüller said belatedly.

"Relax," Buell said.

"The CIA doesn't even have domestic jurisdiction."

"Relax."

His hairline suddenly beaded with perspiration, Altmüller took a step toward the agent who held the needle.

"Sit down," Buell said quietly, coldly.

Numbed by confusion and weakened by fear, Altmüller stared at the silenced pistol that had appeared almost magically in Buell's right hand.

"Sit down."

"No."

"Don't forget your fiancée in the kitchen."

Altmüller glared at him.

"We only want to ask you some questions."

Opening his mouth and then closing it without speaking, Altmüller sat down.

"Roll up your sleeve," Buell said.

Altmüller made no move to obey.

Raising the pistol, Buell put a bullet in the back of the couch, two inches from the big man's shoulder.

Shaken, Altmüller rolled up his sleeve.

The other agent took a length of rubber tubing from the attaché case and tied it tightly around Altmüller's biceps. In seconds the dark vein bulged out of the smooth skin just above the crook of the arm. The agent picked up the syringe, punched the needle through the vein, pulled it back slightly, drew blood into the syringe where the yellow fluid turned orange, then shot the drug into Altmüller's body.

As the smaller agent began to put away the medical equipment, Altmüller looked at Buell and said, "Ask your questions and get the hell out of here."

"The drug won't take effect for another minute or so," Buell said, still covering the big man with the pistol.

A minute late Altmüller's eyelids drooped. His mouth sagged partway open. He leaned back against the couch and let his hands fall, palms up, at his sides. His voice was weak, distant: "Oh . . . Jesus . . . Christ!"

Buell put away his pistol and took a sheet of paper from his wallet. It was a list of forty names. He took a felt-tip pen from his shirt pocket, uncapped it, and held it next to the first name on the list. Standing over Altmüller, he said, "Do you know a federal marshal named Frank Jaekal?"

Glassy-eyed, Altmüller did not respond.

Buell asked the same question again, in a firmer, louder voice this time.

"No," Altmüller said weakly.

"Do you know a federal marshal named Alan Coffey?"

"No."

"Do you know a federal marshal named Michael Morgan?"

"Yes."

Buell drew a line through that name.

On the couch Altmüller began to twitch uncontrollably.

"Better hurry along," the other agent told Buell.

Buell read out the remaining thirty-seven names, one at a time, until he had finished the list. Fourteen of the forty names were familiar to Altmüller. Calling the names at random, Buell went through the list a second time in order to double-check it, and he found Altmüller's responses did not change.

"It's really hitting him now," the smaller agent said.

Altmüller had fallen on his side on the couch. His eyes were wide and sightless. Clear fluid bubbled at his nostrils. He mumbled and murmured and chewed at his tongue. His body snapped and twisted like a flag in the wind.

"It's a damned good drug," the smaller agent said, "except for the side effects."

Altmüller fell off the couch and thrashed violently on the floor. His tongue was bleeding, and his chin was painted red.

"Will these convulsions kill him?" Buell asked. He watched the big man roll and twist; he was intensely interested.

"No," the smaller agent said. "Unless he was under a doctor's care, he might injure himself severely. But the drug isn't deadly."

"I see."

"But that's academic, of course."

"Yes, of course," Buell said. He drew his pistol and shot Altmüller twice. He put the gun away.

"Let's wrap him in that rag rug," the other agent said.

When they had the corpse rolled into a neat cocoon, they carried it out to the kitchen.

Connie Eaton was sitting on a straight-backed chair, a strip of cloth adhesive tape over her mouth. Her wrists were handcuffed behind her back. She didn't struggle when she realized what was in the rug. She didn't try to scream, and she didn't faint. Instead, all the life drained out of her pretty eyes; she stared ahead as if she were mesmerized, catatonic.

The agent who wore eyeglasses said, "No need to carry him down to the basement. I found a better place to put him." He led them across the room to a food freezer that stood in an alcove beside the back door. The freezer was practically empty. "Good?"

"Perfect," Buell said.

They dumped Altmüller's body into the frosted bin and were just closing the freezer lid when the telephone rang.

"Probably for us," Buell said. He went to the wall phone by the refrigerator, picked up the receiver, and said, "Hello?"

"Buell?"

"Yes, sir."

"This is the Spokesman."

"Yes, sir." He explained how things had gone with Altmüller.

The Spokesman said, "Too bad about the woman."

"Yes, it is."

"But why haven't you disposed of her too?"

"She must have a family."

"She does," the Spokesman said.

"And if she disappears for a few days, they'll have the police looking for her. They're bound to come to Altmüller."

"Yes. You're right. What will you do? Take her somewhere and make it look like an accident?"

"That would be best," Buell said. "Does she live alone?"

"According to my information, she does. I see what you have in mind. You can take her back to her apartment and make it look like the work of a burglar."

"Yes, sir. Do you know her address?"

The Spokesman gave it to him. "But I have another job for you, first. There's a federal marshal named William Peyser. Lives near Maryland Park. Not far from where you are now." He gave Buell the exact address. "Get to Peyser as soon as you possibly can and run him through the Altmüller program."

"Will Peyser be alone?"

"To the best of my knowledge, yes. He has no children. His wife died four months ago, so he shouldn't have a girl friend."

Buell stroked his chin with his long, pale fingers. He had a musician's hands, and he was fairly good on the piano. "Then I can leave one man here with the woman. Two of us can deal with Peyser."

"When you've had time to wrap things up in Maryland Park, I'll give you a call there. I want to know which names on that list were strangers to both Altmüller and Peyser."

"Yes, sir."

"I'll have additional instructions for you when you're finished at Mr. Peyser's place."

"Fine."

"Wait there for my call."

"Yes, sir."

The Spokesman hung up.

Putting the receiver back on the hook, Buell turned and looked at the woman.

She stared through him.

To the agent who wore eyeglasses, Buell said, "Jerry, you stay here with Miss Eaton. Jim and I have another job to take care of. It's just over in Maryland Park. We shouldn't be gone very long. When we get back we'll deal with her."

Jerry took off his raincoat and tossed it onto the kitchen counter. "She's so pretty. I wish she hadn't been here."

The smallest man said, "*How* do we deal with her?"

"The boss says to take her back to her apartment and make it look like some burglar killed her." Buell watched her eyes and saw no spark of fear.

"Sounds reasonable," Jerry said.

Buell smiled. He had a sharp, saturnine face as pale as dusting powder. "I have a better idea."

"What's that?"

"We take her back to her apartment, just like the boss says. But we don't make it look like the work of a burglar." Buell paused to see if she was listening. She gave him no sign. "We make it look like the work of a rapist."

Emotion, like dark fish in a gelid sea, flickered deep in the woman's eyes.

Buell knew that look, that well-concealed but still-visible terror. He had seen it in the eyes of countless women—and men—when he'd been a rifleman in Vietnam years and years ago.

"Good idea," Jerry said, grinning.

The smallest man agreed.

Kweichow Province, China

On the morning of his twenty-first birthday, Chai Po-han soared up through the familiar nightmare. In his dream he lay upon a padded table in a room with an extremely low ceiling. Every aspect of the room was white: chalky white, star-white, so fiercely white that the eye rebelled at the sight. The eye—affronted by this unnatural, unbroken, flat and glaring whiteness—attempted to peer through the ceiling, walls, and floor as if, after all, they were merely constructed of veined alabaster. But the eye could not deceive itself. And what sort of place was so inhumanly white and sterile? Instantly he knew that he had died and that now he was stretched out upon a table in some celestial morgue, beyond the veil of life. Soon the gods would come to dissect his soul and judge its worthiness. His Communistic soul. His atheistic soul. Why in the name of all his ancestors had his people—and he himself— embraced Maoism? Opiate of the masses: what folly! There *were* gods, ultimate beings who urinated on the soul of the dead Chairman. And when the dissection was completed, when the gods saw the worm of atheism curled within his heart, Chai Po-han would suffer eternal torture. Pages from the *Quotations of Chairman Mao* would be ground up and mixed with dung, and he would be forced to dine on this mixture for the rest of time. To sharpen his humiliation, he would find the dung always tasted better than the other half of his menu. Or perhaps he would be reincarnated first as a slug, then as a cockroach, then as a snake . . . And now, in the ethereal silence, the gods came: men in green gowns, green surgical masks, and green caps, men like linen dragons. They circled him. He saw one of them raise a scalpel. White light winked along the cutting edge. In a moment the dissection would begin. His dead flesh would part bloodlessly, and his stilled heart would open to reveal the worm of faithlessness. Then: one form of damnation or the other, no question about it. And the scalpel rose, descended, touched his translucent skin and grew through it like a thorn through a rose petal . . .

Chai Po-han sat up on his meager straw mattress, a scream caught like bloody phlegm in the back of his throat. Then he heard the soft, furtive rustling of sleeping men turning on their straw beds on all sides of him, and he realized where he was: the agricultural commune in the cursed Province of Kweichow, well north of the minor city of Ssunan. He swallowed the scream and felt it slide thickly down his throat.

Lying back, closing his eyes, he tried to recover his breath and slow his heartbeat.

The night wind rattled the glass in the warped window frames of the long stablelike building.

Why, he asked the darkness, was he plagued with this hideous, repeating nightmare?

The wind abruptly gentled down, and the window glass stopped rattling—as if the darkness were saying that it did not want to talk with him.

Was the cause of his bad dream to be found in his visit to the United States? The dream had begun immediately after that, around the middle of February, and it had been replayed nearly every night since then. In that land of unproscribed churches and cathedrals and synagogues and temples, had he begun to doubt the Maoist creed of godlessness which had freed China and made it great? No. Most certainly not. Surely a lifetime of atheism could not be cast off after one brief encounter with those who were religious. Such faith was not a bacterium that could infect a man once he had but taken a few breaths of tainted air.

But how else was he to explain this dream which he threw out each morning and which returned like a boomerang each night?

He got up and dressed in the coarsely woven gray pajama-suit which had been folded at the head of his bed, on top of the thatched box that contained his personal belongings. Although there was little light in the communal sleeping quarters, Chai made his way into the central aisle without stepping on anyone, and he walked to the far end of the building where there were several windows flanking the main entrance.

The glass was discolored and flecked with imperfections, but it was clean; and he was able to look down through the foothills to the River Wu which shimmered in the waning moonlight. A thin, pale yellow line edged the horizon: dawn was not far off.

How would he celebrate this anniversary of his birth? he wondered. Working in the terraced rice paddies? Or perhaps he would be assigned to the construction crew that was erecting— laboriously and solely by manual labor—new dormitories, barns, machinery sheds, and grain storage silos.

What a stifling place this is! What a hole!

Just months ago, during his visit to the West, he had spoken to American and French journalists who had been to China and who praised the communes. They had all seen Liu Ling Commune in Shensi and were impressed. Chai was proud of his people and had talked about Liu Ling as if he had been there. He had explained about the Chairman's enormous program which moved millions of young people to the countryside every year in order to keep them from becoming bourgeois, in order to have them "revolutionized" by the peasants, in order to have them completely "reeducated" as they could be only by sharing the simple life of the countryside. He had been so eloquent. At the time, however, he had not known that Liu Ling was a showplace, an atypical unit of the system, highly polished for the benefit of foreign newsmen and diplomats. Now, a veteran of the Ssunan Commune, Chai understood that those foreign journalists had been deceived, that he had been deceived, that most of the communes were slave labor camps where the inmates remained for the most part voluntarily because they had been made to believe that they were not slaves but heroes who were shaping the future of China.

He wanted out of here. Badly. But to leave on his own, to go where the government had not sent him, would be disastrous. He would not be arrested, of course. He would not be beaten or publicly shamed. Rather, he would be ostracized by every Party coordinator in every town and district throughout China. He would be able to get no work at all and little if any subsidization. Then he would know *real* poverty, and he would beg to be given a place on a commune, any commune at all—even this hole north of Ssunan.

He shuddered.

He had not been born to this.

Chai Po-han was the eldest son of Chai Chen-tse, who was one of the most powerful men in the country. The elder Chai was director of the Central Office of Publications, which had total control over every form of print and broadcast media within the People's Republic of China. Chai Chen-tse was respected—and feared.

In his father's shadow Chai Po-han had moved through the highest strata of Chinese society. He had studied media theory and language in Peking and had been greatly honored when he was chosen as the student representative to the group of publishers that was sent to tour the United States during the first half of February, and then France during the latter half of the same month.

He could never have foreseen that the trip to the United States would be his downfall.

The trouble had begun just three days before his group had been scheduled to leave Washington for Paris. During dinner that evening Chai had become drowsy and slightly sick to his stomach. Soon after the dessert and coffee had been served, he asked to be excused from the table, and he returned to his hotel room. The tour had been full of conferences, lectures, expeditions to publishing houses and printing plants and television stations, receptions . . . His exhaustion was not remarkable—although he thought it was somewhat odd how suddenly and forcefully it had caught up with him. No sooner had he undressed and passed water and climbed into bed than he was fast asleep.

He had learned the next part of the story second-hand:

An hour later his roommate, Chou P'eng-fei, had been stricken by the same exhaustion and had returned to their room. According to Chou (liar of liars), Chai had not been in the room at that time. Surprised but not alarmed, Chou had gone to sleep. When he woke the following morning, Chou saw that Chai had returned and was asleep in the other bed. And then Chou realized that his roommate stank of whiskey. He thought of ignoring it, thought of helping to conceal Chai's reactionary behavior. But Chou (liar of liars) said that he quickly realized his duty was to Maoism and Chinese honor rather than to his friend. Shocked, Chou had gone immediately to see Liu Hsiang-kuo, who was the security chief for the tour group. Chou and Liu returned to the hotel room and woke Chai with some difficulty.

And the rest of it he remembered all too clearly:

He *had* been in an incredible state. He had slept in his clothes, which were soaked with perspiration. He reeked of whiskey. And worst of all, preposterous as it seemed, impossible as it seemed, he was sleeping with a pair of lacy women's panties, very Western panties, clutched in his hands.

He insisted that he had slept the night through, that he had not been out of the room, that he knew nothing of the whiskey or the panties.

Liu Hsiang-kuo said that it would be easier to believe the peace offerings of the worst war-mongering, running-dog imperialist who had ever lived than it would be for him to believe Chai's story of mysterious victimization and ultimate innocence. Liu Hsiang-kuo said that he would rather sleep with vipers and eat with tigers and live with scorpions than turn his back to Chai Po-han.

Chai Po-han said that apparently Liu Hsiang-kuo thought he was lying about all of this.

Liu Hsiang-kuo said this was exactly, wonderfully true.

For the remainder of their stay in the United States and for the entire two weeks they spent in France, Chai Po-han was watched closely. He was never allowed to go anywhere by himself for fear that female pawns of the capitalists would convert him into a mad, raging counterrevolutionary by cleverly manipulating his genitals. One could not guess what techniques these Western women knew—although one had surely heard the shocking stories. So Chai was informally but rigorously guarded. And on their return trip to Peking, when their aircraft stopped to refuel in Chungking, Chai Po-han was taken from his group and given orders to report to the Ssunan Commune forthwith so that, by associating with working peasants, he could be "reeducated in Maoist thought and purged of his counterrevolutionary and nonrevolutionary interests and weaknesses."

He had been framed, and now that he'd had enough time to

think about it, he knew why. His father was a great and much-respected man—but he had enemies just the same. The elder Chai was far too powerful for anyone to risk an overt attack on him. He knew too much about other high government officials to allow himself to be purged from the Party. He would not hesitate to use his knowledge to destroy anyone who attempted to usurp his authority. However, these faceless cowards might attempt to ruin Chai Chen-tse by discrediting his eldest and favorite son. That was the only explanation for these astounding events in Washington.

Soon after he had reported to the Ssunan Commune, Chai had sent word to his father that Chou P'eng-fei—and perhaps Liu Hsiang-kuo as well—had drugged him at dinner, soaked him with whiskey while he was unconscious, and placed a pair of Western women's decadently lacy underwear in his hands while he slept all unawares. Two weeks later a letter had arrived from the elder Chai, in which he assured his son that he had faith in him and knew he had been tricked; Chai Chen-tse also promised that his son would be ordered home from Ssunan before many weeks had passed. Relieved, Chai Po-han had waited for these new orders to come—had waited and waited and waited. Two days ago he had received another letter from his father, who assured him that he would soon be brought East from the wasteland of Kweichow. But he was no longer certain that his father could arrange it. And after six and a half months at Ssunan, he knew he would never again be happy living *anywhere* in the People's Republic, for his trust in Maoism and the dictatorship of the proletariat had been broken by too many fourteen-hour days of brutal, semi-enforced labor.

Now, beyond the discolored window glass, dawn had come while he stared at the River Wu and thought over his predicament. And now, outside of the commune director's quarters, the gong sounded which signaled the beginning of a new workday.

Behind Chai, the other men of this dormitory—a fraction of the comrades, both women and men, who lived at Ssunan—got to their feet and stretched. They rolled up their thin mattresses and bound them with cord and hung them from specially rigged poles so that—if a storm should come and rain should wash across the dormitory floor—their beds would not be prey to a capricious Nature. One by one, then in twos and threes, they dressed and went outside, heading toward the men's latrines. When he could not delay any longer, Chai Po-han followed them.

From the latrines they filed to an open-air kitchen, where they were given two bowls each: one filled with rice and large chunks of stewed chicken, the other containing orange slices and pieces of hard yellow bread. Here and there young courting couples sat together to eat, although they maintained a respectable yard of open space between them. For the most part the peasants ate together, the students ate together, and a third group of nonstudent transferees from the cities ate in circles of *their* friends.

Chai was sitting in one of these circles, finishing his breakfast, when the commune director brought him a large envelope. "For you, Comrade." The director was a short, squat man with an enormous chest and thick biceps. He never smiled. Now he seemed to be frowning more deeply than he usually did.

Chai took the envelope. "What is it?"

"You are being transferred from Ssunan," the director said.

Chai quickly opened the envelope.

K'ang Chiu-yeh, Chai's closest friend at the commune, stopped eating. He set his bowls aside on the earth and came up onto his knees. He shuffled closer to Chai and said, "Transferred to where, my friend?"

"Back to Peking," Chai said.

"How wonderful!"

Chai said nothing.

"But you should rejoice!" K'ang said. "And instead, you look at me as if you've just found weevils in your rice." He laughed. Unlike the director, K'ang had a marvelous smile and used it often.

Five months ago it would have been the most wonderful news that Chai could have received. But not now. He said as much.

"But that makes no sense," K'ang said. "Certainly, it would have been better if it had come five months ago. But it is no less a good thing for having come late."

Chai looked at his friend and felt a great sadness well up in him. K'ang had been a medical student at Shanghai University before his name had appeared on a list of thirty-seven thousand young people who were to leave Shanghai in order to serve the proletariat and the Maoist cause in the Fifty-Year Farm Program. K'ang was not going home; he would not leave Ssunan for years and perhaps not ever. K'ang did not have a powerful father; therefore, his duty would remain with the Fifty-Year Farm Program.

"What is the matter?" K'ang asked him.

Chai said nothing.

K'ang shook him by the shoulder.

Chai thought of the thousands of displaced young men and women who were in no better position than K'ang. Tens of thousands of them. Hundreds of thousands . . . Now, instead of laughing aloud at his transfer as he would have done five months ago, Chai Po-han began to weep.

He was going home.

TWO

transit, and had passed through customs, with the aid of the
. . . Norwegian, or Italian. Customs ... was new. Committee

TOKYO: FRIDAY, 2:00 P.M.

The International Date Line made it all very complicated. In order to minimize the effects of ordinary jet lag compounded by the radical change of clock-calendar time, David Canning allowed himself only five hours of sleep in Honolulu, rose at six in the morning, had an early breakfast, and read a paperback novel until it was time for him to go to the airport. His flight for Tokyo departed shortly after noon. Aboard the plane, he ate a light lunch and drank two martinis. Then he settled back for a nap, and because he had not allowed himself a full night's sleep in Honolulu, dozed off almost as soon as he closed his eyes. He was asleep when the jet crossed the International Date Line, switching instantly from Thursday to Friday. After nearly a five-hour nap he woke forty minutes out of Tokyo and had a third martini while the aircraft worked into its landing approach. They touched down in Japan at two o'clock Friday afternoon, which was seven o'clock *Thursday* evening in Hawaii and midnight Thursday-Friday in Washington, D.C.

Just after he had passed through customs, with the aid of his State Department credentials, Canning saw the first Committee agent. Any Westerner would have found it impossible to run a surveillance on Canning in this airport without his noticing it. In the predominantly Asian crowd, the man's pallor and height made him as obvious as a dead fly atop an uncut wedding cake. He was standing near the boards that listed the departures and arrivals, and he stared openly at Canning.

Canning stared back at him and nodded.

The agent looked through him.

Smiling grimly, Canning walked out into the crowded main hall of the terminal. He sensed rather than felt the man fall into step behind him, and he walked with his shoulders tensed.

But there would be no killing here—and for the same reason that they could not possibly run a secret surveillance of him. The killers were tall and white, and they could not count on anonymity to help them escape through the hundreds of incoming and outgoing passengers. Furthermore, the Japanese were generally not as apathetic about crime as were most Americans. They admired tradition, stability, order, and law. Some of them would surely give chase to anyone who tried to commit murder in a public air terminal. And although the Japanese police—stationed throughout the building—relied for the most part on the sort of nonviolent techniques of the British bobbies, they were capable of swift and terrible action when it was necessary. The Committeemen, therefore, would merely follow him to be certain that he went to the Imperial Hotel, where, having had his real and cover names for more than twenty-four hours, they would surely have traced his Otley reservation. Then, at the hotel, in the comparative privacy of a corridor or an elevator, or perhaps in his own room, they would make a hit.

Or try.

He wouldn't be an easy target.

Outside the terminal, there were more people than cabs at the taxi line. Most of them were Westerners who had too much luggage or not enough self-confidence to use the city's bus system. Canning walked to the back of the line, stepped off the curb, and put down his suitcases. He held up three fingers and waved them prominently at the taxis that were just turning into the approach lane: this was a sign that told the drivers he would pay three times the meter price, and it was often the only way to get a cab in Tokyo, where the drivers worked as much as sixteen hours a day for quite modest wages. He got a taxi at once, much to the consternation of the people who had been waiting there some time before he arrived.

"*Konnichiwa,*" the driver said, smiling at him as he climbed into the taxi.

"*Konnichiwa,*" Canning said, smiling back at him. The automatic cab door closed and locked behind him. He asked the driver to take him to the Imperial Hotel.

The Committee agent also knew the three-fingered trick. His taxi followed immediately behind Canning's cab.

The driver spoke no English, and Canning spoke only a few words of Japanese; therefore, the ride into the city was silent, and he had nothing to do but take in the scenery—what there was of it. On both sides of the road there were shabby houses, unpainted warehouses, gray factories, gasoline stations, and power lines. There were no cherry trees, landscaped gardens, or flower-encircled temples as seen in all popular illustrations of the Orient.

The tourist guidebooks did not lie; there was great beauty in Tokyo, but it existed in pockets, like oases in the desert of urban sprawl. This was possibly the only city in the world where great mansions could flourish with shacks on both sides of them. The imperturbable Japanese, so quick to smile and so eager to help strangers, had somehow managed to transform the planet's most crowded and polluted metropolis into one of the most pleasant capitals in the world. The Tokyo Tower came into view, a monstrous blot on the skyline, taller than the Eiffel Tower which had inspired it, yet just incongruous enough to be charming. Then they entered the narrow, unbelievably congested streets of the central city area that made the busy avenues of midtown Manhattan seem like quiet country lanes. As usual, the pollution index was high: the gray-yellow sky hung so low that it looked like a roof spanning the boxlike high-rise buildings. At first Canning had a vague but quite discomforting feeling of suffocation; however, that soon turned into a not unpleasant sense of hivelike protection. Then they breezed along Hibiya Park, weaved wildly from lane to lane, and stopped with a squeal of brakes directly in front of the magnificent Imperial Hotel.

The taxi driver said "*Domo, domo*" when he was paid; and the hotel doorman welcomed Canning with a smile and nearly perfect

English. He picked up Canning's two suitcases, and Canning followed him inside.

The Committee agent entered close behind them. He didn't trail Canning all the way across the huge lobby to the front desk. Instead, he sat on one of the comfortable divans where tourists of all nationalities were consulting maps and guidebooks, and he remained there while Canning checked in. In fact, he stayed there, his legs crossed, his hands folded on his lap, when Canning boarded the elevator with the bellhop a few minutes later.

Canning waved at him as if telling him to hurry before the lift doors slid shut.

The agent merely stared at him, blank-faced, humorless as an alligator.

He thinks he doesn't have to follow me any farther because I'm trapped now, Canning thought.

And maybe he's right.

Five minutes later Canning tipped the bellhop and was alone in his room. It was a fairly large room, well furnished, with a nice big Japanese-style bathroom. There was a walk-in closet, a linen closet, and a locked door with a brass key in it. He used the key and found another door beyond; this one locked from the far side and apparently connecting to the adjoining room. He closed the door on his side, locked it again, and used the desk chair to form a wedge between the floor and the knob. At the main door he slipped the chain latch into place and made certain that the night lock was properly engaged. Switching on the lights as he went, he crossed the room and drew the heavy maroon-and-white brocade drapes over the windows that faced out on Hibiya Park.

He looked at his watch: three o'clock.

He went into the bathroom and used the toilet.

He washed his face in cold water.

He looked at his watch: five minutes past three.

He combed his hair.

He came back out into the main room, went to the windows, parted the drapes, and watched the people walking and cycling through Hibiya Park.

He sat down on the edge of the bed.

He listened to the hotel sounds.

He looked at his watch: three-twelve.

Where in the hell was Tanaka?

SEOUL, KOREA: FRIDAY, 3:00 P.M.

General Lin Shen-yang, chief of the Internal Security Force for the People's Republic of China, leaned back in the large oval-shaped copper washtub and sighed as more hot water was poured into his bath. He closed his eyes and breathed in the steam. When the woman began to scrub his chest with a soft-bristled brush and rose-petal soap, he opened his eyes and smiled at her. He touched her cheek and said, "You are a perfect jewel of great value."

She blushed with happiness and said, "I am pleased that my Tai-Pan is so happy with me."

"Delirious."

The scent of rose petals was so rich that he felt almost drunk with it.

"But I am praised too much. I am no jewel. I am just an old, faithful cow." Her lovely face was set in a scowl, as if she were castigating herself for not being the precious jewel that he thought she was.

"If you are an old cow, then what am I?" he asked as her small hands dropped the brush and began to scoop up water with which to rinse his chest.

"You are Tai-Pan of this house," she said. "Master of this house and my master too."

"An old dinosaur," he said.

"Not at all old," she said, dismayed.

Teasing her, he said, "But if you are old, then so must I be."

She frowned more fiercely than ever. "Well, I am young, then. I change my mind. I am a *young*, faithful cow." She finished rinsing his chest. "Because you are not old."

He was, in fact, sixty-four years old. He had been a young lieutenant at Mao's side when Chiang had been driven from the mainland many years ago, and he had been in a position of power within the People's Republic ever since. He was a squat, powerfully built man, with a closely shaven head, deep-set black eyes, a wide nose, lips broad and flat like strips of hammered metal, and a round, blunt chin. He did not look sixty-four years old or even fifty-four. And he felt like a young man—especially when he was with her.

Her name was Yin-hsi, and she was lovely beyond words. Her oval face was graced with a wide, sensuous mouth and almond-shaped eyes as clear and dark as the night between the stars. Her hair was piled high atop her head and held in place by antique jeweled pins that were the same sapphire shade as her silk robe. Her skin was far silkier than the robe: warm yellow-brown, taut, scented with a delicate Western perfume. She was only twenty-three years old, young enough to be his granddaughter.

In 1949 her real grandparents and her mother—who was then still a child—had fled to Taiwan with Chiang Kai-shek's followers. Her mother had grown up on the island and had married Yin-hsi's father there. The newlyweds had then emigrated to South Korea, where, in the aftermath of the United Nations' war against North Korea, there were many golden opportunities. Her father had become a moderately successful businessman, and her mother had settled down to raise a family, one son and two daughters.

Yin-hsi had been born in Seoul, and her parents had raised her much as Chinese girls had been raised before Mao's revolution. She had never been meant for factory work or for farm work on some dust-choked commune. She was too soft for that, too delicate, too like a flower of flesh and hair. She had none of the virtues of an emancipated Communist woman—but those were not the only virtues that a woman might rightfully cultivate. Yin-hsi's great strength lay in her desire to serve her master, be he her husband or only her owner. She gloried in giving her Tai-Pan all the pleasure she could produce with her woman's knowledge, obedient nature, personal devices, and body. And because this was what she had been educated to do, Yin-hsi was a very great credit to her father, mother, and to herself.

After extensive and prolonged negotiations, General Lin had purchased Yin-hsi six years ago, shortly after she had turned seventeen. He had given many tasteful gifts and considerable cash to her father. He had promised to treat her well always and to keep her always unspoiled. He had bought a four-room, gracefully designed pine bungalow two doors from her family, and there he had set her up in housekeeping with a female servant and all the necessities. Before Yin-hsi, there had been another mistress of whom the general had grown weary. He didn't think he would ever grow weary of his Yin-hsi, even if he were to live well into his eighties.

The general considered himself to be a good Communist, yet he did not feel guilty about owning another human being. This was, of course, an inexcusable sin in the eyes of other Communists. General Lin knew, however, that he owned the girl only in the most abstract sense. He never treated her as a slave; and he had impressed upon her that if she should ever want to quit this life in favor of the more modern and conventional path of marriage and suburban life, he would free her instantly upon her request.

Nevertheless, had any officials in China known about Yin-hsi, General Lin would have been stripped of his authority and drummed out of the Party. Quite likely, he would also be put on trial and found guilty and sentenced to prison or to "reeducation" on a pig farm.

Which would have been terribly tragic, for the general really was a good Communist. He believed that the Party had fed, clothed, housed, and educated the masses better than any capitalistic system could have done. He deeply desired a lasting Communistic future for China.

What he did not believe in or desire was the joyless, sexless, robotistic Communism that had grown out of the Maoist State. Mao Tse-tung had always been a crushing bore and a prude: a brilliant and admirable political leader but a rather shallow human being. Lin had been close enough to him to see this much from the start of the revolution. But to think that in just a few short decades Mao and his most ardent followers had managed to lead an entire nation of nearly a billion people into voluntary sexual self-denial and outright self-repression! Incredible! And more than incredible, he thought, it was nonrevolutionary. Criminal. If you allowed yourself to be programmed as an asexual automaton, you were no different from capitalism's programmed worker-drones who had been propagandized into denying themselves the full rewards and joys of their own labors.

From the beginning of his association with the Maoist cause,

General Lin had rejected asexuality and had, indeed, assiduously cultivated his erotic drives. At sixty-four he was still an extremely active man—and quietly proud of it.

His cover was perfect. He had been made chief of the Internal Security Force in 1951, and from the earliest days of the ISF he had done field work just like the agents who were answerable to him. He was the ISF's leading expert on South Korea and made regular monthly undercover missions into that country, often remaining there for a week or ten days at a time. This activist role was applauded by the Party's highest executives. As they saw it, any general who took the same risks as those he required of his subordinates was in no danger of being corrupted by power or by a sense of elitism. (And, in fact, this was part of the reason why he had always worked in the field as well as behind the desk.) He was, they said, an excellent example of revolutionary Communism at work. Accepting this constant praise with calculated modesty, the general continued his field work in South Korea, where, until such a time as the Korean dictator could be overthrown, he could enjoy a vigorous and very non-Maoist sex life beyond the sight and suspicion of his superiors.

"I am a failure," Yin-hsi said.

"Are you fishing for more compliments?"

"I am a failure."

"That isn't true."

"It is true."

"Why is it true?"

"You think too much."

"How does that reflect on you?"

"If I were a good woman to you, I should be able to take your mind off all your troubles. But I am no good. I am a failure. You sit there frowning, worrying."

He stood up in the bath while she dried him with a large, thick towel. "I frown only because I can think of no way to be with you more often."

She tilted her head and looked at him coquettishly. "Are you telling the truth?"

"Yes."

"This is why you were frowning?"

"Yes."

"Then I am not a failure?"

"Indeed, you are too much of a success."

Smiling, she finished drying him.

"Stand before me," he said.

She did, her arms at her sides.

He removed the jeweled pins from her hair. Rich, shining, dark crescents of hair fell about her face.

"You desire me?" she asked.

"Perhaps."

"Only perhaps?"

"I have not decided."

"Oh?"

"I have high standards."

She looked down at his thick erection and giggled.

"Ah, woman," he said in mock exasperation. "Where is your modesty? Have you no shame?"

She pouted and said, "I am a failure."

Laughing, he untied the sash of her robe and slipped the silk from her. Her sweet breasts quivered before him. He took them in his gnarled, scarred hands and gently massaged them.

"Should I turn down the bed?" she asked.

"Yes—unless you want to be taken on a brick floor."

"You would bruise me?"

"If necessary."

"But you would not like me with bruises."

"Then I would leave you."

"Oh?"

"Until the bruises had vanished."

"You are a cruel man," she said teasingly.

"Oh, terribly cruel."

She crossed the softly lighted room to the low-standing bed and pulled back the quilted blankets. The sheets were yellow silk. She stretched out on them, her golden thighs slightly parted, the shaven petals of her sex visible in dust-soft shadows. Her hair was fanned across both pillows. Smiling at him, she put the tip of one finger against her right breast and murmured wordlessly as the nipple rose and stiffened under it.

So beautiful! he thought. So exquisitely beautiful!

She patted the mattress beside her.

The general was a good, unselfish lover. He did for her all the things he wanted her to do for him; and after they had spent nearly an hour preparing each other, he mounted her. His compact, muscular body was powerful yet gentle in the act. She had no need to pretend a long, shuddering climax, for it came to her almost as soon as he began to thrust within her. And a few minutes after she had convulsed beneath him a second time, he groaned softly and emptied his seed deep into her.

"Tai-Pan," she said.

He kissed her neck.

Later they sat up in bed and sipped mint tea which she had made in a silver pot. They ate miniature cakes sprinkled with honey, raisins, and toasted almonds.

When he was full of cakes, he got out of bed and retrieved a small box and a long beige envelope from his clothes. He placed the envelope on the mirrored tray atop her vanity and brought the box back to the bed. He gave it to her and said, "An imperfect gift for a perfect woman."

As delighted as a child, she put down her teacup and unwrapped the box. She withdrew from it a long, fine-linked gold chain at the end of which was suspended a single jade teardrop. Carved in the stone were the basic features of a lovely oriental woman. "Oh," she said breathlessly, "it is the most beautiful thing I have ever seen."

"It is nothing."

"But it is magnificent!"

"It is unworthy of you."

"I am unworthy of it."

"You deserve far more."

"You are too generous."

Gradually, each allowed himself to be flattered. Yin-hsi slipped the chain around her neck, and the jade fell between her smooth, heavy breasts. They agreed that the jewelry was perhaps the most beautiful piece of its kind in the world—and that it looked more beautiful between her breasts than it could have looked on any other woman who had ever lived. Both of them blushed and smiled.

After they had sipped brandy for a few minutes, he said, "How have your household funds been holding up? Am I giving you enough to meet the bills?"

She was surprised, for he had never asked about this during the last six years. "More than enough. You are too generous with me, Tai-Pan. I have accumulated a large surplus in the bank. Would you like to see my records?"

"No, no. The surplus is yours."

"I manage the accounts well. You can be proud of me."

He kissed her cheek. "Today I am leaving an envelope which contains four million Korean won." At the current exchange rate, four hundred and fifty won equaled one United States dollar.

"That is too much!" she said.

"Is it sufficient to run the house for one year?"

"Perhaps two years! And stylishly!"

"Good. I would not want you to be in need of anything."

Worry lines appeared in her face. "You are not going away for an entire year?"

"I hope not."

"But maybe?"

"Maybe forever."

The worry lines deepened. She bit her lower lip. "You are teasing me."

"There is serious trouble in Peking."

She waited.

"A great danger," he said, thinking of the Americans and their Dragonfly project. "Perhaps the problem will be quickly dealt with. If not . . . Many of my people will die, and there will be months of chaos, disorder."

"Do not go back," she said.

"I am Chinese."

"So am I!"

"I am a Communist."

"You cannot really believe in Communism, not deep in your heart."

"But I do. I do not expect you to believe, but I do. And a man cannot run away from his philosophy."

"You love Communism more than you love me."

"I have been with you six years," he said softly. "And I love you more than I have ever loved a woman. But Communism has been my entire life, and to deny it now would be to deny myself."

Tears shimmered on her eyelashes.

"Do not cry."

She cried.

He raised his voice and became sharp with her. "You are disgracing your family. You are supposed to improve my spirits, not deflate them. What manner of concubine are you? Either you will stop crying at once, or I will punish you severely."

She rolled off the bed and ran from the room.

Leaning back against the pillows, he tossed off the rest of his brandy and managed to hold back his own tears. Damn these Americans! What fools! What maniacs!

Ten minutes later she returned and climbed into bed with him. Her eyes were clear. She had refreshed the light coat of makeup that she wore. "I am a failure," she said.

"Oh, yes. Oh, yes, yes, yes," he said with mock severity. "You are such a failure, a terrible failure. Oh, yes!"

Her smile was weak; her lips trembled.

He put one hand on her firm breasts.

She said, "Must you return today?"

"Within the hour. I should never have left Peking in the middle of such a crisis. But I had to see you once more and be sure that you were provided for. If I get back tonight, I will not have been *too* derelict in my duties."

Without another word she slid down in the bed until her face was in his lap. She began to kiss him there. A few minutes later she said, "Do you desire me again?"

"Would you have me say no when the proof of the lie is in your hand?" he asked.

"Indisputable proof," she said, squeezing his erect member.

"Come to me."

Soon after they had finished, he got out of bed and began to dress. When she started to get up too, he said, "No. Lie down. I want to look at you while I dress. I want to take away with me the picture of you naked on my bed."

She smiled for him.

"At the end of a year," he said, "consider yourself free. Wait twelve months, but no longer."

She said nothing.

"Do you understand me?"

"Yes," she said all but inaudibly.

"I will most likely return in a month."

She nodded.

He hugged her to him once more before he left. Outside, as he walked away along the pine-shrouded alley toward the lower slopes of Seoul, he felt as if some creature with razored talons had torn him open and scooped out the contents of his chest.

In the house, in the bedroom, Yin-hsi felt even more miserable than her Tai-Pan. She sat on the edge of her bed, her slender brown shoulders hunched, her face in her hands. She wept and shuddered and cursed herself. She knew that she would never see him again. She wished that she had told him what awful things she had done, and she could almost hear the conversation that might have been:

—*Tai-Pan, you do know that no other woman could love you as well and deeply as I love you?*

—*You're a good woman, Yin-hsi.*

—*Try not to hate me.*

—*Why should I hate you?*

—*I am a wretch. I have betrayed you to your enemies.*

—*What game is this?*

—*It is true.*

—*What enemies?*

—*They came here to see me.*

—*When?*

—*Months ago. In the winter.*

—*Who were they?*

—*A South Korean and an American. They wanted me to help them destroy you . . . somehow. I don't know how. I never learned how it was to be done. I refused. They said they would kill my mother and my father. They said they would rape and kill my sister, murder and mutilate my brothers. At first I didn't believe them. But they convinced me that they were the kind of men who would do anything. They raped me and hurt me badly in other ways. Very badly. They frightened me, Tai-Pan. And in the end, awful wretch that I am, I cooperated with them. I betrayed you.*

But it was pointless to imagine a confession that had not been made. She had *not* spoken to him about these things, not even when she suspected that, somehow, this crisis in Peking was connected with the men who had first come to see her last winter. It was in this current crisis that Shen-yang was to be destroyed. Somehow.

Some way. She was certain of it, yet she had kept her silence. Fear was stronger than affection. Terror drove out love. After he had given her so much pleasure, while his warm semen was still oozing from her, she had let him walk out the door to his fate without giving him one word of warning.

She loathed herself.

She wished that she had the courage to commit suicide. But she knew that she was too much of a coward to even prick her skin. She would collapse at the sight of blood.

She sat on the edge of the bed, her feet on the cool brick floor, and she wept.

And she prayed that however her master was to be destroyed, he would go quickly, with dignity, and without pain.

WASHINGTON: THURSDAY, MIDNIGHT

In the book-lined first-floor study of his elegant townhouse in the Georgetown section of the capital city, Robert McAlister poured himself a third bourbon on the rocks and returned with it to his desk. He sat down and had time for one sip before the telephone rang. It was the call that he had been waiting for since ten o'clock. He said, "Hello, Mr. President."

"I'm sorry to be late, Bob."

"That's all right, sir."

"It's this flare-up in the Mideast."

"Certainly."

"Ever since they discovered those new Israeli oil deposits, it's been a nightmare."

"Yes, sir."

The President sighed and clicked his tongue. "Any progress on your end of the Dragonfly mess?"

"Not much," McAlister said. "It's been a bad day right from the start—thanks in part to your Mr. Rice."

The President clicked his tongue against his teeth again. "Andy? What did Andy do?"

McAlister closed his eyes and held the glass of bourbon against his forehead. "I'm sorry, sir. It's a small thing. Inconsequential, really. I shouldn't even have mentioned it. But I'm so tensed up—"

"I want to know." He clicked his tongue.

"Well, he was supposed to round up a dozen federal marshals—"

"He didn't?"

"He did. But he didn't call them until around ten o'clock last night. Now, some of them weren't scheduled for duty, and they'd made plans for an extra-long weekend. They went home yesterday and packed suitcases and loaded up campers . . . and then had to unload and unpack when Rice called them late last night. They weren't happy this morning, and the apologies were mine to make." He lowered the glass of bourbon to the desk. "Oh, what the hell, it's really nothing. I'm just frustrated by all of this, and I'm trying to find a convenient punching bag."

"No, you're right, Bob. There was no reason he couldn't have called the marshals before five yesterday. I'm going to mention this to Andy in the morning." *Click!* went his tongue.

"Well, it really is petty of me. After everything that has happened today, the murder and all—"

"Murder?" the President asked.

"You don't know about that?"

"I've been tied up on this Mideast thing."

McAlister swallowed some bourbon. "The best investigative lawyer I have is a man named Bernie Kirkwood."

"I've met him. He's done a great job for you these last six months," the President said. He didn't click his tongue.

What was he doing instead? McAlister wondered. Boring at his ears? Drumming his fingers on the desk? Or perhaps he was picking his nose—

"Bob? Are you there?"

"Sorry, sir. Woolgathering."

"Bernie Kirkwood."

"Yes, sir. Early this afternoon Bernie came up with what we thought was a damned good lead. He was working on a list of names—scientists with experience in biological-weapons research. And he discovered that a man named Potter Cofield had once worked for Dr. Olin Wilson. Furthermore, Cofield had received a promotion at the Pentagon almost entirely on the recommendation of Wilson."

"Ah," the President said.

"Next, Bernie learned that Dr. Cofield had retired from his job at the Pentagon two years ago."

"How old was he?"

"Fifty."

"It's possible to retire from government service that young."

"Yes, sir. But Cofield wasn't the kind of man to pack it up and lie in the Caribbean sun. Bernie studied his record and talked to a few of Cofield's friends. The man lived for his research."

"I see."

"So Bernie, two other lawyers, and the federal marshal who's protecting them, went to talk to Cofield. He was dead."

"How?"

"Stabbed repeatedly in the chest and throat."

"My God!"

McAlister swallowed some bourbon. He felt lousy. "His house had been torn up a bit. As if a burglar had been going through the drawers looking for cash and valuables."

"But you don't think it was a burglar?"

"The place hadn't been torn up *enough*. It was a very hasty job, a cover, nothing more. Besides, Cofield still had his wallet, and there was seventy dollars in it."

"Any clues?"

"We brought in the FBI," McAlister said. "They've got some of the best forensic men combing the house. But I don't have much hope that anything'll come from that. For one thing, we can't trust everyone in the FBI. And for another, these killers are professionals. They don't leave fingerprints."

"What about the police?"

"We didn't inform them," McAlister said. "If we had, the press would have been crawling all over the house. And sure as hell, someone from the *Times* or the *Post* would pick up on the whole Dragonfly mess by tomorrow morning."

"They're good reporters," the President said.

"One other thing about Cofield."

"What's that?"

"He was killed no more than half an hour before we got to him."

The President clicked his tongue: he had come full circle. "So it isn't just a case of The Committee routinely killing off the men who worked with Wilson."

"That's right. Cofield was killed because the other side knew we wanted to talk to him. And the only way they could know that is if they've got someone inside my organization."

"Who?"

"I haven't any idea." He rattled the ice cubes in his glass and wished he could put the phone down to go get another drink. He was ordinarily a light drinker, but these last several months had given him a taste for Wild Turkey.

After clicking his tongue twice, the President said, "What are you going to do?"

"Just be careful, watch everyone closely, and hope the damned son of a bitch will trip himself up sooner or later." Ordinarily, he was no more of a curser than a drinker. But that had changed too.

"It's not likely that he will," the President said after a few seconds of thought. "Trip himself up, I mean."

"I know. But I don't see how else I can handle it."

"What about the agent that Berlinson killed out there in Carpinteria? Anything on him yet?"

"No leads at the moment. Not on him or his partner. We're verifying the whereabouts of every current and ex-agent, but this is going to take a good deal of time."

"Have you heard from Canning?"

"His cover is blown."

"But how is that possible?"

"I don't know," McAlister said wearily. "The only people who knew about him were me, you, and Rice."

"Where is he now?"

"Tokyo."

"Then it's about time for us to send his name along to the Chairman."

"No, sir. Canning just arrived in Tokyo. He's a full day behind schedule, thanks to some trouble he ran into in Los Angeles." He quickly explained about that.

"Yes, Bob, but now that his cover has been blown, I don't see any reason for us to keep his identity a secret from the Chairman until the very last minute."

"Well, sir, the Chairman's going to want to know *how* Canning will be arriving in Peking. You can tell him our man will be aboard one of the two dozen authorized flights from Tokyo to Peking. But I'd like to keep that a secret until the plane is in the air."

"Okay," the President said. "We'll send all the data except the name of the flight—and we'll stat that by satellite as soon as it takes off from Tokyo. Which flight is it?"

"For now," McAlister said, "I'd like to keep it a secret from you as well as the Chairman, sir."

The President hesitated, sighed, and said, "Very well. Is there anything else?"

Once more the President had stopped clicking his tongue. McAlister was happier when he could hear that sound, for then he didn't have to wonder what the man was *doing*. He longed for another series of clicks. He thought: I'm going mad. And he said, "Sir, there's something I believe we have to do, but it's beyond my jurisdiction. Are you open for a suggestion?"

"I'm always open for suggestions."

"Arrest A.W. West."

There was a long silence on the line.

"Sir," McAlister said, "we strongly suspect that he's one of the men behind The Committee, behind Dragonfly. Arresting him might throw the organization into confusion. That might buy us time. And they might panic, start making mistakes."

"We have no proof against him," the President said sternly. "We may suspect that West is behind it, but we have nothing that would convince a judge."

"Then arrest him for the Kennedy assassinations. We *know* that he was one of the people who financed all of that."

"We have circumstantial proof. Only circumstantial proof. We may *know* that he was part of a conspiracy, but again we have nothing to show a judge, nothing concrete. Furthermore, I thought we had all made a policy decision not to open that can of worms and throw the country into a turmoil."

McAlister sagged in his chair.

"Do you agree, Bob?"

"Yes, sir," he said, exhausted. The bourbon was getting to him. His mind was clouded.

"I'll leave instructions with my secretary to put you through to me at any hour. If something comes up, call me at once."

"Yes, sir. And, Mr. President?"

"Yes?"

"If you have any speaking engagements over the next few days—cancel them."

"I have none," the President said soberly.

"Don't even go for walks on the White House grounds."

"And stay away from windows too?"

"Sir, if you were assassinated now, we'd be thrown into such turmoil that we'd never be able to stop Dragonfly—if it's stoppable under any conditions."

"You're right, of course. And I've had the same thoughts myself. Did you take my advice about a bodyguard?"

"Yes, sir," McAlister said. "There are five men stationed in my house tonight."

"FBI?"

"No, sir. I don't trust the FBI. These are Pinkerton men. I hired them out of my own pocket."

"I suppose that's wise."

McAlister sipped some of the melted ice in his glass. "We sound like true psychotics, thoroughbred paranoids. I wonder if we're ready for an institution?"

"Someone once said that if you think everyone is out to get you, and everyone *is* out to get you, then you're not a paranoid but merely a realist."

Sighing, McAlister said, "Yes, but what are we coming to? What are we coming to when wealthy men can hire the assassination of the President—and get away with it? What are we coming to when private citizens and crackpot elements of the CIA can find the means to wage biological warfare against a foreign country? What are we coming to when all this can be happening—and you and I are so relatively calm about it, reasonable about it?"

"Bob, the world isn't going to hell in a handbasket—if that's what you're saying. It got pretty bad there for a while. But we're straightening it up, cleaning it up. That's what my administration is all about."

And how many times have I heard that before? McAlister wondered.

The President said, "Bit by bit we're putting it all back together, and don't you forget that."

"I wonder," McAlister said. He was seldom this morose, and he realized that Dragonfly was the final catalyst necessary to start major changes in him. He didn't know what those changes might be; they were still developing. "Sometimes I think the world just gets crazier and crazier. It certainly isn't the world that I was taught about when I was a young man in Boston."

"You're just tired."

"I suppose."

"Do you want me to relieve you? Would you like someone else to take over the agency?"

McAlister sat up straight. "Oh, Christ, no! No, sir." He wiped one hand across his face. "I can't think of any other poor son of a bitch"—and here he was cursing again—"who could have stood up to these last six months as well as I have. That's not egomania—it's just fact."

"I have faith in you."

"Thank you."

"We'll get through this."

"I hope you're right."

"I want to be informed the moment there are any major developments. And if you don't call me, if nothing comes up, I'll still give you a ring around five o'clock tomorrow afternoon."

"Yes, sir."

"Get some rest."

"I'll try."

"Goodnight, Bob."

"Goodnight, sir."

The President clicked his tongue and hung up.

While McAlister was on the telephone with the President, Andrew Rice was in his car, cruising around one of the unofficial red-light districts of Washington. He drove slowly past a couple of blocks of cocktail lounges, cheap bars, adult movie theaters and bookstores, boutiques, pawnshops, and shuttered delicatessens. Young and generally attractive girls, alone and in groups of two or three, stood at the curb near the bus stops. Although they were dressed and posed provocatively, many of them were trying to look—for the benefit of the police, who were not deceived but pretended to be—as if they were waiting for a bus or a cab or their boyfriends. They were all prostitutes; and Rice had already driven through the area once before in order to study and compare the merchandise. Finally, he turned a corner, pulled his Thunderbird to the curb, stopped near two flashily dressed young girls, and put down the automatic window on the passenger's side.

A tall blonde in a tight white pantsuit and a short red vinyl jacket leaned in at the open window. She smiled at him and said, "Hello there."

"Hi."

"Nice night, after all that rain."

"Yes, it is."

She looked him over, studied the leather-upholstered interior of the car. She said nothing more.

"Ah . . ." His hands were slippery with sweat. He was gripping the wheel so hard that his knuckles were bloodless; they poked up sharp and hard in his fat fingers. "I'm looking for someone."

"What's his name? Maybe I know him."

You rotten bitch, he thought. He took his wallet from his inside jacket pocket. "How much?"

She pretended to be confused. "For what?"

"You know."

"Look, mister, so far as I know you're a cop. And I ain't going to proposition no cop, no way."

"Sex," he said.

"Not interested," she said, turning away from the window.

"Hey! What about your friend?" He nodded at the girl behind her.

"I'll ask her."

The other girl came to the window. She was a petite brunette, in her late teens or early twenties. She was wearing tight jeans and a long-sleeved white sweater and a short buckskin jacket. "Yeah?"

"How much?"

"You just did that routine with Velma."

"Okay, okay." Embarrassed, he told her what he wanted.

She appraised the car and said, "Seventy bucks."

"Okay."

"You have a motel room, or what?"

"I thought maybe we could use your place," he said.

"That's ten extra."

"Okay."

"Eighty—in advance."

"Sure."

She went over to the blonde, and they talked for almost a minute. Then she came back, got in the car, and gave him her address.

She had three rooms and a bath on the fourth floor of a thirty-year-old apartment house. There was a new wall-to-wall carpet in every room, including the kitchen; but she didn't have much furniture. What pieces she did have were expensive and in good taste.

In the bedroom, when they had both undressed, he said, "I'll stand up. You get on your knees."

"Whatever makes you happy." She got down before him and took his penis in one hand.

Before she could bring it to her lips, he chopped a knee into her chin and knocked her backward. As she fell he tried to imagine that she was not a hooker, that she was McAlister, that he was beating McAlister. He kicked her alongside the head and laughed when her eyes rolled back. He imagined that he was kicking McAlister and David Canning and the President and everyone else who had ever gotten the best of him or held authority over him. He even imagined that he was kicking A.W. West—and that made him feel best of all. He stopped kicking her and stood over her, gasping for breath. Then he dropped to his knees beside her and touched the bloody froth at her nostrils. Sighing contentedly, he began to use his fists.

TOKYO: FRIDAY, 3:15 P.M.

Someone knocked gently on the door, three times.

Canning stood up. He put one hand under his coat and touched the butt of the pistol in his shoulder holster.

The knocking came again, somewhat louder and more insistent than it had been the first time.

Keeping one hand inside his jacket, he turned away from the door which opened on the hotel corridor. The knocking came from the other door, the one that connected to the adjoining room. He walked over to it and stood against the wall. When the knocking sounded a third time, quite loud now, he said, "Who is it?"

"Tanaka." The voice was rather soft and high-pitched, just as McAlister had described it.

That didn't mean it was Tanaka.

It could be anyone.

It could even be the man who had followed him from the airport, the man who had watched him board the elevator.

"Are you there?"

"I'm here."

"Open up."

Whether or not it was Tanaka, he couldn't just stand here and wait for something to happen; he had to *make* it happen.

"Just a minute," he said.

He drew his pistol and stepped to one side of the door. He pushed the chair out from under the knob and out of the way. Then he twisted the brass key, pulled the door open, stepped past it, and shoved the silenced barrel of the Colt against the trim belly of a strikingly lovely young Japanese woman.

"I'm so happy to meet you, too," she said.

"What?"

"A gun in the stomach is so much more interesting than a plain old handshake."

"Huh?"

"A saying of Confucius."

He stared at her.

"Ah, and you're so articulate!"

He blinked. "Who are you?"

"Lee Ann Tanaka. Or would you like me to be someone else?"

"But . . ."

"Yes?"

He looked at her face carefully and saw that she fit the description that McAlister had given him. A tiny scar marked the left corner of her upper lip—although it was only as wide as a hair and half an inch long, certainly not a souvenir of a fight to the death with broken bottles. High on her left cheek there was a tiny black beauty mark: the "mole" for which McAlister had advised him to look. Finally, her hair was full, rich, and as black as raven wings. McAlister's only sin was one of omission.

"Are you going to kill me?" she asked.

"Of course not."

"Oh, then you were worried about my heart."

"What are you talking about?"

"My heart."

He shook his head.

She said, "Fear is good for the heart. Speeds it up. Gives the heart muscles much-needed exercise. Cleans out the system. How nice of you to be worried about my heart, Mr. Canning."

He put the pistol back in his holster. "I'm sorry."

"But my heart *needed* the exercise!" she said.

"I'm sorry for almost shooting you."

"Was it that close?"

"Close enough."

She put one hand to her breast. "Now you're giving my heart too damned much exercise." She stepped back a pace and said, "Do you have any luggage?"

"Two pieces."

"Bring it."

He fetched the suitcases and followed her into the adjoining room. It was a large, airy bedchamber decorated with imitations of old Japanese rice-paper watercolors and with genuine eighteenth-century Japanese furniture.

"This won't be good enough," he said.

In the middle of the room she stopped and turned to look back at him. "What won't be good enough?"

"Someone will be watching the door to my room."

"Right you are, Mr. Canning. You're under surveillance."

"If I don't come out and make a target of myself, sooner than later there are some goons who'll break in there and try to get me."

"Break right into your room?"

"One way or the other."

"What is Japan coming to? It's as bad here as in the States."

"And if I'm not in my room," Canning said, "they'll know that I didn't go out the front door. And they'll know I *couldn't* have climbed out onto the window ledge with two heavy suitcases. So the first place they'll look is in here."

She clapped her hands. "Marvelous!"

"What's marvelous?"

"Your magnificent exhibition of deductive reasoning," she said brightly. She gave him a big, very pretty smile.

He felt as if he had stepped into a whirlwind. He didn't quite know how to deal with her, and he couldn't understand why McAlister had put him in the hands of a woman, any woman, and especially *this* woman. "Look, Miss Tanaka, when these men don't find me next door, they'll simply come over here. They'll find me here. And they'll shoot me."

"Ah, I have confidence in you," she said. "You're much too fast on the draw for them." She rubbed her stomach where he'd held the gun on her.

"Miss Tanaka—"

"They won't shoot you," she said. "Because you won't be here." She turned and walked toward what he thought was the bathroom door. Over her shoulder she said, "Come along."

"Where to?"

"You'll see."

He followed her out of the bedroom onto a narrow railed deck that overlooked the first-floor living room of a two-floor suite. A bathroom and another bedroom opened onto the deck, and a carpeted spiral staircase wound down to one corner of the living room. A huge crystal chandelier hung from the roof of the gallery.

Downstairs, she turned to him and said, "They will not be expecting you to enter a room on one floor and immediately come out of a room on the floor below."

"I believe you've got something," he said.

"Charm," she said.

"Excuse me?"

"Come along."

At the front door of the suite, she reached for the brass knob, then let go of it, turned, and put her back to the door. She held one finger beside her lips. *"Sssshh!"*

He put down his suitcases and listened to the voices in the hotel corridor.

"Don't go for your gun," she said, grinning at him. "It's just the bellhop moving new guests into the room across the hall. Killing them might be exciting, but it would accomplish nothing." She closed her eyes and listened to the voices beyond the door.

He was standing no more than two feet away from her, and he did not close *his* eyes. For the first time since he'd seen her upstairs, he had an opportunity to study her face, to look beyond the hair-line scar on her upper lip and the beauty mark on her left cheek. Her forehead was broad and seamless. Her eyebrows were two natural black crescents, and her eyes were deeply set for an oriental face. She had a pert nose, very straight along the bridge, delicate nostrils; and her breathing was as quiet as the flight of a moth. With her high perfect cheekbones, aristocratic haughtiness, and shockingly ripe mouth, she might have been one of those high-priced fashion models who periodically took Manhattan, Paris, and London by storm. Her flawless complexion was the shade of aged book paper, and the sight of it somehow made him feel all warm and loose inside.

And what of the body that went with a face like that? he thought.

He looked down at the rest of her. But she was wearing a long belted trenchcoat that concealed everything except the crudely defined thrust of her breasts and the tininess of her waist. When he looked up again, he found that she was watching him.

Her eyes were large and clear. The irises were as black as her hair. They fixed on his eyes and seemed to bore straight through him, pinning him like an insect to a velvet specimen tray.

He blinked.

She didn't blink.

Suddenly his heart was beating so hard that he could hear it. His mouth was dry. He wanted to sit down somewhere with a drink and knit his nerves together again.

"Now," she said.

"Now what?"

"Time to go."

"Oh," he said thickly.

She turned away from him and opened the door. She leaned out, looked left and right, then went into the hall.

Picking up his suitcases, he followed her. He waited while she locked the suite, and then he trailed her down the corridor and through a brightly marked door into a concrete stairwell.

"We don't want to go out through the lobby," she said. "They think you're in your room, and they won't be expecting you down there—but one of them might be lurking about just the same. I have a rented car parked near the hotel's side entrance."

Their footsteps echoed flatly off the concrete walls.

At every landing Canning expected to see a man with a gun. But there was no one on the stairs.

Once he had to call a stop to catch his breath. His shoulders ached from the weight of the bags; he rubbed the back of his neck and wished he were sitting in a hot bath.

"Would you like me to take one of those?" she asked, pointing at the suitcases.

"No, thank you."

"I'm stronger than I look."

"That's what McAlister told me."

She grinned again. She had fine, brilliantly white teeth. "What else did he say about me?"

"Well, he said that the scar on your upper lip came from a fight you were in."

"Oh? A fight?"

"Some mean bastard carved you with a broken bottle."

Laughing lightly, she turned and went down the stairs, two at a time. She was almost skipping.

He plodded.

Outside, she helped him put his suitcases in a sparkling white Subaru, then went around and got in behind the wheel. When she drove away from the curb, the tires smoked and squealed, and Canning was pressed back into his seat.

He turned around and looked out the rear window. But it was soon evident that they had not been spotted and followed by any of The Committee's agents.

"Where are we going?" he asked, facing front again.

"Hotel New Otani."

"Where's that?"

"Not far."

To Canning's way of thinking, even one block was too far. The frenzied Tokyo traffic was not like anything he had seen before—or like anything he wanted to see again. There did not appear to be any formal lanes along which traffic could flow in an orderly manner; instead, strings of automobiles and trucks and buses crisscrossed one another, weaved and tangled with insane complexity. And the motorbikes, of course, zipped in and out between the larger vehicles, as if their operators had never been told about pain and death.

Initially, Canning felt that Lee Ann Tanaka drove like a certifiable maniac. She swung from one informal "lane" of cars into another without looking to see what was coming up behind her; and other cars' brakes barked sharply in her wake. Repeatedly, she stopped so suddenly and forcefully that Canning felt as if he were being cut in half by his seatbelt. She accelerated when there was absolutely nowhere to go, somehow squeezed in between trucks and buses that appeared to be riding bumper-to-bumper, gave a score of pedestrians intimations of mortality, and used the car's horn as if she thought this was New Year's Eve.

Gradually, however, Canning realized that she knew precisely what she was doing. She smiled continually. She did not appear to be frightened by the dozens of near-collisions—as if she knew from experience the difference between destruction and a millimeter. Evidently she was as at home in the streets of Tokyo as he was in his own living room.

He said, "How long does it take to become a carefree driver in this traffic?"

She shrugged. "I don't know."

"Well, how long have you been driving here?"

"Since the day before yesterday."

"Oh, sure."

She glanced sideways at him. "I'm an American," she said somewhat sharply. "I was born and raised an American. I'm as American as you are. I was never in Japan in my life—until the day before yesterday."

"Oh God," he said miserably.

"I flew in from San Francisco. Took a written test and an eye exam at the licensing bureau's airport office. Rented this car and been winging it ever since." As she spoke she swerved out of her lane, cut off a city bus and beat it through the intersection under a changing light.

"I thought you'd driven here all your life."

She cornered hard, nearly running down several pedestrians who had edged out from the sidewalk. "Thanks for the compliment! It's really not as awful as it looks from the passenger's seat."

"I'll bet."

"The only time it gets hairy is around nine in the morning and five in the afternoon. Just like in any American city. And you know what the Japanese call the peak traffic hours?"

"I couldn't guess."

"*Rushawa.*"

"Rush hour?"

She spelled it for him, switching lanes twice between the first and the final letters.

He smiled appreciatively. "But since you *haven't* driven here all your life—do you think you could *slow down?*"

She whipped the car to the right, stood on the brakes, stopped the car on a hundred-yen coin, and switched off the engine.

Lifting his head from his knees, Canning said, "Jesus! I only asked you to slow down—"

"We're here," she said brightly.

"What?"

"The Hotel New Otani."

Dazed, he glanced up just as the uniformed doorman opened the door of the Subaru. The man leaned in, smiled at Canning, offered a hand to help him out of the low-slung little car, and said, "*Konnichiwa,* sir!"

Afternoon, yes, Canning thought. But was it good? And could it be the same afternoon that he had got off a plane from Honolulu? So much seemed to have happened in the frenetic company of Miss Tanaka. *Days* seemed to have passed. "*Konnichiwa* yourself," he said.

As they followed the doorman and Canning's luggage into the hotel, Lee Ann took his arm and said, "We don't have to register. I've done that already. We're traveling as Mr. and Mrs. J. Okrow. I figure that once The Committee's agents know they've lost you at the Imperial, they'll start checking other hotels—but not for married couples. And if they manage to get their hands on the hotel register—well, the name Okrow sounds *Western* to the Japanese desk clerk at the Otani, but it probably will sound *Japanese* to most Westerners."

"It does to me."

"You see!"

"You think of everything," he said, genuine admiration in his voice.

"I try to," she said, beaming up at him and squeezing his arm in a fine imitation of wifely pleasure and devotion.

The room she had booked for them was attractive and spacious. Two double beds dressed in white chenille and boasting dark caned headboards were set against one wall. A matching caned nightstand stood between the beds and held a twin-necked lamp, a telephone, and menus from the hotel's restaurants. On the other side of the room, there was a combination desk-dresser with a wall mirror above it. There was also a color television set on its own wheeled cart. Two Danish-style armchairs stood on opposite sides of a small round coffee table. The wallpaper was pebble-textured and cream-colored, except for the wall opposite the windows: *that* was decorated with an abstract brown and green and white mural of mountains and bamboo fields. In the bathroom—with separate tub and shower stall, sun lamps, and bidet —there was a full bottle of whiskey and another of vodka standing on the makeup counter. A small refrigerator hummed to itself in the niche under the sink, and it was stocked with a variety of soft drinks.

Taking off his suit jacket, Canning said, "You must think I'm a real boozer."

"I like to drink, myself."

"The agency never bought me whiskey before."

"You haven't been playing it right." She sat down in one of the armchairs and folded her hands in her lap. "You like the room?"

Hanging his jacket in the foyer closet, Canning said, "Well, it isn't as nice as the George V in Paris or the Sherry-Netherland in New York. But I suppose it'll do."

She was looking quite pleased with herself. "We've got to spend the next sixteen or seventeen hours in here. Can't take a chance of going out to dinner or breakfast and being spotted by your friends from the Imperial. We'll have food sent up. So . . . If we're going to be imprisoned, we might as well have all the comforts."

He sat down in the other armchair. "We're going to Peking in a French jet?"

"That's right."

"Tell me about it?"

"Didn't Bob McAlister tell you about it?"

"He said you would."

She said, "It belongs to Jean-Paul Freneau, a very classy art dealer who has headquarters in Paris and branch offices throughout the world. He deals in paintings, sculpture, primitive art—everything. He's a valued friend of the Chairman."

Canning made a face. "Why would the Chairman maintain a close friendship with a rich, capitalistic French art dealer?"

Lee Ann had the rare habit of looking directly at whomever she was talking to, and now her black eyes locked on Canning's. A shiver went through him as she spoke. "For one thing, now that China is at last moving into the world marketplace, she needs contacts with Western businessmen she feels she can trust. Freneau has helped to arrange large contracts for the delivery of Chinese handicrafts to the Common Market countries. More importantly, Freneau has helped the Chairman to buy back some of the priceless Chinese art taken out of the country by followers of Chiang Kai-shek in 1949. Every time some wealthy Nationalist puts a piece or a collection on the market, Freneau is there with the highest bid. He's the agent for Red China in its attempt to keep the Chinese heritage from being spread throughout the private collections of the West."

"And why is Freneau so willing to cooperate with the CIA?"

"He isn't," she said. "He's cooperating with Bob McAlister. They've been friends for years."

"When do we leave?"

"Tomorrow morning at nine."

He thought for a moment. Then: "I guess the only other thing is the list of names. The three agents we have in China."

"You really want me to go through that now?"

He sighed. "No. I guess tomorrow on the plane is soon enough. But I do want to know about you."

She raised her eyebrows. "Oh?"

"You're a surprise."

"How?"

"When McAlister described Tanaka . . . Well, I didn't think . . ."

Her lovely face clouded. "What are you trying to say? That you don't like working with someone who isn't a nice lily-white WASP?"

"What?" He was surprised by the bitterness in her voice.

"I am as American as you are," she said sharply.

"Wait a minute. Wait a minute. It isn't your ethnic background that bothers me. I just wasn't expecting a woman."

Gradually her face unclouded. "That's exactly Bob McAlister's sense of humor."

"So tell me about yourself."

"If we're going to sit here and jabber much longer, I want a drink." She stood up and took off her trenchcoat. She was wearing a red silk blouse and a long black skirt, and she looked better than any woman he had ever seen. "Can I get you something?"

"Whatever you're having," he said.

She came back from the bathroom a few minutes later and handed him his glass. "Vodka and orange soft drink."

He clinked glasses with her in a wordless toast. After he had taken a good swallow of the concoction, he said, "Once in the car and then again just a few minutes ago, you got very hot under the collar when you thought I was questioning your Americanism. Why so sensitive?"

Hesitating for a moment, pausing to sip her drink, she finally said, "I'm sorry. It's a problem I have, a psychological problem I understand but can't lick." She took another drink. She seemed unwilling to say anything more, then suddenly explained it with a rush of words that came almost too fast to be intelligible: "My mother was Japanese-American, and my father was half Japanese and half Chinese. He owned a small shop in San Francisco's Chinatown. In 1942, about the middle of May, they were taken from their home and put in a concentration camp. You must know about the camps where Japanese-Americans were kept during World War Two. They called them 'assembly centers' but they were concentration camps, all right. Barbed wire, armed guards, machine-gun posts guarding them . . . They spent more than three years in the camp. When they got out, after V-J Day, they found my father's store had been stripped of merchandise and rented to someone else. He received no compensation. They had also been evicted from their home and lost their personal possessions. They had to start all over again. And it wasn't easy—because banks and businessmen just weren't in the mood to help any Japanese-Americans."

Leaning forward in his chair, Canning said, "But you aren't old enough to have lived through that."

"I'm twenty-nine," she said, her eyes never wavering from his. There was a thread of fear woven through those black irises now. "I wasn't born until well after the war. That's true. But I was raised in an emotionally torn household. My parents were quietly proud of their Asian ancestry, but after their ordeal in the camp they were anxious to prove themselves 'native' Americans. They became over-Americanized after that. They even stopped writing to relatives in the Old World. They taught me Chinese and Japanese in the privacy of our home, but they forbid me to speak it outside the home. I was to speak only English when I was out of their company. I was twenty-four before anyone but my mother and father knew I was multilingual. And now I seem to have this need to prove how American I am." She smiled. "About the only good thing to come of it is a very American drive to achieve, achieve, achieve."

And she had achieved a great deal by the age of twenty-nine. While she was still twenty she had graduated from the University of California. By twenty-five she'd obtained a master's and a doctorate in sociology and psychology from Columbia University. She had done some speech-writing for a successful Vice-Presidential candidate, and it was in that capacity that she had met and become friends with Bob McAlister and his wife. When she was twenty-six she had applied for a position with the CIA, had passed all the tests, and had backed out at the last minute when she'd accepted a proposal of marriage from one of her professors at Columbia. The marriage had failed a few months ago, and she had been more than available when McAlister had asked for her help in the Dragonfly investigation.

"I took the oath and signed the secrecy pledge the first time I applied for work with the agency," she said. "So there was really no technical reason why Bob couldn't tell me everything and ring me in on this."

Canning stood up and said, "Another drink?"

"Please."

When he came back with two more vodka atrocities, he said, "I'm damned glad he did ring you in. You're the most efficient partner I've ever worked with."

She didn't blush or demur, and he respected her for that. She just nodded and said, "That's probably true. But enough about me. Let's talk about you."

Canning was not the sort of man who liked to talk about himself, and especially not to people whom he had just met. Yet with her he was talkative. She sat with her head tilted to the left and her mouth slightly open as if she were tasting what he said as well as listening to it.

Around seven o'clock they stopped drinking and talking long enough for her to order their dinner from room service. While she did that, he took a hot shower, brushed his teeth, and shaved.

When he came out of the bathroom in fresh slacks and a T-shirt, the room-service hot cart was set up and the food was ready.

While he was in the shower, she had changed into a floor-length silk lounging robe which had a peaked hood after the fashion of a monk's habit. The silk was forest-green, with a decorative gold zipper all the way down the front. She was striking, exotic.

They ate *mizutaki,* the white meat of the chicken stewed in an earthenware pot and flavored with many herbs. When the chicken was gone, they drank the excellent broth. This was accompanied by piping hot *sake* which was delicious but which—Lee Ann explained—tasted like a spoiled sauterne when it was cool. For dessert, there were mandarin-orange slices and shredded almonds. To finish the meal and stretch out the evening, there were six small bottles of *Kirin,* the excellent lager that was an equal to the best European beers.

At some point they adjourned to one of the beds, where they stretched out side by side, each with a bottle of *Kirin.* The conversation continued nonstop, and Canning found that the sound of her voice was like a tranquilizer.

Shortly before ten o'clock she went to use the bathroom, and when she came back she was nude. She was exquisite. Her breasts were small but perfectly shaped, upthrust, with nipples as dark as baker's chocolate. Her stomach was as flat as that of a young boy. Her navel was convex rather than concave: a sweet, protruding nubbins. Her pubic thatch was thick and dark, and her legs were as smooth and sinuous as any he had ever seen in Las Vegas showrooms or in the Crazy Horse Saloon or in the airbrushed pages of *Playboy.* Yet for all of this, there was something childlike and vulnerable about the way she stood before him.

He said, "Are you sure?"

"Yes."

"Maybe it's the wine."

"No."

She switched off all but one light.

"I'm too old for you."

"You're younger than you are. And I'm older than I am."

"It's so fast."

"That's the American way. I'm an American woman, and American women get what they want. I want you." She knelt on the bed beside him. "Relax. Enjoy. Remember that we could be in Peking when Dragonfly is detonated. We could be dead tomorrow."

"Is that the only reason for this?" he asked.

"No. I like you."

He reached for her.

She stretched out on top of him.

He tasted her mouth.

After a while she undressed him.

His erection was like a post. When she touched it he felt a quick flash of guilt and remembered Irene. But that passed, and he slipped into a pool of sensation.

Afterward, she got two fresh bottles of *Kirin*. They sat up in bed, drinking. They touched one another, gently, tentatively, as if to reassure themselves that they had been together.

At some point in the night, after the *Kirin* was gone, when she was lying with her head upon his chest, he said, "I told you about my son."

"Mike."

"Yes. What I didn't tell you was that he thinks of me as a murderer."

"Are you?"

"In a sense."

"Who have you killed?"

"Agents. The other side."

"How many?"

"Eleven."

"They would have killed you?"

"Of course."

"Then you're no murderer."

"Tell him that."

"The meek don't inherit the earth," she said. "The meek are put in concentration camps. And graves."

"I've tried to tell him that."

"But he believes in pacifism and reason?"

"Something of the sort."

"Wait until he finds most people won't listen to reason."

He cupped one of her breasts. "If I told him about Dragonfly, Mike would say the world has gone mad."

"I think poor Bob McAlister feels that way. At least a little bit. Don't you think?"

"Yes. You're right."

"And of course, it hasn't gone mad."

"Because it's always *been* mad."

She said, "You know why I wanted you?"

"Because I'm handsome and charming?"

"A thousand reasons. But, maybe most of all—because I sensed violence in you. Death. Not that you're fond of death and violence. But you accept it. And you can deal it."

"That makes me exotic, exciting?"

"It makes you like me."

He said, "You've never killed anyone."

"No. But I could. I'd make a good assassin if I believed the man I was to kill *had* to die for the good of mankind. There are men who need to die, aren't there? Some men are animals."

"My liberal friends would think *I'm* an animal if they heard me agree with you," he said. "But then, so would some of my conservative friends."

"And your son. Yet without you and a few others like you, they'd all have fallen prey to the *real* animals a long time ago. Most men who can kill without guilt are monsters, but we need a few decent men with that ability too."

"Maybe."

"Or maybe we're megalomaniacs."

"I don't know about *you*," he said. "But I don't *always* think I'm right. In fact, I usually think I'm wrong."

"Scratch megalomania."

"I think so."

"I guess we're just realists in a world of dreamers. But even if that's what we are, even if we *are* right, that doesn't make us very nice people, does it?"

"There are no heroes. But, Miss Tanaka, you're plenty nice enough for me."

"I want you again."

"Likewise."

They made love. As before, he found in her a knowledge and enthusiasm that he had never known in a woman, a fierce desire that was beyond any lust that Irene had ever shown. None of the very civilized, very gentle lovers he had had were like this. And he wondered, as he swelled and moved within her, if it was necessary to see and accept the animal in yourself before you could really enjoy life. Lee Ann rocked and bucked upon him, gibbered against his neck, clutched and clawed at him, and worked away the minutes toward a new day.

At twelve-thirty he put through a call to the desk and asked for a wake-up message at six the next morning. Then he set his travel clock for six-ten.

Lee Ann said, "I gather you don't trust Japanese hotel operators."

"It's not that. I'm just compulsive about a lot of things. Didn't McAlister warn you?"

"No."

"I have a well-known neatness fetish which drives some people crazy. I'm always picking up lint and straightening pictures on the walls . . ."

"I haven't noticed."

Suddenly he saw the room-service cart, covered with haphazardly stacked, dirty dishes. "My God!"

"What's the matter?"

He pointed to the cart. "It's been there all night, and I haven't had the slightest urge to clean it up. I don't have the urge now, either."

"Maybe I'm the medicine you need."

That could be true, he thought. But he worried that if he lost his neuroses, he might also lose that orderliness of thought that had always put him one up on the other side. And tomorrow when they got into Peking, he would need to be sharper than he had ever been before.

HSIAN, CHINA: FRIDAY, MIDNIGHT

Steam blossomed around the wheels of the locomotive and flowered into the chilly night air. It smelled vaguely of sulphur.

Chai Po-han walked through the swirling steam and along the side of the train. The Hsian station, only dimly lighted at this hour, lay on his right; aureoles of wan light shimmered through a blanket of thin, phosphorescent fog. The first dozen cars of the train were full of cargo, but the thirteenth was a passenger cab.

"Boarding?" asked the conductor, who stood at the base of the collapsible metal steps that led up into the car. He was a round-faced, bald, and toothless man whose smile was quite warm but nonetheless unnerving.

"I'm transferring from the Chungking line," Chai said. He showed the conductor his papers.

"All the way into Peking?"

"Yes."

"And you've come from Chungking today?"

"Yes."

"That's quite a trip without rest."

"I'm very weary."

"Come aboard, then. I'll find you a sleeping berth."

The train was dark inside. The only light was the moonlike glow which came through the windows from the station's platform lamps. Chai could not really see where he was going, but the conductor moved down the aisle with the night sureness of a cat.

"You're going the right direction to get a sleeping berth," the toothless man said. "These days the trains are full on their way out from the cities, on their way to the communes. Coming in, there are only vacationers and soldiers."

In the sleeping cars, where there were no windows, the conductor switched on his flashlight. In the second car he located a cramped berth that was unoccupied. "This will be yours," he said in a whisper.

All around them, three-deep on both sides, men and women snored and murmured and tossed in their sleep.

Chai threw his single sack of belongings onto the bunk and said, "When will we reach Peking?"

"Nine o'clock tomorrow evening," the conductor said. "Sleep well, Comrade."

Lying on his back in the berth, the bottom of the next-highest mattress only inches from his face, Chai thought of his home, thought of his family, and hoped that he would have good dreams. But his very last thought, just as he drifted off, was of Ssunan Commune, and instead of pleasant dreams, he endured the same nightmare that had plagued him since the end of winter: a white room, the gods in green, and the scalpel poised to dissect his soul . . .

3

WASHINGTON: FRIDAY, 3:00 P.M.

Andrew Rice ate a macaroon in one bite while he waited for
McAlister's secretary to put the director on the line. He finished
swallowing just as McAlister said hello. "Bob, I hope I'm not
interrupting anything."

"Not at all," McAlister said guardedly.

"I called to apologize."

"Oh?"

"I understand that you had to sweet-talk those federal marshals
because I called them so late Wednesday evening."

"It's nothing," McAlister said. "I soothed everyone in a few
minutes. It didn't even come close to a fistfight."

"Yes, but with everything you've got on your shoulders right
now, you don't need labor problems too."

"Really, I was being petty. I should never have mentioned it to
the President."

"No, no. He asked me to call and give you an explanation. And
you deserve one. Besides, the truth of it will let me off the hook, at
least somewhat." He took another macaroon from the bag in his
desk drawer and turned it over and over in his fingers as he spoke.

"Fredericks at Justice was supposed to send me a list of marshals in the D.C. area, and he took his time about it. His messenger didn't get to my office until nearly six o'clock."

"I see."

"Then, of course, I wanted to get some background material on each of the marshals so we could be damned sure that none of them had past connections with the CIA. By the time I had twelve men I was sure I could trust, most of the evening had disappeared. If Fredericks had gotten that list to me earlier . . . Well, I should have been on the phone to him every fifteen minutes, pushing and prodding. I wasn't, so part of the blame is mine."

McAlister said, "Now I'm doubly sorry that I mentioned this to the chief."

"As I said, you deserved an explanation." He waved the macaroon under his nose. "Any new developments?"

"Unfortunately, no," McAlister said.

"Your man should reach Peking shortly."

"Then the fireworks start."

"Let's hope not," Rice said, meaning something much different than McAlister would think he meant. "Sorry again about any problems I may have caused you."

"Sure. Be seeing you."

"Goodbye, Bob."

The moment he hung up he popped the macaroon into his mouth and instantly ground it to a sweet paste.

He felt pretty good today. For one thing he had worked off most of his nervous tension with that whore last night. She was his first woman in four months and the first he had ever picked up in Washington. He had always felt that he would be risking too much by taking his satisfaction here in the capital. In Washington D.C., where the juiciest gossip and the main topic of conversation was nearly always about politicians, even a prostitute was likely to be somewhat politically aware; there was always the chance that even a seldom-photographed Presidential aide would be recognized on the street. But his need had been too great to delay, and he'd had no time or excuse for a trip to New York, Philadelphia, or Baltimore. And after all, the affair had gone well: she had been attractive; she hadn't recognized him; and she'd helped him to get rid of the awful pressure that had been building within him. Now, this morning, the news about Dragonfly had suddenly taken a turn for the better, and Rice felt as well as a five-foot-ten, two-hundred-eighty-pound man could ever feel.

"Mr. Rice?"

He swallowed another macaroon, pressed an intercom button, and said, "Yes?"

"Mr. Yu is here."

"Send him right in."

Mr. Yu Miao-sheng, Formosa's ambassador to the United States, was a short, wiry man who wore excellent Hong Kong suits and thick wire-framed glasses. He smiled quite a bit; and his teeth were very sharp, almost canine.

Rice greeted him at the door, and they shook hands. "Please have a seat, Mr. Yu."

"Thank you, Mr. Rice."

"Can I get you something to drink, Mr. Yu?"

"Would you possibly have any dry sherry, Mr. Rice?"

"Certainly."

"Dry Sack, perhaps?"

"I believe it is."

"Could I possibly have some of that over ice?"

Rice got the drink, put it on the coffee table, and sat in the armchair opposite the ambassador. When Mr. Yu had taken a sip of his drink and smiled approval, Rice said, "How was your meeting with the President?"

"Very strained," Mr. Yu said. He was quite amused by this; he laughed softly. "The President insisted that I knew something about a CIA plan to overthrow the government of the People's Republic of China. And I insisted that I knew nothing. We were both adamant, but we managed to behave like statesmen."

Rice smiled. "I am happy to hear that."

Frowning, Mr. Yu said, "However, the President made one point which causes me great concern."

"Oh?"

"According to intelligence reports from which he quoted, the Russians are now aware of Taiwan's preparations for war."

"Yes."

"And the Soviet army is making preparations of its own."

"That's true enough; however, there is really nothing to worry about, Mr. Yu."

"But might not the Russians sweep in from the west and take a substantial part of the homeland before we can secure and defend it? The Russians are far better armed, far better prepared for war than are the Communist Chinese. You must know that if the Russians decided to take such risks—even if they were to forsake nuclear weapons—they would be too powerful an adversary for our Taiwanese forces."

"Yes, of course. But remember that mainland China is a vast country. The Russians will need weeks if not months to consolidate their gains in the west. Before they can get near Peking or the other eastern cities you will seize in the invasion—well, we will have taken care of the Russians."

Mr. Yu blinked stupidly for a long moment. Then: "There is a Dragonfly for Russia too?"

"Something of that sort," Rice said. "We hadn't planned to launch *that* operation for a few years. But if the Russians take advantage of the confusion in China to acquire some new territory, we'll have to advance our schedule."

"I am amazed."

Rice smiled tolerantly. "Now, tell me, how are things coming along in Taipei?"

"I received a coded message from the capital just this morning," Mr. Yu said. "We are virtually one hundred percent prepared."

"Excellent."

"Two thousand paratroopers will be in the air within three hours of your go-ahead signal. Within nine to twelve hours they will have seized every one of Communist China's nuclear weapons."

"The seaborne troops?"

Pausing only to take an occasional sip of sherry, Mr. Yu spent the next ten minutes discussing the preparations which had been made for the invasion. When he had nothing more to report, he said, "As you can see, we need no advantage except the confusion caused by the plague in Peking."

Rice said, "I, too, have received a coded message."

"From Taipei?"

"From Peking."

"Sir?"

"Dragonfly is on the move at last," Rice said. "He will arrive in Peking around nine o'clock Saturday night, their time."

Mr. Yu was delighted. He slid to the edge of his chair. "And when will he be triggered?"

"As soon as possible," Rice said. "Within twenty-four hours of his arrival in the capital."

"I will alert my people." Mr. Yu finished his sherry and got to his feet. "This is a momentous occasion, Mr. Rice."

"Momentous," Rice agreed as he struggled out of his chair.

They shook hands.

At the door, Rice said, "How are your wife and daughters, Mr. Yu?"

"Quite well, thank you, Mr. Rice."

"Will you give them my best, Mr. Yu?"

"I certainly will, Mr. Rice."

"Good day, Mr. Yu."

"Good luck, Mr. Rice."

WASHINGTON: FRIDAY, 6:00 P.M.

After giving the President a progress report by telephone at five o'clock, McAlister had gone straight to dinner. He was not at all hungry, but dinner gave him an excuse for drinks. By six he was at his favorite corner table in an expensive Italian restaurant that was popular with Cabinet officials, White House aides, senators, congressmen, and reporters. This early in the evening, there were very few customers. McAlister sat alone with his back to the wall, the *Washington Post* in front of him and a glass of iced bourbon ready at his right hand.

As it had been for more years than he liked to think about, the news was sprinkled liberally with insanity, with signs of a society enduring a prolonged attack of schizophrenia. In Detroit three men had been killed when a group of young Marxist factory workers, all of whom earned salaries that provided them with a Cadillac-standard of living, planted a bomb under a production-line conveyor belt. In Boston an organization calling itself The True Sons of America was taking credit for a bomb explosion in the offices of a liberal newspaper, where a secretary and bookkeeper were killed. And in California the left-wing Symbionese Liberation Army had surfaced once again. Eight SLA "soldiers" had crashed a birthday party in a wealthy San Francisco suburb and murdered two adults and five small children. They had kidnapped three other children, leaving behind a tape recording which explained that after much consideration and discussion among themselves about what would be best for the People, they had decided to stop the capitalist machine by either murdering or "reeducating" its children. Therefore, they had kidnapped three children for reeducation and had slaughtered those for whom they had no available SLA foster parents.

McAlister picked up his bourbon and finished nearly half of it in one long swallow.

In the past he had read this sort of news and had been appalled; now he was *outraged.* His hands were shaking. His face felt hot, and his throat was tight with anger. These SLA bastards were no different from the crackpots who were behind the Dragonfly project. One group was Marxist and one fascist, but their methods and their insensitivity and their self-righteousness and even their totalitarian goals were substantially the same. Was it possible for even the most single-minded liberal to support fair trial, mercy, and parole for these bastards? Was it possible for anyone to try to explain their behavior as having its source in poverty and injustice? Was it possible, even now, for anyone to express equal sympathy for killers and victims alike? He wished it were possible to execute these people without trial . . . But that would be playing right into the hands of men like A.W. West—who, of course, deserved the same treatment, the same quick and brutal punishment, but who would probably wind up administering it to the left-wingers. None of these people, revolutionaries or reactionaries, deserved to live among men of reason. They were all animals, throwbacks, forces for chaos who had none but a disruptive function in a civilized world. They should be sought, apprehended, and destroyed—

Yes, but how in the hell did that sort of thinking mesh with his well-known liberalism? How could he believe in the reasonable world his Boston family and teachers had told him about—and still believe in meeting violence with violence?

He quickly finished the last of his bourbon.

"Bad day, was it?"

McAlister looked up and saw Fredericks, an assistant attorney general at the Justice Department, standing in front of his table.

"I thought you were pretty much a teetotaler," Bill Fredericks said.

"Used to be."

"You ought to get out of the CIA."

"And come over to Justice?"

"Sure. We whittle away hours on anti-trust suits. And even when we've got a hot case, we aren't rushed. The wheels of justice grind slowly. One martini a night eases the tension."

Smiling, McAlister shook his head and said, "Well, if you've got it so damned easy over there, I wish you'd make an effort to help take the pressure off me when you get the chance."

Fredericks blinked. "What'd I do?"

"It's what you *didn't* do."

"What didn't I do?"

McAlister reminded him of how long he'd taken to send that list of federal marshals to Andrew Rice.

"But that's not true," Fredericks said. "Rice's secretary called and asked for the list. No explanations. Very snotty. Wanted to have it sooner than immediately. National security. Fate of the nation at stake. Future of the free world in the balance. Danger to the republic. That sort of thing. I couldn't get hold of a messenger fast enough, so I sent my own secretary to deliver it. She left it with Rice's secretary." He stopped and thought for a moment. "I *know* she was back in my office no later than four o'clock."

McAlister frowned. "But why would Rice lie to me?"

"You'll have to ask him."

"I guess I will."

"If you're dining alone," Fredericks said, "why don't you join us?" He motioned to a table where two other lawyers from Justice were ordering drinks.

"Bernie Kirkwood is supposed to join me before long," McAlister said. "Besides, I wouldn't be very good company tonight."

"In that case, maybe *I* better join you, Bill," Kirkwood said as he arrived at McAlister's table.

Kirkwood was in his early thirties, a thin, bushy-headed, narrow-faced man who looked as if he'd just been struck by lightning and was still crackling with a residue of electricity. His large eyes were made even larger by thick gold-framed glasses. His smile revealed a lot of crooked white teeth.

"Well," Fredericks said, "I can't let any newsmen see me with *both* of you crusaders. That would start all sorts of rumors about big new investigations, prosecutions, heads rolling in ·high places. My telephone would never stop ringing. How could I ever find the time I need to nail some poor bastard to the wall for income-tax evasion?"

Kirkwood said, "I didn't know that you guys at Justice ever nailed anyone for anything."

"Oh, sure. It happens."

"When was the last time?"

"Six years ago this December, I think. Or was it seven years last June?"

"Income-tax evader?"

"No, I think it was some heinous bastard who was carrying a placard back and forth in front of the White House, protesting the war. Or something."

"But you got him," Kirkwood said.

"Put him away for life."

"We can sleep nights."

"Oh, yes! The streets are safe!" Grinning, Fredericks turned to McAlister and said, "You'll check that out—about the list? I'm not lying to you."

"I'll check it out," McAlister said. "And I believe you, Bill."

Fredericks returned to his own table; as he was leaving, the waiter brought menus for McAlister and Kirkwood, took their orders for drinks, fetched one bourbon and one Scotch, and said how nice it was to see them.

When they were alone again, Kirkwood said, "We found Dr. Hunter's car in a supermarket parking lot a little over a mile from his home in Bethesda."

Dr. Leroy Hunter, McAlister knew, was another biochemist who had connections with the late Dr. Olin Wilson. He had also been on friendly terms with Potter Cofield, their only other lead, the man who had been stabbed to death in his own home yesterday. He said, "No sign of Hunter, I suppose."

Kirkwood shook his woolly head: no. "A neighbor says she saw him putting two suitcases in the trunk of the car before he drove away yesterday afternoon. They're still there, both of them, full of toilet articles and clean clothes."

Sipping bourbon, leaning back in his chair, McAlister said, "Know what I think?"

"Sure," Kirkwood said, folding his bony hands around his glass of Scotch. "Dr. Hunter has joined Dr. Wilson and Dr. Cofield in that great research laboratory in the sky."

"That's about it."

"Sooner or later we'll find the good doctor floating face-down in the Potomac River—a faulty electric toaster clasped in both hands and a burglar's knife stuck in his throat." Kirkwood grinned humorlessly.

"Anything on those two dead men we found in David Canning's apartment?"

"They were each other's best friend. We can't tie either of them to anyone else in the agency."

"Then we're right back to square one."

Kirkwood said, "I called the office at six o'clock. They'd just received a telephone call from Tokyo. Canning and Tanaka took off in that Frenchman's jet at five P.M. Friday, Washington time—which is nine o'clock tomorrow morning in Tokyo."

McAlister handed him a section of the *Washington Post.* "Let's make a pact: no more talk about Dragonfly until after dinner. The world's full of *other* interesting crises and tragedies. I would advise, however, that you skip all that negative stuff and look for the harmless human-interest stories."

Nodding, Kirkwood said, "You mean like 'Hundred-Year-Old Man Tells Secret of Long Life.' "

"That's it exactly."

"Or maybe, 'Iowa Man Grows World's Largest Potato.' "

"Even better."

The waiter returned, interrupting their reading long enough to take two orders for hearts of artichokes in vinaigrette, cheese-filled ravioli, and a half-bottle of good red wine.

Just before the artichokes arrived, McAlister was reading about a famous Christian evangelist's ideas for the rehabilitation of the thousands of men in American prisons. The evangelist wanted to surgically implant a transponder in each prisoner's brain so that the man could be monitored by a computer. The computer would not only keep track of the ex-prisoner but it would listen in to his conversations wherever he might be—and give him an electric shock if he used obscene language or tried to break the terms of his parole. The minister thought that, indeed, such a device could benefit a great many Americans who had never been to prison but who had engaged in hundreds of minor violations of the law all of their lives. The evangelist also felt—and said that he was certain God agreed with him—that the punishment for various crimes should be brought into line with the nature of the original transgression. For example, a rapist should be castrated. A thief should have some of his fingers chopped off. A pornographer should have one eye poked out because it had offended God. A prostitute—

"What in the hell?" Kirkwood's voice was uncharacteristically breathless, quiet.

McAlister looked up from his section of the newspaper. "It can't be as bad as what I'm reading."

After he'd taken a moment to reread a paragraph, Kirkwood said, "Last night, right near here, a prostitute was badly beaten by one of her johns."

"Don't read about prostitutes," McAlister said. "Read something uplifting. I'm reading about this evangelist—"

"She couldn't talk very well because her mouth was swollen," Kirkwood said. "But she was plucky. While they worked on her at the hospital, she insisted on trying to tell the cops a few things about her assailant. Do you know what this john kept saying, over and over, while he beat up on her?"

"I guess you're going to tell me."

"He kept saying, 'You can't stop Dragonfly, you can't stop Dragonfly.' "

They stared at each other.

Finally Kirkwood said, "The police think he was just raving, that it doesn't mean anything."

"Maybe it doesn't."

"Maybe."

"I mean even to us."

"Maybe."

"Could be coincidence."

"Could be."

McAlister said, "Let me see that."

Kirkwood handed the newspaper to him.

After he had read a few paragraphs, McAlister said, "Did she give a description of the man?"

"Top of the second column."

McAlister read what the girl had told the police: her assailant had been fat, she meant really fat, three hundred pounds or more, and he was middle-aged, sloppily dressed, didn't belong in that expensive car, probably stole the car, she didn't know what kind of car, maybe a Cadillac or a Continental, all those luxury cars looked the same to her, she knew nothing about cars, she just knew he was fat and strong and kept saying she couldn't stop Dragonfly, whatever in the hell that was . . . With each word he read, McAlister felt the blood drain out of his face.

Kirkwood leaned over the table and said, "Hey, do you recognize this guy?"

No. It was impossible. It was crazy. It made no sense. He would never have taken such a risk.

Rice?

No.

Rice?

McAlister began to remember things and to connect them: Rice had been so eager to know whom McAlister was sending to Peking, even more eager than the President had been; the Committeemen had tried to kill Canning at his apartment within a couple of hours after Rice had been given his name; and Rice had lied about Bill Fredericks and the list of federal marshals who lived— Good Christ, the federal marshals!

"Bob? Are you there?"

The waiter brought their hearts of artichokes and the half-bottle of red wine.

McAlister sat very still: stunned.

The moment the waiter had gone, Kirkwood said, "You look like you've been pole-axed."

Softly, McAlister said, "I don't know . . . I may be wrong and . . . I *have* to be wrong! It would be such a foolish thing for him to do! What a risk to take in his position! Yet if he's as unbalanced, as completely crazy as he'd have to be to get involved in this, and if he's feeling the pressure half as much as I'm feeling it, he just might . . ." His voice trailed off.

Frowning, Kirkwood said, "What in the name of God are you talking about?"

McAlister stood up. "We don't have time for dinner." He dropped his napkin and turned away from the table.

"Bob?"

McAlister hurried toward the front of the restaurant, weaving between the tables, nearly running.

Bewildered, Kirkwood followed close behind him.

PEKING: SATURDAY, 11:00 A.M.

In the second-floor study of a stately old house in Peking, a man sat down at a large mahogany desk and unfolded a sheet of paper. He placed the paper squarely in the center of the green felt blotter. It was a list of numbers which had been transmitted by laser wireless in Washington, bounced off a relay satellite high over the Pacific Ocean, and picked up by a receiver in this house.

The man at the desk smiled when he thought that the Chinese counterintelligence forces had surely monitored and recorded this same transmission at half a dozen different points along the Eastern Seaboard. Even now a score of code specialists would be trying to break down the numbers into some sensible message. But none of them would ever crack it, for there was no intrinsic alphabetic value to the numbers. They referred to chapters and page numbers within a certain book which was known only to the man in Washington and the man in this house.

He poured himself some whiskey and water from the bottle and pitcher that stood on the desk.

He opened the center drawer of the desk and took from it a pencil and a small brass pencil sharpener. Holding both hands over the wastebasket in order to keep the shavings from falling on the carpet, he put a needlelike point on the pencil and then placed it beside the list of numbers. He dropped the brass gadget into the desk, closed the drawer, and dusted his hands together.

Still smiling, he tasted his whiskey.

He was savoring the moment, drawing out the thrill of anticipation. He was not at all worried, for he knew precisely what the message would be, what it *had* to be. He felt fine.

At last he turned around in his chair and took a copy of Kenneth Grahame's *The Wind in the Willows* from the bookshelves behind him. This was the 1966 slipcased Grosset and Dunlap edition, illustrated by Dick Cuffari. In Washington, Andrew Rice had had the same edition at hand when he'd composed the message which had come in on the laser wireless.

The first line of Rice's message read:

8000650006

The man at the desk opened *The Wind in the Willows* to Chapter Eight, which was titled "Toad's Adventures." He counted to the sixty-fifth line from the start of that chapter and then located the sixth word in that line. He picked up the pencil and wrote:

snapdragon

He drank some more of the whiskey. It was excellent, due in large measure to the water with which he had cut it. You had to mix fine whiskey with the proper water; otherwise, you might just as well drink vinegar or moonshine—or that absolutely terrible rice wine which the Chinese fermented and served with such great pride. He had gone to considerable trouble to obtain the right water for this whiskey, and now he took time to enjoy it. After another sip, which he rolled on his tongue, he said "Ahhh," and put down his glass.

The second line of the number code read:

10003210004

Consulting *The Wind in the Willows*, he found that the fourth word in the three-hundred-twenty-first line of the first chapter was "fly." He wrote that down and looked at what he had thus far:

snapdragon fly

He crossed out the first four letters and drew the rest of it together in one word:

dragonfly

He had another sip of whiskey.

600030007

He worked that out rather quickly and wrote the word "to" after "dragonfly."

600030008
10002100003
11000600010

Gradually he worked his way down through the list of numbers, taking time out to sample his drink, now and then reading a passage out of which Rice had plucked a word. In half an hour he had decoded the entire message:

dragonfly to be used
as soon as possible
stop
within twenty-four
hours maximum
essential
stop
city will be unsafe
for ninety-six hours
after dragonfly
is triggered
stop
save self
but staff must be
abandoned
stop
risk all
end

Humming softly and tunelessly, the man at the desk read the brief message several times, savoring it as he had savored the whiskey. Then he put it through the paper shredder and watched the pieces flutter into the wastebasket.

The largest and yet quickest war in history was about to begin.

FAIRMOUNT HEIGHTS, MARYLAND: FRIDAY, 7:40 P.M.

"I still don't see what the hell Sidney Greenstreet has to do with this," Bernie Kirkwood said, leaning over the back of the front seat as the sound of the car's engine faded and the night silence closed in around them.

Burt Nolan, the six-foot-four Pinkerton bodyguard who was behind the wheel of McAlister's white Mercedes, said, "Do you want me to come in with you, sir?"

"There won't be any trouble here," McAlister said. "You can wait in the car." He opened the door and got out.

Scrambling out of the back seat, Kirkwood said, "I suppose I'm allowed to tag along."

"Could I stop you?" McAlister asked.

"No."

"Then by all means."

They went along the sidewalk to a set of three concrete steps that mounted a sloped lawn.

"You've been damned close-mouthed since we left the restaurant," Kirkwood said.

"I guess I have."

"The description in the newspaper . . . You recognized the man who beat up on that hooker."

"*Maybe* I did."

At the top of the three concrete steps, there was a curving flagstone walk that led across a well-manicured lawn and was flanked on the right-hand side by a neatly trimmed waist-high wall of green shrubbery.

"Who is it?" Kirkwood asked.

"I'd rather not say just yet."

"Why not?"

"It's not a name you toss around lightly when you're discussing sex offenders."

"When *will* you toss it around, lightly or otherwise?"

"When I know why Beau called him 'that Sidney Greenstreet.' "

The house in front of them was a handsome three-story brick Tudor framed by a pair of massive Dutch elm trees. Light burned behind two windows on the third floor. The second floor was dark. On the ground level light shone out from stained, leaded windows: a rainbow of soft colors. The porch light glowed above the heavy oak door and was reflected by the highly polished pearl-gray Citroën S-M that was parked in the driveway.

"Who is this Beau Jackson?" Kirkwood asked as McAlister rang the doorbell.

"Cloakroom attendant at the White House."

"You're kidding."

"No."

"This is an accountant's neighborhood."

"What kind of neighborhood is that?"

"Right below a doctor's neighborhood and right above a lawyer's."

"It isn't exactly what I was expecting," McAlister admitted.

"What does he do on the side, rob banks?"

"Why don't you ask him?"

"If he does rob banks," Kirkwood said, "I'd like to join up with his gang."

A dark face peered at them through a tiny round window in the door. Then it disappeared, and a moment later the door opened.

Beau Jackson was standing there in dark-gray slacks and a blue sport shirt. "Mr. McAlister!"

"Good evening, Mr. Jackson."

"Come in, come in."

In the marble-floored foyer, McAlister said, "I hope I'm not interrupting your dinner."

"No, no," Jackson said. "We never eat earlier than nine."

McAlister introduced Kirkwood, waited for the two men to shake hands, and said, "I'm here to talk to you about a man you once compared to Sidney Greenstreet."

Jackson's smile faded. "May I ask why you want to talk about him?"

"I think he's involved in a major criminal conspiracy," McAlister said. "That's all I can tell you. It's an extremely sensitive and top-secret matter."

Jackson pulled on his chin, made up his mind in a few seconds, and said, "Come on back to my den."

It was a large, pleasantly stuffy room. On two sides bookshelves ran from floor to ceiling. Windows and oil paintings filled the rest of the wall space. The desk was a big chunk of dark pine full of drawers and cubbyholes; and the top of it was littered with copies of *The Wall Street Journal*, *Barron's*, and other financial publications.

Picking up a *Journal*, Kirkwood said, "You don't rob banks, after all."

Jackson looked puzzled.

"When I saw this beautiful house, I said you must rob banks on the side. But you're in the stock market."

"I just dabble in stocks," Jackson said. "I'm mostly interested in the commodities market. That's where I've done best." He pointed to a grouping of maroon-leatherette armchairs. "Have a seat, gentlemen." While they settled down, he looked over the bookshelves and plucked several magazines from between the hardbound volumes. He returned and sat down with them. To McAlister he said, "Evidently you've learned who Sidney Greenstreet was."

"Bernie told me," McAlister said. "Greenstreet was one of the all-time great movie villains."

"A fat man who was seldom jolly," Jackson said. "His performance as Kasper Gutman in *The Maltese Falcon* is one of the greatest pieces of acting ever committed to film."

"He wasn't bad as the Japanese sympathizer in *Across the Pacific*," Kirkwood said.

"Also one of my favorites," Jackson said.

"Of course," Kirkwood said, "he wasn't always the villain. He did play good guys now and then. Like in *Conflict*, with Bogart and Alexis Smith. You know that one?"

Before Jackson could answer, McAlister said, "Bernie, we *are* here on rather urgent business."

The black man turned to McAlister and said, "When I referred to Mr. Rice as 'that Sidney Greenstreet,' I meant that he is very cunning, perhaps very dangerous, and not anything at all like what he seems to be. He pretends liberalism. At heart he is a right-wing fanatic. He's a racist. A fascist." Jackson's voice didn't rise with the strength of his judgments or acquire an hysterical tone; he sounded quite reasonable.

"Mr. Rice? Andrew Rice? You mean the President's chief aide?" Kirkwood asked weakly. He looked as if he were about to mutter and drool in idiot confusion.

Ignoring Kirkwood, certain that he was on the verge of learning something that he would have preferred not to know, McAlister stared hard at Jackson and said, "You're making some pretty ugly accusations. Yet I'm sure that you don't know Rice personally. You probably don't know him even as well as I do—and that's not very well at all. So what makes you think you know what's in his heart?"

Back in the early 1960s, Jackson explained, he had reached a point in his life when he finally felt secure, finally knew that he had gotten out of the ghetto for once and all. He had plenty of tenure on the White House domestic staff. He was making a damned good salary. His investments had begun to pay off handsomely, and he had been able to move into a good house in the suburbs. He had been successful long enough to have accepted his new position, and he had gotten over the lingering fear that everything he had worked for might be taken away from him overnight.

"All my life," he told McAlister, "I've enjoyed books. I've believed in continuous self-education. In 1963, when I moved to the suburbs, I felt financially secure enough to devote most of my spare time to my reading. I decided to establish a study program and concentrate on one subject at a time. Back then, I was most interested in racial prejudice, having been a victim of it all of my life. I wanted to understand the reasons behind it. The psychology behind it. So I worked up a reading list, both fiction and nonfiction, and did considerable research. Eventually I was led to these two magazines owned by a man named J. Prescott Hennings."

"I know of him," McAlister said.

Jackson said, "He's published some of the most hateful racist propaganda ever committed to ink and paper in this country. It's not all directed against blacks. Hennings despises Jews, Puerto Ricans, Chicanos . . ."

"I've seen copies of the magazines, but I've never bothered to read one of them," McAlister said.

Jackson picked up the first magazine in his lap and opened it to an article titled "Negro Mental Inferiority." He handed it to McAlister and said, "Here's a little something written by Andrew Rice in 1964."

Reading the first several paragraphs, McAlister winced. He passed the magazine to Kirkwood.

Jackson gave another one to McAlister. "Here's an especially nasty little number titled 'Has Hitler Been Maligned?'"

"Christ!" McAlister said, feeling sick to his stomach. Glancing only perfunctorily at the article, he quickly passed it on to Kirkwood. Weakly, he said, "Well . . . People *do* change."

"Not as radically as this," Jackson said. "Not from a fanatical fascist to a paragon of liberal virtue." He spoke with conviction, as if he'd had considerable time to think about it. "And people certainly don't change so *quickly* as Rice appears to have done. That paean to Hitler was published exactly one year before Harvard University Press issued his *Balancing the Budget in a Welfare State*, which was a best seller and which was overflowing with *liberal* sentiment."

Skimming through the Hitler article, Kirkwood said, "This is the work of an Andrew Rice who belongs in a nice little padded cell somewhere."

"Believe me," Jackson said gloomily, "that Andrew Rice is the same one who is today advising the President." He opened another magazine to an article titled 'The Chinese Threat,' and he gave this to McAlister. "In this one Rice advocates an immediate nuclear attack on Red China in order to keep it from becoming a major nuclear power itself."

Shocked for reasons Jackson couldn't grasp, McAlister read this piece from beginning to end. By the time he had finished it, he was damp with perspiration. "How could he ever have become accepted as a major liberal thinker when he had a background like this?"

"He published eleven of those articles, the last in October of 1964," Jackson said. "They all appeared in magazines with terribly small circulations."

"And even then, not everyone who received a copy read it," said Kirkwood.

"Right," Jackson said. "My guess is that no one who read those magazine pieces also read his liberal work beginning with the Harvard book. Or if a few people did read both—well, they never remembered the byline on the articles and didn't connect that work with the book. As the years passed, the chance of anyone making the connection grew progressively smaller. And when Rice *did* move into a position of real power, it was as a Presidential aide. Unlike Cabinet members, aides do not have to be confirmed by the Senate. Because Rice doesn't have an engaging or even particularly interesting personality, he hasn't been much of a target for newspapermen. No one has combed through his past; they all go back to the Harvard book and never any further."

As he wiped the perspiration from his face with his handkerchief, McAlister said, "Why haven't you blown the whistle on him?"

Jackson said, "How?"

"Call up a reporter and put him on the right track. Even give him your copies of the magazines."

"Too dangerous."

"Dangerous?"

Sighing, Jackson said, "Do you think for a minute Rice could have gotten away with this change of face if Prescott Hennings didn't want him to get away with it?"

"You're suggesting a conspiracy?"

"Of some sort."

"To accomplish what?"

"I don't know," Jackson said.

McAlister nodded.

"But I'm beginning to think you know."

Staring straight into the black man's eyes, McAlister said nothing.

Jackson said, "I'd wager that if I hustled some reporter with this stuff, Hennings would have conclusive proof that the very famous *liberal* Andrew Rice was not the same Andrew Rice who wrote those articles way back when. And then yours truly would be marked as a slander monger. I've got a nice job and a big earned pension that's coming to me in a few years. When it comes to my financial solvency, I'm as morally bankrupt as the next man."

McAlister folded his handkerchief and returned it to his pocket. "Rice isn't a very common name. Even if Hennings did have some sort of trumped-up proof, it wouldn't be believed."

"Mr. McAlister, forgive me, but even if the proof was conclusive, Rice would remain as a Presidential aide—and I'd get bounced out of the cloakroom on my ass. Do you think all those liberals, Democrats and Republicans, who have praised Rice to the skies are suddenly just going to admit they were deceived? Do you think the President will admit Rice made a fool of him? If you think so, then you're more naïve than I would have thought. There will be a lot of somber speeches and statements about giving a man a second chance and about the marvelous capacity for change that Rice has shown. Hearts will bleed. Pity will flow like water. The conservatives won't care if Rice goes or stays. And the liberals would rather argue that a child killer can achieve sainthood even in the act of murder than admit they were wrong.

"I believe that Rice probably has taken a long-term position in order to achieve power with which he can score points for right-wing programs—while he professes liberal aims. It's an ingenious tactic. It requires consummate acting skill and monumental patience, and it's more dangerous to our system of government than any screaming, shouting frontal attack of the sort that right-wingers usually make. But it's much too complicated for most Americans to understand or worry about. They like their politics nice and simple. Actually, *I'm* not even so sure that it's anything to worry about. I'm not so sure he can do all that much damage. If he's got to maintain his liberal image, he can hardly begin pressing for the Hitlerian laws and schemes he wrote about in those articles for Hennings' magazines."

Getting to his feet, McAlister said, "That's quite true."

"But now I'm not so sure," Jackson said, standing, stretching, watching McAlister closely. "Since you came here like this, you must think Rice is involved in something very big and very dangerous."

McAlister said, "I'd appreciate it if you kept this visit to yourself."

"Naturally."

"Could I have a few of those magazines?"

"Take them all," Jackson said.

Kirkwood scooped up all eleven issues.

At the front door, as they were shaking hands, McAlister said, "Mr. Jackson, I can only repeat what I said on Wednesday: you're sure full of surprises."

Jackson nodded and smiled and shuffled his feet, putting on a bit of that refined Stepin Fetchit routine which he used to such great effect at the White House.

"Would you and your wife consider joining Mrs. McAlister and me for dinner some evening soon?"

"I believe that would be most interesting," Jackson said.

"I believe you're right."

On the way down the flagstone walk to the car, neither McAlister nor Kirkwood said a word.

On all sides of them, the grass looked bluish-white, pearly in the October moonlight.

A teenage boy and a pretty blonde were leaving the house next door, just starting out on a big date.

A child's laughter came from the front porch of the house across the street.

McAlister felt as if the sky were going to collapse on him any second now. He walked with his shoulders hunched.

When they were both in the car again and the Pinkerton man had started the engine, McAlister turned to Kirkwood and said, "It was your group that got the Cofield lead."

"That's right."

"And the Hunter lead too."

"Yes."

"How are you using your investigators?"

"Some of the other teams are working a sixteen-hour day. But I've got my men divided into three different eight-hour shifts so we can pursue our leads around the clock."

"Who are the federal marshals guarding your team?"

"Right now, on the four-to-midnight grind, it's a man named Bradley Hopper. Midnight to eight in the morning, it's John Morrow. During the day shift, when I'm on duty with two assistants, we've got a marshal named Carl Altmüller."

After six months with this man as his chief investigator, McAlister was no longer in awe of Kirkwood's ability to remember every detail of his work, even the full names of the guards who were assigned to him. "Which one of them was on duty when the Potter Cofield lead began to get hot?"

Kirkwood said, "Altmüller."

"What do you know about him?"

"Not much. I chatted him up when he first came on duty. Let me see . . ." He was quiet for a few seconds. Then: "I think he said he wasn't married. Lived in—Capitol Heights somewhere."

"Capitol Heights, Maryland?" McAlister asked.

"Yeah."

He turned to Burt Nolan, the Pinkerton man. "That's not very far from here, is it?"

"No, sir."

"Better get to a phone, look in the book, see if there's a full address listed for him," McAlister said.

Nolan pulled the Mercedes away from the curb.

Leaning up from the back seat, pushing one thin hand through his bushy hair, Kirkwood said, "You think that Carl Altmüller is working for Rice?"

"Rice assigned the marshals," McAlister said. "He chose them. And once he had a list of possibilities sent over to him from Justice, he needed six hours to call the first one of them. Now, what do you think he was doing all that time?"

Kirkwood's glasses had slid so far down his nose that they were in danger of falling off. He looked startled as McAlister pushed them in place for him. "Well . . . I guess he was trying to find a man—or men—he could buy. It took six hours."

Nolan found a telephone booth at the corner of a shopping-center parking lot, and Kirkwood went in to look through the book. While he was out of the car, McAlister said, "Burt, I hope you remember that you've taken the agency's secrecy oath."

"I haven't heard a thing," Nolan said.

When Kirkwood came back a minute later, he said, "Altmüller is listed." He gave Nolan the address. To McAlister he said, "Isn't it dangerous for us to walk in on him all by ourselves?"

"He won't be expecting anything," McAlister said. "And Burt here has a gun of his own."

"Begging your pardon, sir," Nolan said, keeping his eyes on the busy highway, "but I think that you might be getting me in over my head. I'm not a public law officer. That secrecy oath didn't give me any police powers. I've been hired to protect you, but I can't go looking for trouble."

"Then," McAlister said, "I'll borrow your gun. Bernie and I can go it alone."

Burt took a long moment to consider all the angles of that. He accelerated around a panel truck and pulled back into the right-hand lane. His broad face was expressionless in the lights of the oncoming cars. Finally: "I'd have to take the gun out of my holster and lay it on the seat. Why would I do that?"

"Maybe while we were parked at the telephone booth, you saw someone approaching the car, someone who looked suspicious," McAlister suggested.

"That's a possibility. I wanted to be ready for him. But maybe after this person proved to be no threat, I left the gun on the seat where it would be handy. And then you picked it up without my seeing."

Smiling, McAlister said, "I suppose you could make a mistake like that."

"Everyone makes mistakes," Burt agreed.

Kirkwood didn't like the sound of it. He shifted nervously and said, "I think we should get some help."

Turning around to look at the younger man once more, McAlister said, "I'd like nothing better, Bernie. But who in the hell could we trust?"

Kirkwood licked his lips and said nothing.

PEKING: SATURDAY, 1:00 P.M.

The air terminal in Peking was a hulking neo Stalinist building with cold marble walls and floors and altogether too much gilt trim around the ceilings. Ranks of fluorescent lights cast stark shadows; but there was not a speck of dust or a smear of grease to be seen in any corner. Even on Saturday afternoon there were no more than sixty or seventy travelers using the facilities. Of these, the most eye-catching were three beautiful North Vietnamese women who were dressed in white silk trousers and brightly colored, flowered silk *odais*. North Vietnamese and Cambodian women, Canning thought, were among the most beautiful in the world: petite, extremely delicate and yet shapely, with very fine-boned faces, enormous dark eyes, and thick black hair. These three—as they stood waiting for cups of tea at one of the carts that dispensed free refreshments—contrasted pleasantly with the inhuman architecture and with the generally drab clothing of the Chinese around them.

A smiling, pretty Chinese woman of about thirty-five met Lee Ann and Canning when they got off the Frenchman's jet. Her long hair hung in a single braid behind her. She wore baggy blue pants, a baggy white shirt, and shapeless khaki jacket. She was all crisp efficiency as she escorted Canning and Lee Ann through customs, gave their luggage to a baggage handler, and led them out into the terminal's great hall, where Alexander Webster, the United States' first *fully* accredited ambassador to the People's Republic of China, was waiting for them.

Webster was an imposing figure. At six foot three, he was two inches taller than Canning. He was conscious of his posture; he stood stiff and straight to emphasize his height. His neck was thick, not with fat but with muscle. His shoulders and chest were unusually broad; and although he was a bit heavy in the stomach, he managed to hold it in well. His face was like the marble bust of some famous Roman centurion: square chin, bulging jaws, firm mouth, straight nose, eyes set back like ornaments on a deep shelf, and a formidable brow. Only two things kept him from looking like a roughneck: his expensive and stylish New York suit, which he wore as if he were a model; and his wavy silver hair, which softened the sharp angles of his rather brutal face. All in all, he appeared to be a former football star who, when he had lost his physical edge, had left the game and set out upon a brand-new career as a banker.

"Welcome to Peking," Webster said, bowing slightly to Lee Ann and shaking hands with Canning. His voice was not hard and gravelly, as Canning had expected, but soft and easy and deep and spiced with a trace of what had once been a lush Louisiana accent. "Miss Tanaka, if all CIA operatives were as lovely as you, we'd have won the espionage war decades ago. Who on earth would want to fight with you?"

"And if all our ambassadors were as gracious as you," Lee Ann said, "we'd have no enemies."

Outside, there was no limousine waiting for them. Webster explained that the use of "decadent forms of transportation" within the People's Republic had recently been denounced and forbidden by Party edict—although Chinese diplomats in Washington and at the UN in New York relied increasingly upon custom-ordered black Cadillacs. "Western governments don't have an exclusive right to hypocrisy," Webster observed.

Instead of a Cadillac, there was a Chinese-made vehicle that resembled a Volkswagen microbus. Inside, behind the driver's seat, there were two benches, one along each wall. Lee Ann and Canning sat on the right and faced Webster across the narrow aisle. The seats were uncomfortable: thinly padded and upholstered in canvas. But there were windows on both sides, and they would at least be able to see the city as they passed through it.

The driver, a State Department career man whom Webster introduced as James Obin of St. Louis, finished loading their luggage aboard. Then he got behind the wheel and started the tinny engine.

As the microbus began to move, Webster said, "Security was so tight on your flight that I didn't even learn what plane you were on until it was airborne."

"Sorry if you were inconvenienced," Canning said. "But it was necessary."

"There were several attempts on his life before he even got to Tokyo," Lee Ann said.

"Well then, I can understand the tight security," Webster said.

"But what I *can't* understand is why you had to come all the way out from the States in the first place. McAlister could have wired me the names of these three deep-cover agents of ours. I could have worked with General Lin to locate and interrogate them."

"I'm sure you could have handled it," Canning said. "But if we had wired the names, General Lin's Internal Security Force would have intercepted them. No matter how complicated the code, they would have broken it—and fast."

"But they're going to learn the names anyway, sooner or later," Webster said.

"Perhaps they won't have to be told all of them. If we find the trigger man the first time out, we can withhold the other two names from Lin." He quickly outlined the procedure he would insist upon for the pickup and the interrogation of the three agents.

Webster grimaced and shifted uncomfortably on the bench. "The general won't like that."

"If he doesn't accept it, then he doesn't get any of the names. He has absolutely no choice in the matter—and I'll make that plain to him. I'm not a diplomat, so I don't have to waste time being diplomatic. It'll be your job to smooth his feathers."

"He's not an easy man to deal with."

Canning said, "Yes, but since he's in the counterintelligence business himself, he ought to be able to understand my position even if he doesn't much like it. Although my primary concern is to find the trigger man and learn from him who Dragonfly is, I've a second duty nearly as important as the first. I have to keep the ISF from cracking open the agency's entire network in the People's Republic."

"I'll do what I can to help."

"Did the polygraph arrive safely?"

"Yesterday morning."

"Good."

"It's quite large."

"It's not a traditional lie detector. It's actually a portable computer that monitors and analyzes all of the subject's major reactions to the questions he's asked. The newest thing."

"It's locked in a tamper-proof steel case," Webster said. "I suppose you have the key?"

"Yes." It had been in the packet of Theodore Otley identification and expense money that McAlister had given him in Washington. "When do we meet General Lin?"

"An ISF car is following us right now," Webster said, pointing through the rear windows of the microbus. A jeeplike station wagon trailed them by a hundred yards. "By this time they'll have radioed the news of your arrival to the general's office. Knowing how polite and thoughtful the Chinese are, I'd say Lin will give you fifteen or twenty minutes at the embassy to freshen up before he comes knocking."

They were now cruising along an avenue at least three times as wide as Fifth Avenue in New York. There were no automobiles and only a few trucks, vans, and buses. But there were thousands of bicycles whizzing silently in both directions. Many of the cyclists smiled and waved at Canning, Lee Ann, and the ambassador.

"Are all the streets this wide?" Lee Ann asked.

"Many but not most," Webster said. "These ultra-wide thoroughfares are the newest streets in Peking. They were built after the revolution. Once they were completed and opened, the Party was able to classify the *old* main streets—which were often very broad—as lanes and alleyways. Today, most domestic and *all* foreign traffic moves on these new arteries."

"But why did they build new and bigger streets when they didn't have cars enough for the old ones?" Lee Ann asked. "Two-thirds of this avenue is empty."

"The old streets were dotted with religious shrines and literally hundreds of magnificently ornate temples," Webster said, enjoying his role as guide. "Some of these were destroyed in the revolution and some, later, by Party edict. But the Communists realized that the temples—although they were shameful reminders of a decadent past full of excess and injustice—were priceless works of art and history. Cooler heads prevailed, thank God, and the destruction ceased. They opted for an alternate program. They built these thoroughfares, restructuring the city away from the temples. As a result, many of the old landmarks are tucked away behind fences in quiet pockets of the city where they can't have a corruptive influence on the masses." Webster was amused by all of this, and he winked at Lee Ann as if they were adults tolerating the eccentricities of slow-witted but pleasant children.

"Incredible," Lee Ann said.

Canning said, "Not really. We do the same thing."

Webster frowned. "What do you mean?"

"We build and redesign our cities to hide the ghettos from ourselves, rather than the churches."

"You know, you're right!" Lee Ann said.

"Well," Webster said stiffly, "I don't see even the most remote similarity. And if I were you, I wouldn't express that sort of an opinion in front of someone like General Lin. He would be delighted to spread your thoughts far and wide, to the detriment of the United States' image in Asia." He turned away from them and stared out at the hordes of cyclists.

Lee Ann glanced at Canning and raised her eyebrows.

He just shrugged.

Peking was a city of eight or nine million, capital of the largest nation on earth—yet it was more like a small town than like a metropolis that was four thousand years old. There were no neon signs. There were no skyscrapers. There was nothing that looked like a department store or theater or restaurant—although there were surely all of these things in the city, tucked away in squat and official-looking brick buildings. Beyond the broad avenues and occasionally glimpsed spires of the forbidden temples, there were tens of thousands of gray houses with gray and yellow rooftops; they stretched like a carpet of densely grown weeds over all the city's hills, encircling countless small gardens of trees and shrubbery.

The United States Embassy was in one of the city's three diplomatic compounds that were reserved for foreign missions in order that they might be kept apart from the Chinese people. The compound contained a large seven-story office building which was shared by the seven foreign delegations quartered there. The compound also contained seven spacious, boxy four-story pink-brick houses where the diplomats and their staffs lived. The United States Embassy was no larger, no smaller, no different at all from the other six, except that the Stars and Stripes flew from a low flagpole beside the front door.

"Here we are," Webster said jovially, apparently no longer miffed at Canning. "Home sweet home."

The higher you went in the house, the more important you were in the diplomatic scheme of things. The first floor contained the drawing room, dining room, kitchens, and bedrooms for the servants who had been imported from Washington. Four secretaries also had quarters on this first level. The second floor contained the bedrooms for the ambassador's staff. The third floor was where Webster's chief aide and private secretary had rooms—and it was here as well that important visitors from the States were put up. The top level, of course, was Webster's private domain—except when the President, Vice-President, or Secretary of State came to China, in which case Webster opened a separate three-room suite for his guests. Lee Ann and Canning did not rate the suite—or a room behind the kitchen. They were given separate bedchambers on the third floor.

Canning's room might have been in a house in Washington, New York, or Boston. No concession had been made to the Orient. The furniture, all shipped in from the States, was heavy, dark pine, Colonial. The walls were white and hung with oil paintings of George Washington, Thomas Jefferson, and Abraham Lincoln. There was a framed copy of the Declaration of Independence hanging just to the right of the door.

The bathroom, however, was decidedly Chinese-modern. The tub, sink, and toilet were all made from a dark-brown, glossless ceramic material that resembled mud. The fixtures were not stainless-steel or even chrome-plated; instead, they were cast-iron, dull and pitted and spotted with incipient rust—except for the water faucets, which were all rough-cut copper pipe. There was no place for him to plug in his electric razor near the mirror; however, the embassy staff had thoughtfully provided an extension cord which was plugged into and dangled from the socket that for some inscrutable reason had been let into the wall three feet above the tank of the commode.

He shaved lightly, washed his face and hands, put on a clean shirt, strapped his shoulder holster back in place, and put on his suit jacket. He took the pistol from the holster and switched off both safeties; then he dropped it back into the leather pocket.

The telephone rang. It was Webster. "General Lin arrived a few minutes ago. He's extremely anxious to get moving."

"We'll be right down," Canning said.

The end of the assignment was in sight.

He was suddenly depressed.

What would he do when this was finished? Go back to Washington? Back to the White House assignment? Back to the lonely apartment on G Street? Back to his son's scorn and his daughter's indifference?

Maybe he would ask Lee Ann to stay with him in Washington. She was what he needed. In a short time she had not only patched up his lover's ego, but she had also made him feel decent and clean again. She had given him back the self-respect that he had allowed Mike to bleed from him. Would she stay with him? Would she say yes? She had insecurities of her own, problems to work out; and she needed help with them. Maybe he was precisely what she needed too. Maybe . . .

He squeezed his eyes shut for a moment, trying to clear his head, and he told himself that he was not to worry about any of these things. He must stick to the moment, stick to the problem at hand, approach it single-mindedly. If he didn't find the trigger man, if Dragonfly was detonated while he was in Peking, then he would not be going back to anywhere or anything. And neither would Lee Ann. They would either be victims of the plague—whatever it turned out to be—or they would be inmates of a Chinese political prison.

TAIYÜAN, CHINA: SATURDAY, 2:00 P.M.

Just outside the city of Taiyüan, in the Province of Shansi, two hundred and ten rail-miles from Peking, the train clattered onto a lay-by. The brakes squealed; the passenger car trembled. The steel wheels shot sparks into the clouds of steam that rushed back from the locomotive's vents and pressed, briefly, against the coach window next to Chai Po-han's face.

Chong Shao-chi, the man in the seat beside Chai, was the manager of a large grain-storage facility near Anshun. He was en route to the capital, where he was to speak before a gathering of agricultural specialists who were interested in his novel and successful ideas about rodent control. He was quite excited—not because of the speech so much as because his aged parents lived in Peking. This was his first homecoming in seven years. Tonight his family was holding a great feast in his honor: cold gizzard and liver, hundred-year eggs, green-bean noodles, fried noodles, buns with silver threads, wheat-packet soup, sesame cakes, fried bread, fried hot peppers, mushrooms, sweet and sour fish, fried eel, three-glass chicken, beef in oyster sauce, and much more—a feast indeed! Therefore, the moment the train came to a full stop, Chong said anxiously, "What is the trouble? Can you see? Have we broken down?"

"I can't see anything," Chai said.

"We *can't* have broken down. I must get to Peking no later than nine. My family has planned a feast! They—"

"You've told me," Chai said, not unkindly.

"Maybe we have just stopped to refuel."

"I don't see any fuel tanks," Chai said.

"Please, no breakdown. I have lived well. I am a loyal Maoist. I don't deserve this!"

A minute later the toothless man in charge of this coach and the two sleeping cars behind it entered at the front and clapped his hands for attention. "We will be delayed here for half an hour. There is a long train outbound from Peking on these tracks. Once it has passed, we can continue."

Chong stood up and caught the toothless man's attention. "Will we arrive late in Peking?"

"No. This is a scheduled lay-by."

Chong collapsed into his seat and sighed with relief.

When the outbound train came along ten minutes later, it roared by within a few feet of Chai's window. It was nearly overflowing with young people on their way to the communes. Colorful posters affixed to the flanks of the cars proclaimed the joy and dedication of the young Maoists within. But Chai could not see all that much joy or dedication to the Fifty-Year Farm Plan in those faces that peered back at him from the passing cars. Oh, yes, occasionally there was someone grinning rapturously at the thought of serving the People; but the vast majority of them showed nothing but resignation and, occasionally, despair.

Chai sympathized with them. He ached with pity for them. And he thought, miserably: I have become a reactionary, an anti-Maoist, and an enemy of the People.

Deep down within, he knew that his pity was for himself as well as for these strangers flashing past. It was not merely self-pity for what he had been through—the sixteen-hour days of brutalizing labor, the weeks he had been assigned to collect human waste for use as fertilizer on the rice paddies, the weevils in his food, the fevers which had swept the communes when there was no medicine to combat them—but he was also full of self-pity for those things he felt he might yet suffer. If his father died, or was removed from power, what would become of him? If his father could not protect him, would he be sent back to the Ssunan Commune? Yes. Definitely. There was no doubt about it. He was only temporarily safe, safe only so long as his father's heart continued to beat, safe only so long as his father's enemies in the Party remained weak. Within the next few years he would be back in the country again, a slave laborer again. He was afraid for himself, and he despaired of his future.

There *had* to be a way out.

And of course there *was* a way out.

He saw the door to escape. But to open it and pass through was no simple matter. It was a monumental step, a denial of his past, his family, everything. It was a decision that he would have found impossible, a change in outlook he would have thought despicable, before Ssunan.

Leave China.

Forever.

No. It was *still* unthinkable.

Yet . . .

Was a return to Ssunan any more reasonable? Did he wish to end up like Chong Shao-chi, this miserable man beside him? Did he want to be forty years old, a champion killer of rats, whose greatest pleasure in seven years was a one-night reunion with his family?

Remembering his trip to America, Chai suddenly saw that there was one great flaw in the social system of the United States—and one great flaw in China's system as well. In the United States, there was an unreasonable selfishness, a destructive desire to possess more and more things and to obtain more and more power through the acquisition of more and more money. In China, there was an equally unreasonable self*less*ness; the Party was so concerned about the welfare of the masses that it overlooked the welfare of the individuals who composed the masses. In the United States, there had seemed to be no peace and contentment, for life there was a frantic process of accumulation and consumption and reaccumulation to fuel a new round of consumption . . . Yet in the United States you *could* live outside the system; selfishness was not dictated by the government or demanded by the people. And even if the greedy capitalistic rabble roared around you—was that not better than to live in the People's Republic, where you had little or no choice, where the self was denied and virtue was not a choice but a requirement?

If only, he thought as he watched the commune-bound train pass, there were some country in the world where the two systems had been merged, where the flaw in each canceled out the flaw in the other.

But there was no such place. That was a child's dream and always would be.

How terrible to be raised to have a fierce belief in your government and society, only to be given the wit, knowledge, or experience to suddenly see that the system was unjust, imperfect. Chai saw that he had been forced by his society to make certain decisions which that same society had taught him were decadent and shameful.

But there was only one escape from an intolerable future, and it was far from the perfect answer: leave China.

Now.

Soon.

But how?

As the outbound train finished passing and their own train began to move once more toward Peking, Chai Po-han wrestled with his conscience and tried to make himself accept the only future that made any sense at all.

5

CAPITOL HEIGHTS, MARYLAND: FRIDAY, 9:05 P.M.

McAlister took Burt Nolan's pistol from the seat. He held the gun above the dashboard and studied it in the purplish-white light that filtered into the Mercedes from a nearby mercury-vapor street-lamp. He found the red safety and flicked it off.

Nolan watched none of this. He stared intently out of his side window at the houses across the street.

Shoving the gun into his coat pocket, keeping his right hand on the butt, McAlister opened his door and got out of the car.

Unarmed but game, Bernie Kirkwood climbed out of the back seat and followed his boss across the sidewalk.

Carl Altmüller's house was a small two-story Colonial saltbox, pale-gray, with black shutters and trim. A neat, matching gray-and-black saltbox garage stood at the top of the sloping driveway. The garage doors were closed. The house was dark; apparently Altmüller was not at home.

McAlister felt somewhat foolish stepping into this peaceful scene with his shoulders tensed and a loaded gun in his pocket. Nevertheless, he kept his hand on the gun butt.

The doorbell was set beneath a clear three-watt night light. The chimes produced a four-note melody that sounded like distant Christmas bells striking up "Joy to the World."

No one came to the door.

"Maybe it's his night for macramé lessons," Kirkwood said.

McAlister rang the bell again.

Nothing. No one. Silence.

"He could be at a prayer meeting," Kirkwood said. "Or counseling a troop of boy scouts."

Ringing the bell a third time, McAlister said, "Have you ever considered a career as a comedian?"

"No. You think I should?"

"Well, it would be *something* to do after I've fired you."

"Yeah. We could form a team. You'd be the straight man."

"I don't intend to fire myself."

"Yeah," Kirkwood said, "but you won't last long without me."

Turning away from the front door, McAlister said, "Come on. Let's have a look around."

"Around what?"

"The house."

"Why?"

"I want to find a way in."

"You're going to break and enter?" Kirkwood asked, shocked.

"I won't break anything unless it's necessary. But I damned well am entering."

Kirkwood caught him by the arm. "Let's get a warrant first."

"No time for that."

"You don't sound like the Bob McAlister I know."

"I've changed," McAlister said, feeling hollow inside, chilled. "Probably for the worse. But I've had no choice." He pulled free of Kirkwood's hand. "Bernie, do you realize the trouble we're in if Rice is one of these Committeemen?"

"It's a major scandal," Kirkwood said, pushing his damp woolly hair back from his forehead.

"It's more than that. We're sitting on a time bomb. Bernie, look, suppose *you* were a Committeeman with a cover as a famous liberal thinker. Suppose *you* were a fascist who was the right-hand man to a liberal President who trusted you. You could see, in the years ahead, thousands of opportunities to subtly misuse your power to fascistic ends. You were just beginning . . . How would you conduct yourself? What would your first priority be?"

Kirkwood thought about it for a moment, then said, "Protecting the power I've finally gotten. Which would mean protecting my cover. I'd lay low. Play it cool. Go easy."

"And is that what Rice is doing—supposing he *is* a Committeeman?"

"No. He's taking big risks. Like trying to use federal marshals to monitor our investigations. If one of the marshals rejected his offer and told us about it, Rice would have a lot of explaining to do."

"Exactly," McAlister said. "And when he told me that Bill Fredericks hadn't been very cooperative in arranging for the marshals, Rice had to know there was a good chance I'd catch him in his lie."

"You think he no longer cares whether he's caught or gets away with it?"

"It looks that way to me. Which means Dragonfly will be used soon. So soon, in fact, that Rice figures even if we nail him, we won't have time to make him tell us Dragonfly's identity. We won't have time to stop the project before detonation."

"But he'll end up in jail just the same," Kirkwood said. "Is he fanatical enough to spend the rest of his life in prison for a cause?"

"Maybe he doesn't think he'll go to trial, let alone to prison."

"I don't follow you."

"My imagination may be running wild. I'm beginning to see some very ugly possibilities. Like . . . Maybe the Dragonfly project, as big as it is, just isn't the whole bundle. Maybe it's only one element in a much larger scheme."

"Such as?"

"Maybe Rice is taking these risks because he expects his people to seize control of the United States government during or immediately after the crisis in China. If that was what he was anticipating, he would have no fear of jail."

Kirkwood was dumbfounded. He looked up at the stars, then at the quiet houses across the street. "But that's . . . Well . . . I mean . . . For God's sake, that's screaming paranoia!"

"Paranoia?" McAlister said wearily. "That's just a way of life, like any other. These days, it's just another way to get along."

"But how could they do it? How could they seize the government?"

"I don't know."

Kirkwood stared at him.

"Go back to the car."

Kirkwood didn't move.

"Keep Burt company."

"We aren't compatible."

"I can handle this myself."

"I'll go with you anyway."

"It's breaking and entering, remember?"

Kirkwood smiled grimly. "If we get sent to the same prison, we can share a cell."

They circled the house, looking for a barrier that was flimsier than the solid-oak front door. They tried the first-floor windows, but those were all locked. The rear door was as formidable as the front door. Finally, on the north side of the house, they came upon a set of four French doors, and these looked flimsy enough.

Because there were no lights in the house next door, they didn't try to conceal what they were doing. McAlister wrapped Kirkwood's woolen scarf around his right fist and smashed one of the foot-square panes of glass in the first door. He reached through, fumbled around for several seconds, but was unable to find the lock. He broke another pane—and found no lock. He moved to the second door and broke two more panes before his trembling fingers located the cool metal latch.

They went into the house, glass crunching under their shoes.

After he found a wall switch and turned on the dining-room light, Kirkwood said, "By the way, what in the hell are we looking for?"

"I've been waiting for you to ask. We're looking for a corpse."

Kirkwood blinked. "One corpse in particular? Or will we take anything we can find?"

"Carl Altmüller."

"Are you serious?"

"Deadly."

"But why would they kill him?"

"Maybe they didn't need him any more."

"But if Altmüller is already theirs, if they've bought him and put him in their pocket—"

"The Committeemen are fanatics," McAlister reminded him. "So far as we know, however, Altmüller's just an ordinary guy who happened to be in a position where they needed someone but where they could not place anyone. So maybe they bought him. But because he really wasn't one of them, they wouldn't trust him. You can never be sure that money will keep a man's mouth shut. But a bullet in the head does the job every time."

"*Jesus,* you sound like a cold son of a bitch!" Kirkwood said, shivering slightly.

"Sorry." He *felt* cold too.

"Why didn't you tell me this outside?"

"If you'd thought there was a corpse in here, you'd have gone straight to the police. You'd have *insisted* upon a warrant."

"Of course."

"And we don't have time."

Kirkwood locked eyes with him for a moment, then sighed and said, "Where do we start looking?"

Heading for the door of the dining-room closet, McAlister said, "Check the front room. When we've finished downstairs, we'll go upstairs together."

Grim-faced, repeatedly clearing his throat, Kirkwood went into the living room and turned on more lights. He came back within a few seconds and said, "I think I've found a clue."

"Clue?"

"Buckets of blood," Kirkwood said shakily.

"Buckets" was an exaggeration, although there was certainly a cup or two of it. Or, rather, there *had* been a cup or two. Gouts of blood had spattered the sofa; but now it was dried into a maroon-brown crust. There was even more blood, also dry and crusted, on the floor in front of the sofa.

"Looks like you were right," Kirkwood said.

Kneeling on the floor, rubbing his fingertips over the blood crust on the sofa, McAlister said, "And maybe I wasn't."

"What do you mean?"

"Altmüller worked with you just this afternoon, didn't he?"

"You know that he did."

"Did he look healthy to you?"

"Sure. Yeah."

"He was definitely alive?"

"What are you driving at?"

"When was the last time you saw him?"

Kirkwood thought. Then: "Five-thirty."

"The earliest he could have been killed here in his own home was six o'clock. Not even three and a half hours ago." He patted the stains on the sofa. "If that were the case, this blood would still be damp. Even wet—congealed but wet. At the very least, this stuff has been here for a couple of days."

The house was crypt-quiet except for the soft ticking of an antique mantel clock.

Reluctantly, Kirkwood touched the stains. "Whose blood is it?"

"Altmüller's."

Kirkwood swayed on the balls of his feet. "But you just said—"

"I'll explain when we find the corpse."

"Upstairs?"

McAlister got to his feet. "They wouldn't kill him and lug him up all those steps. He's in the kitchen or basement."

"I'd still like to think he's just spending the evening at a prayer meeting."

In the kitchen McAlister found a smear of dried blood on the lid of the freezer. "Here we go." He opened the lid.

A rolled-up rag rug was stuffed into the freezer, and there was obviously a body inside of it.

"Help me get him out," McAlister said.

As they lifted the rug out of the freezer, thin plates of frozen blood cracked and fell away from the rags and hit the floor and shattered into thousands of tiny shards.

McAlister peeled the rug back from one end of the corpse until the face was revealed. `Dark, sightless eyes, webbed with ice crystals, gazed up at him. "Carl Altmüller."

Surprised, Kirkwood said, "But Altmüller has blue eyes, and he isn't as old as this man!"

"This is Carl Altmüller," McAlister repeated adamantly. "The man you're describing is the one who killed Altmüller and has been impersonating him since Thursday morning. I'd bet on it." He was shaking inside with both fear and rage.

"Then Altmüller wasn't bought."

"That's right."

"Are all our federal marshals impostors?"

"The Committee would need only one or two men planted in our offices."

"But there might be another one?"

"Yes."

"Now what?"

"We go to the agency headquarters and pull a photograph from the files. Then *I* go to the White House while you get your ass to the hospital."

"Hospital?"

"You're going to show the photograph to a young woman of the streets who has fallen on bad times recently."

Kirkwood said, "Oh, yeah."

PEKING: SATURDAY, 2:00 P.M.

General Lin Shen-yang was in the embassy drawing room, pacing back and forth, when Canning and Lee Ann came down from the third floor. He was not at all what Canning had been expecting. By all Western standards, of course, he was somewhat on the short side, as were most of the Chinese. But he was not also slender and wiry like many Chinese men; instead, he was broad and muscular, and he had the face of a barbarian warrior. He did not move with the serenity or perfect grace of an oriental; rather, his manner was aggressive, quick, extremely energetic. The moment that they entered the room he strode toward them.

Stubbing his cigar in an ashtray, Webster got out of an easy chair and made the introductions.

The general and Lee Ann conversed in Chinese for more than a minute. From the way she was smiling, Canning could tell that Lin was flattering her.

Then the general turned to Canning and shook hands. In nearly unaccented English he said, "There are two vans waiting outside. I've got six soldiers in the one. We'll ride in the other. We have no time to waste, and I would appreciate it if you were to give me the names of your deep-cover agents in the Peking area."

"Not quite so fast," Canning said. "I've got a few things to explain."

"Then explain," the general said impatiently.

"There is a certain procedure we will follow," Canning said. "I'll give you only one name at a time. Together we'll go and arrest that man and bring him here to the embassy." He pointed to the polygraph that stood in its steel security case in the center of the room. "We will interrogate him here, using that machine. If he is not the trigger man for Dragonfly, he will remain here in the embassy until he can be flown back to the United States on one of our own aircraft. Then we will proceed to the second name. And then to the third. I will not turn any of these agents over to you—not even the trigger man for Dragonfly."

Incredibly, the general nodded and said, "Perfectly understandable. I would insist upon the same terms if our roles were reversed."

Amazed, Canning said, "That's quite reasonable of you." His opinion of the general rose considerably.

"I do not wish to waste time in pointless arguments," Lin said. "I will only warn you that if this Dragonfly should be used, the People's Republic would have no recourse but to declare war against your country."

Canning nodded.

"We are not frightened of your nuclear weapons," the general continued. "You have surely heard of the network of tunnels that honeycomb all of Peking. Because of much practice and regular drills, the entire populace can be underground in seven minutes."

Canning had, indeed, read of this fabulous creation. It was an entire underground city: fuel depots, power plants, kitchens, stores of food and clothing, medical stations, living quarters . . . Every thirty or forty feet, along every major street and most of the minor ones as well, there were steps leading down into this vast undercity. Every apartment house, store, theater, restaurant, and office building had one, two, or even three entrances to the system of nuclear-proof tunnels. The concrete warrens reached out more than twenty miles beyond the city limits, into the green country- side, a perfect escape route constructed by the People's Liberation Army back in the 1960s. Although they both knew that the tunnels would not be much good when the city was attacked by chemical-biological weapons, Canning said, "I believe we understand each other, General Lin."

"Then what is the first name?" Lin asked.

WASHINGTON: FRIDAY, 10:50 P.M.

Her name was Heather Nichols, and she was in bad shape. Her long hair was pinned back from her face, damp with perspiration. Her left ear was swollen and bruised. She had a long cut on her left jaw. Her lips were split, swollen into thick purple ridges. Tubes disappeared into her nostrils, which were thoroughly braced with wooden splints and bloody gauze. Her right eye was swollen completely shut. Her left eye was open, although barely; and she watched him with suspicion and perhaps hatred.

The intern said, "She can't talk at all. She lost several teeth. Her gums are badly lacerated, and her tongue's cut. Her mouth is swollen inside as well as out. I really don't think—"

"Can she write?" Kirkwood asked.

"What?"

"Can she *write?*"

"Well, of course she can write," the intern said.

"Good."

"Though not at the moment, of course." His voice gained a note of sarcasm. "As you can see, the fingers of the poor girl's left hand have been well broken. Her right arm is taped to that board, and she's got an I.V. needle stuck in there."

"But the fingers of her right hand are free," Kirkwood said.

"Yes, but we don't want to pull the needle loose," the intern said obstinately.

"Give me your clipboard."

Heather's one good eye darted quickly from one to the other, hating both of them.

"I think you're exciting her too much," the intern said. "This is all highly irregular to begin with and—"

Kirkwood snatched the clipboard out of his hand, ignoring his protests. There was a pen attached to the clipboard. He put the board at Heather's side and closed her fingers around the pen.

She dropped it.

"She's been feeding intravenously for two hours now," the intern said. "She hasn't been able to move that arm, and of course her fingers are numb."

Kirkwood leaned close to the girl and said, "Miss Nichols, you must listen to me. I've got a photograph in this envelope. It might be of the man who did this to you. I need to find out for sure. If it *is* him, we'll be able to get other evidence, and we'll put him behind bars."

She continued to glare at him.

"Do you understand me?"

She said nothing.

He put the pen in her hand.

This time she held on to it.

He fumbled with the manila envelope for a moment, extracted the eight-by-ten glossy of Andrew Rice. He held it up in front of her; his hand was shaking.

She stared at it.

"Is this the man?"

She just kept staring.

"Miss Nichols?"

The intern said, "I must object. This is all too much for her. She's isn't up to—"

"Heather," Kirkwood said forcefully, "is this the man who beat up on you?"

Her hand moved. The pen skipped uselessly across the sheet of paper. Then she got control of it, scribbled for a moment, and at last wrote one word:

yes

THE WHITE HOUSE: FRIDAY, 11:05 P.M.

McAlister and the President were sitting at opposite ends of a crushed-velvet couch in a small office off the chief executive's bedroom. The only light came from the desk lamp and one small table lamp; the room was heavy with shadows.

The President was wearing pajamas and a dressing gown. He was cracking his knuckles, one at a time, being very methodical about it. He smiled every time one of them popped with especially good volume. "Bob, if what you tell me is even half true—"

The telephone which stood in the middle of the glass-and-chrome coffee table rang twice.

"It'll be your man," the President said.

McAlister picked up the receiver.

The White House operator said, "Mr. President?"

"Bob McAlister."

"I have a call for you, Mr. McAlister. It's a Mr. Bernard Kirkwood."

"Put him through, please."

Bernie said, "Are you there?"

"Did you see her?" McAlister asked.

"Yes. She says it was Rice."

"She's positive?"

"Absolutely. Now what?"

"You want to go home to bed—or do you want to be in on the end of it?" McAlister asked.

"Who could sleep tonight?"

"Then get over here to the White House. I'll leave word at the gate that you're to be let through."

"I'll be there in ten minutes."

McAlister hung up and turned to the President, who had thrust his left hand under his pajama shirt and was scratching his right armpit. "That was Kirkwood, sir. The girl has positively identified Rice as the man who assaulted her."

The President took his left hand out of his pajamas. Then he thrust his right hand into them and furiously scratched his left armpit. His handsome face was bloodless. "Well. Well, well!" He stopped scratching his armpit and stood up. "Then I guess we have no choice but to proceed according to the plan you outlined a few minutes ago."

"I see no alternative, sir."

"What a sewer."

"Yes, sir."

"They've brought us down to their level."

McAlister said nothing.

The President scratched his nose, then the back of his neck. "Where do you want Rice? Here?"

"The Pentagon would be better," McAlister said. "It's nice and quiet at this hour. There's a security-cleared doctor already on duty there, so we won't have to rout some other poor bastard out of bed."

"The Pentagon it is," the President said, one hand poised before him as if he were trying to think of one more place to scratch.

McAlister glanced at the wall clock: 11:15. "As soon as I leave, would you call Pentagon Security and tell them that I'm to have their full cooperation?"

"Certainly, Bob."

"Then wait half an hour before you call Rice. That'll give me time to reach the Pentagon and get ready for him. Tell him to come to the Mall Entrance and that he'll be met there."

"No problem."

Bending over, McAlister began to gather up the copies of Prescott Hennings' magazines, which were strewn over the coffee table.

"Could you let those here?" the President asked. "I'm not going to be able to sleep tonight. I might as well find out what Andy Rice is really like."

"I'd like to have one issue to throw at him for psychological effect," McAlister said. "I'll leave the rest."

They went out of the office and across the President's private bedroom.

At the door, the chief executive stopped and turned to McAlister. "Bob, it appears you're right about Rice beating up that girl. And it looks like he's behind this Dragonfly business. I hate to admit I've been made a fool of, but I've got to face facts. But one thing . . ."

"Yes, sir?"

"It seems to me that the rest of your theory is a bit too far-fetched. How could these Committeemen seize the government?"

"Assassination," McAlister said without hesitation.

"But the Vice-President isn't a Committeeman, surely."

"Then they'll assassinate him, too," McAlister said.

The President raised his eyebrows.

"They'll assassinate however many they have to—until they get to that man in the line of succession who *is* one of theirs."

The President shook his head no, vigorously. "It's too much killing, Bob. They could never get away with all of it. It's too bizarre."

"I don't know whether it's population pressures, future shock, the end product of a permissive society, or what," McAlister said morosely. "But there are pressures working within this country, pressures that are producing madmen of a sort we've never known before. I think they're capable of anything, no matter how bizarre it seems."

"No," the President said. "I can't go along with that."

McAlister sighed and shrugged. "You're probably right, sir," he said, although he didn't think the President was right at all.

"You're right about Rice and Dragonfly, but you're altogether wrong about the rest of it." He opened the bedroom door, escorted McAlister into the hall, and turned him over to the Secret Service agent who was on duty there. "Get back to me the minute he cracks, Bob."

McAlister nodded, turned, and followed the Secret Service man down the long hall toward the elevator.

PEKING: SATURDAY, 4:00 P.M.

The first CIA deep-cover agent was a sixty-eight-year-old man named Yuan Yat-sen. He had been thirty-nine years old when Mao Tse-tung's soldiers had driven Chiang Kai-shek and his corrupt army from China's mainland, back in 1949. An advocate of Chiang's policies, a successful landlord and prosperous banker, Yuan had lost everything in the revolution. Perhaps he could have rebuilt his fortune on Taiwan. But money was not all that he lost. A band of Maoist guerillas had slain Yuan's wife and three children. His business was half his life—and his family was the other half. Although he fled to Taiwan, he could not manage to pick up the broken pieces of his life and start anew. He loathed Maoists, dreamed of slaughtering them by the tens of thousands; and a thirst for revenge was all that kept him going. He had been perfect for the CIA. In 1950, while he was growing ever more bitter in Taipei, he was approached by agency operatives and signed up for deep-cover work. Near the end of that year he was dropped back onto the mainland, where he assumed a new name and a past that was not linked to Chiang Kai-shek. In the confusion that followed the war, he was able to pass without much trouble. Indeed, he had gradually gained recognition as an educator and a revolutionary theorist. Today he was the third man in the prestigious Bureau of Education Planning.

They had found him in a park near his office, taking an afternoon break with an associate. He had surrendered without resistance.

They were all back in the embassy drawing room. Ambassador Webster sat in an easy chair, smoking one of his long Cuban cigars and watching the proceedings with interest. General Lin paced impatiently and kept looking at his watch. Lee Ann was sitting on a cushioned cane chair in the center of the room, and Yuan Yat-sen was facing her from another chair only three feet away. Electrodes were pasted to Yuan's temples; a sphygmomanometer was wrapped tightly around his right arm, controlled by an automatic device that was part of the computer; brightly colored wires trailed back to the sophisticated polygraph which Canning had taken from its steel security case.

The three-foot-square portable computer monitored Yuan's pulse, blood pressure, skin temperature, rate of perspiration, and brain waves. Furthermore, it listened to his voice and analyzed the stress patterns which were beyond his conscious control. Instantly assimilating these indices, the computer translated them into a purple line that glowed across the center of a small read-out screen. If the line was comparatively still, the subject's answers were close to the truth. If the line began to dance and jiggle, the subject was most likely lying. It was a very complicated yet simple machine; Canning had seen it used, had taken a course in its use, and he trusted it.

Because Yuan Yat-sen spoke no English, Lee Ann would ask all the questions.

Canning turned to her now. "We'll start off with questions we know the answers to. The first one is—'What is your name?' "

She relayed the question to Yuan.

"Yuan Yat-sen," he said.

The purple line vibrated for a moment.

Smiling, Canning said, "Very good. Now ask him to tell you his real name, the name he was born with and not the one he adopted when he became a deep-cover agent."

Lee Ann asked the question.

Yuan said, "Liu Chao-chi."

The purple line did not move.

The questioning led to the Dragonfly project, but for the next ten minutes the purple line rarely moved.

At last Canning switched off the polygraph and said, "Yuan is not the man we want. He doesn't know anything at all about Dragonfly or trigger men."

General Lin said, "You are certain? The machine could be wrong."

"That's not likely."

"He seems like a crafty old man," the general said doubtfully.

"Not crafty enough to deceive a computer," Canning said. "Printed circuitry and microtransistors aren't susceptible to guile."

The general nodded. "Very well. What is the name of your second agent? We are wasting time here."

"I agree that we ought not to waste time," Canning said. "This is a very grave matter. On the other hand, Dragonfly has been ready for activation for months and hasn't yet been used. I don't understand your great impatience, General."

General Lin frowned. "I do not understand it either. But I *feel*—something very wrong. I have nightmares, and recently they have grown worse. I *know* time is running out. I sense it. So . . . The second name, please?"

WASHINGTON: FRIDAY, 11:45 P.M.

Andrew Rice was surprised to hear the President's voice on the other end of the line. "Is something wrong, sir?"

"Yes, Andy, I'm afraid that something is very wrong. The Soviet ambassador paid me a visit a few minutes ago. He outlined their reaction to the Dragonfly project if it should be carried out."

His heart suddenly racing, Rice said, "I see."

"I'm sending a limousine around for you."

"Yes, sir."

"It'll bring you to the Pentagon."

"Yes, sir."

Why not the White House? Rice wondered. But he did not ask, for he knew they had said all that could be said on an open phone line.

"See you within the hour, Andy."

"Yes, Mr. President."

Rice hung up, cursing the goddamned Russians. He expected that they would invade China from the west once the plague had struck in Peking. That was acceptable. That could be dealt with in due time. But this sounded like something much more ominous. Had the Russians given Washington some ultimatum? Were those crazy goddamned Bolsheviks siding with the Chinese? They hated the Chinese! Why would they line up with them? It was craziness!

He dressed hurriedly and was standing in front of his town house, crunching LifeSavers two at a time, when the limousine arrived.

PEKING: SATURDAY, 5:45 P.M.

The second CIA deep-cover agent was a sixty-four-year-old man named Ku K'ai Chih. Like Yuan, he had been a follower of Chiang, and he had lost his entire family and his business in the revolution. Another natural for the CIA. He had returned to the mainland in the spring of 1951, and he had rapidly established himself as an ardent Maoist, organizing a Party unit among the dock workers and seamen in the great eastern ports like Foochow, Shanghai, and Tsingtao. Today he was one of the twelve members of the board of managers of China's merchant marine.

The interrogation went as it had with Yuan: Canning asked the questions in English; Lee Ann rephrased them in Chinese, the subject replied, and the computer analyzed the responses. The purple line seldom wavered.

At the end of fifteen minutes of intense questioning, Canning said, "This one's clean too."

Lee Ann explained to Ku that he would remain at the embassy, would later be flown to the United States for debriefing in full, and then would be returned to Taiwan.

"We are left with the conclusion that the trigger man for Dragonfly must be your third agent," General Lin said.

"It certainly looks that way," Canning said.

"His name?"

Canning hesitated for an instant, then said, "He is Sung Ch'ung-chen. As you may know, Sung is in charge of a branch of your Internal Security Force."

General Lin's yellow-brown face darkened perceptibly. He was extremely mortified by the news that one of his own subordinates was a CIA deep-cover agent. "I know Mr. Sung all too well."

"Shall we go find him?" Canning asked.

"*I* shall go find him," the general said. "I will not require your assistance this time, Mr. Canning. Since Sung is obviously the trigger agent for Dragonfly, the crisis is past. We can arrest him and get to the truth in our own fashion, without your marvelous computerized polygraph." He smiled coldly. "And later, of course, he might also wish to tell us what misguided citizens of the People's Republic cooperated with him in the passing of secret information."

Getting swiftly to his feet, Webster said, "General Lin, may I say that this is a most uncooperative—"

"You may say what you wish," Lin assured him. "But I have no time to stand here and listen." He turned and strode out of the drawing room.

Webster was nonplused. He sputtered helplessly for a moment and finally said, "Well, I told you he was a cunning little man. In spite of all your precautions, your network is blown."

Lee Ann began to laugh.

Canning smiled.

Amazed, Webster said, "I fail to grasp the comic element."

Stifling her laughter, Lee Ann said, "David foresaw just this situation as he was drifting off to sleep last night in Tokyo—that neither of the first two agents we interrogated would be the trigger for Dragonfly. He got up and put through a call to Bob McAlister and asked him to dig up a good fourth name."

"A fail-safe name to keep General Lin honest," Canning said.

Webster nodded slowly. "So . . . Mr. Sung is not one of ours. He's an innocent."

"Exactly," Canning said. "General Lin will arrest him. And I'm afraid that Sung will be tortured for several hours. But eventually the general will realize that Sung is no more a CIA operative than he is himself. Then he will be back here, demanding the name of the *real* third agent."

"And you'll give it to him?" Webster asked.

"Oh, sure."

"But when he *has* the right name, why should he play by the rules any more than he's doing now?"

"Because," Lee Ann said, enjoying herself immensely, "he won't be absolutely certain that the next name David gives him is the real article. He'll have to suspect it's another ringer, a double fail-safe. He'll have wasted so much time on Sung that he won't dare waste more on what might be another hoax—especially not when he's having these nightmares and feelings of imminent disaster. So he'll bring our man here for confirmation, and we won't let him take our man back again."

"Mr. Canning, you have a splendid oriental mind."

"I know. I cultivate it."

"And now what do we do?" asked Webster.

"How about dinner?" Canning asked.

"Certainly. But what a letdown after the tension of this afternoon!"

"I can assure you," Canning said, "this is going to be the tensest dinner of my life."

6

THE PENTAGON: SATURDAY, 12:30 A.M.

The office in E Ring belonged to one Lionel Bryson, a full admiral
in the United States Navy, one-time lightweight boxing champion
of the Naval Academy, father of seven children and one of the
twenty most knowledgeable amateur numismatists in the country.
None of these achievements, all-American as they were, had
earned him a forty-foot-square office in E Ring. He could also
captain any nuclear submarine currently in service. But that ability
had not won him his very own secretary with *her* own connecting
office. Bryson was a very special kind of engineer-architect, a
doctor of marine design. It was his talent for designing magnificent
machines of death, rather than his ability to pilot them, that had
earned him the wall-to-wall plush carpeting, the leather couch and
armchairs, the executive desk, the private telephone line, the
mahogany bookcases, the trophy case, the soundproofed walls and
ceiling, and the heavy blue-velvet drapes at the window-with-a-
view.

Bryson was not here tonight. Which was just as well. He would
not have liked the idea of his office being turned into an
interrogation chamber.

There were four people in the room. An armed marine guard, cleared for top-security matters, was standing to the right of the door; the holster at his hip was unsnapped and the revolver in it looked like a howitzer to McAlister. Major Arnold Teffler, night-duty physician at the Pentagon, was sitting on the couch with his black bag; he was also security-cleared all the way up to eyes-only material. Bernie Kirkwood was slumped in an armchair, his feet propped up on a coffee table, his eyes closed, and his hands folded in his lap. McAlister sat behind Admiral Bryson's desk and played with a scale model of a Trident submarine. No one spoke. They had nothing in common and no reason for being here until the fifth man arrived.

Rice.

McAlister still had a bit of trouble believing it.

The telephone rang.

McAlister grabbed it. "Yes?"

"This is the door sergeant at the Mall Entrance," the man on the other end said. "Mr. Rice just came through here."

"Thank you."

McAlister hung up, got to his feet, and came around from behind the desk. "Gentlemen, we're about to begin."

The marine and the doctor remained where they were.

Bernie Kirkwood stood up and stretched.

A minute passed. Then another.

Someone knocked sharply on the door.

The marine opened it.

Two other marines stood in the corridor, and Andrew Rice stood between them. Rice came into the office and the two marines stayed in the hall and the marine already in the room closed the door behind the President's chief advisor.

Rice looked at the doctor and then at McAlister and then around the room. He seemed perplexed. "Where's the President?"

"He couldn't make it," McAlister said.

"But he called me less than an hour ago!"

"He had some important reading to do."

"What about the Russian—"

"There is no Russian problem," McAlister said.

Frowning, Rice waited and said nothing more.

"Don't you want to know what the President is reading?"

"What sort of game is this?" Rice blustered.

McAlister picked up one of Hennings' magazines from the desk and held it out toward Rice.

The fat man just stared at it.

Kirkwood said, "There's also a most interesting article in Friday's *Washington Post*."

Rice looked at him.

"Some poor hooker got nearly beat to death," Kirkwood said.

At last McAlister had the pleasure of seeing a quick flicker of fear pass through Rice's eyes.

"I haven't any idea what you're talking about," the fat man said.

McAlister said, "We'll see."

THE PEKING RAILROAD STATION: SATURDAY, 8:55 P.M.

Chai Po-han got off the train. Slinging his single sack of belongings over his left shoulder, he walked along the concrete platform, past huge pillars bedecked with political posters, up the skeletal steel stairs, and into the public area of the main terminal.

His mother, father, brother, and one of his three sisters were waiting for him. They all wore different expressions. His father was smiling broadly. His brother was quite solemn, as if to say, "What happened to you might as easily have happened to me." His beloved mother and lovely sister were crying with joy at the sight of him.

It was a very Confucian scene, the kind discouraged by the Party. Love of country must take precedence over love of family.

Chai Po-han began to weep too, although his tears were shed because he knew that once he left China as he planned to do, he would never see any of them again.

PEKING: SATURDAY, 9:00 P.M.

At nine o'clock Canning and Lee Ann went up to their rooms, ostensibly to get a few hours' sleep before General Lin Shen-yang came back to them in a rage. But at her door his goodnight kiss metamorphosed into a long, soft, moist battle of lips and teeth and tongues.

"You aren't really sleepy?" she asked.

"Not in the least."

"Me either."

She got her suitcase, and they went quietly down the hall to his room.

Inside, she said, "I feel like a high-school girl sneaking off on a forbidden date."

He held her and kissed her, but that was not enough. His fingers tugged at the buttons of her blouse and slid behind her to unhook her bra. He held her warm breasts in his hands.

She pulled away from him then and said, "I feel all grimy. Let's have a bath together first."

"In that ugly tub?"

"I'll make it beautiful," she said unabashedly.

And she did: she made it beautiful.

Later they made love on the four-poster bed while George Washington, Thomas Jefferson, and Abraham Lincoln watched.

At the end of it, while he was going limp but was still snug within her, he said, "When we get back to the States—will you come stay with me?"

She smiled. "I think that might be good for me."

"And wonderful for me."

"I could have a talk with that son of yours."

"I don't know," he said. "I've been thinking about him. Maybe most people in the world *should* believe in black and white morality. Maybe they shouldn't ever be fully aware of all the animals ready to prey on them. A handful of people like you and me can do the dirty work to keep the balance. If everyone was aware of the nature of the jungle, not many people would be happy."

"No more talk," she said.

They stretched out side by side and pulled the covers over themselves.

He thought of Dragonfly . . .

But then he thought of Lee Ann and knew that he would always have her, knew it in his bones and blood and muscle, reached out and touched her, and dozed for a while.

THE PENTAGON: SATURDAY, 5:00 A.M.

McAlister felt malarial—worse, cancerous—as if he belonged in the terminal ward of a hospital. Every one of his joints ached. His head ached. His eyes were grainy and bloodshot. He was sweaty and rumpled; his face itched from his beard stubble. His tongue felt swollen, and his mouth was sour. He wanted someone to give him a pill and a swallow of gingerale; he wanted someone to tuck him in and fluff his pillow and sing him to sleep.

Andrew Rice seemed to be in even worse shape than the director. His puffy face was as white as coconut meat. His lips were bluish. His quick little eyes were still little but no longer as quick as they had been; they were eyes that had seen more than they wanted to see; tears of weariness streamed from them constantly. Rice breathed as if he were inhaling all the air in the room, as if he were causing the walls to expand and contract like a bellows. His stubby-fingered hands were at his sides, palms up, motionless.

Yet the son of a bitch would not break down!

For the first time in his life Bob McAlister really knew the meaning of the word "fanatic." Not that he had wanted to really know it. But there it was.

Kirkwood said, "You can't put it off any longer."

Furious, too weak to deal with fury, McAlister got up from the couch and walked over to the armchair from which Rice was actually overflowing. "Damn you, we *know!* We know so much that you can't win! Why not tell us the rest of it?"

Rice stared at him and said nothing.

Wiping a hand across his face, McAlister said, "Rice, if you won't talk, I'm going to have to use a drug on you. A very nasty drug."

Rice stared. Said nothing.

"It's that drug I found the agency using when I became director. It's barbaric. I outlawed it. It's the drug your men used on Carl Altmüller when they were trying to establish a list of other federal marshals who wouldn't recognize him. I saw the needle mark on the man's arm, Rice. It was swollen up like a grape. This drug is so hostile to the human system that the point of injection swells up *like a fucking goddamned grape!*"

Rice was unmoved.

"And now you're forcing me to use it on you."

Licking his cracked lips, Rice said, "I suppose that offends your delicate liberal conscience."

McAlister stared at him.

Rice smiled. He looked demonic.

Turning away from the fat man, McAlister said, "Dr. Teffler, please fill the syringe."

Teffler got up and opened his bag and arranged his instruments on Admiral Bryson's desk. He examined the vial that McAlister gave to him. "What's the proper dosage?"

McAlister told him.

"What is it, Pentothal?"

McAlister snapped at him: "Haven't you been listening? It's a new drug. A damned dangerous drug. Handle it like I tell you!"

Unmoving, his hands still at his sides, Rice watched Teffler apply a rubber tourniquet to his thick arm. He watched his own vein rise through the fat, and he sighed when Teffler swabbed his arm with alcohol-soaked gauze.

McAlister forced himself to watch as the needle stabbed deep and the yellow truth serum squeezed out into Rice's system.

The fat man's eyes rolled back into his head, and almost at once he went into convulsions. He pitched out of the chair and to the floor, where he thrashed helplessly.

Going down on his hands and knees, Kirkwood tried to pin Rice's shoulders. It was all he could do, however, to keep from being thrown like a rodeo rider from a wild mount.

McAlister grabbed at the fat man's twisting legs to keep them from being bruised or broken against the furniture. But he took a solid kick in the stomach and was propelled away.

The marine guard ran over from the door, tried to hold Rice's legs, finally sat on them.

"He'll swallow his tongue!" McAlister gasped.

But Teffler was already there, wedging a smooth metal splint between Rice's jaws. With the splint protecting him from a bite,

Teffler used his fingers to catch Rice's tongue and hold it flat against the floor of his mouth.

Gradually, the fat man grew quiet.

Shuddering uncontrollably, McAlister went out into Bryson's secretary's office and vomited in the wastebasket there.

Oh God Jesus Christ no Jesus oh shit oh shit no!

Bernie Kirkwood came in and said, "Are you all right?"

Braced against the desk, his head hanging over the basket, McAlister said, "Is he dead?"

"Just unconscious."

"Coma?"

"The doctor said it's not."

"I'll be there in a minute."

Bernie went away.

After about five minutes McAlister got up, pulled a handful of paper tissues from the box on the secretary's desk, and wiped his greasy face. He threw the tissues in the reeking wastebasket. There was a water carafe on the desk and it was half full. The water was flat, but it tasted marvelous. He rinsed out his mouth and spat into the can. After all of this he felt no worse than terminal.

He went back into the other room to have a look at Rice.

"At first," Teffler said, "I thought it was anaphylactic shock, a deadly reaction to the drug. But now I think the dosage was just too large for his system."

"It was the normal dosage," McAlister said.

"But as overweight as he is," Teffler said, "he might not react in any normal fashion."

McAlister watched the fat man's belly rise and fall, rise and fall, rise and fall.

"What now?" Kirkwood asked.

"How long will he be unconscious?" McAlister asked the doctor.

Sitting on the floor beside Rice, Teffler took the patient's pulse. He peeled back an eyelid. "No less than an hour. No more than two or three."

"We wait for him to wake up," McAlister said.

"Then?" Kirkwood said.

"We give him another dose of the serum. Half what we shot into him the first time."

"I don't know as I like that," Teffler said sternly.

"Neither do I," McAlister said. "But that's what we're going to do, all right."

Rice stirred at eight o'clock, opened his eyes, looked around, closed his eyes.

He was able to sit up at eight-fifteen.

By a quarter of nine he was nearly his old self. Indeed, he was feeling good enough to smile smugly at McAlister.

At nine o'clock Teffler gave him the second, smaller dose of the truth serum—and by two minutes past nine Andrew Rice was spilling all the secrets of The Committee.

But was it too late? McAlister wondered.

PEKING: SUNDAY, 12:10 A.M.

The telephone burred.

Canning woke, rolled over, and lifted the receiver.

"Guess who is waiting for you down in the drawing room," Ambassador Webster said.

"He's here already?"

"Hasn't poor Mr. Sung suffered enough?"

"I imagine he has," Canning said. "Tell the general we'll be down in ten minutes."

THE WHITE HOUSE: SATURDAY, 11:30 A.M.

The President was shocked at McAlister's bedraggled appearance. He kept saying how shocked he was all the while that McAlister got the tape recorder ready. He stood behind his desk in the Oval Office and clicked his tongue and shook his head and said he felt entirely responsible for the awful way McAlister looked.

For his part, McAlister could not tell if the clicks of the President's tongue were expressions of sympathy—or whether the chief was off on another of his shtik. And not knowing which it was bothered the hell out of him. He said, "It's nothing, sir. I'm fine. It's just about all over now. I've sent an urgent message to Canning. I took the liberty of using your name on it. For his eyes only."

"But from what you've told me—do you think he'll get anything we send to him?"

"Not everyone is involved," McAlister said. "The communications man at the Peking embassy is trustworthy. He'll see that Canning gets it." He ran the tape forward at high speed, watching the white numbers roll around and around on the inch-counter. When he found the numbers he wanted, he stopped the tape, checked them against a list of numbers in his note pad. "You'll want to listen to the entire interrogation later," he told the President. "But right now, I have a few special passages you'll be interested in."

"By all means."

McAlister pushed the *Start* button:

MCALISTER: But even if the Nationalists manage to seize the mainland eventually, it won't be an easy thing. I mean, the Chinese may not have much, but it is a hell of a lot more than they had under Chiang. He was a real despot. They'll remember that. Even without guidance from Peking, they're going to fight—with guns, clubs, even fists. Do you realize how many people are going to die?

RICE: Oh, yes. We've done computer analysis, worked it out in detail.

MCALISTER: And it doesn't bother you?

RICE: No. I look at it like Mr. West does.

MCALISTER: How does Mr. West look at it?

RICE: They aren't people. They're Chinks. Both sides.

MCALISTER: Have you calculated the Russian reaction?

RICE: They'll come in from the west. But they'll never keep the territory they take.

MCALISTER: Why not?

RICE: Because we have something for them too.

MCALISTER: Something like Dragonfly?

RICE: That's right.

MCALISTER: You have a Dragonfly in Moscow now?

RICE: We have a dozen of them, all over Russia. It was much easier to plant those than to plant one man in China. Russia is a more open society than the People's Republic.

The President was stunned at Rice's obvious insanity, stunned that he had been deceived for so long by such a lunatic. His face alternately—and sometimes all at once—registered dismay, surprise, and horror as he fully perceived Rice's lunacy and ruthlessness. But worst of all, in the President's view, was Rice's naïveté, and it was at this that the chief executive winced the hardest. He didn't crack his knuckles once.

McAlister closed his eyes and leaned back in his chair. He had heard all of this before, of course. And now he could see Rice under interrogation: sweat beading on his white face, sweat glistening in his eyebrows and along his hairline, his eyes bulging and bloodshot, saliva drooling from one corner of his mouth, his massive body twitching continuously and sometimes spasming uncontrollably as the drug savaged his central nervous system . . . McAlister felt a long snake of self-loathing uncoil slowly within him. He opened his eyes and stared at the whirling reels of tape; and he began to listen to the content as well as to the tone of Rice's words. And when he listened closely and heard the *evil* in the man—the delusions of grandeur, the ruthlessness, the bigotry and jealousy and mindless hatred—he became so enraged that the snake of self-loathing coiled up in him and went back to sleep.

Rice babbled on and thought that he was dispensing gems of military strategy, wisdom for the ages. He talked about the possibility of nuclear war with the Soviet Union. Neither he nor West nor anyone else in The Committee considered that a major worry. The Committee had Dragonfly's equivalent—with code names like Boris and Ilya—in many Russian missile installations. These Dragonflies carried liquefied nerve gas instead of deadly bacteria. When such a spansule was punctured, the gas would literally explode out of the carrier, expanding at an incredible speed. The personnel of an entire missile installation could be eliminated in seconds by a single Boris planted among them. Even so, some missiles would be launched. Warheads would be exchanged; there was no avoiding it. But Americans should not be frightened of nuclear war, Rice said. They should view it as a potentially necessary and helpful tool. Even a peacemaker like Henry Kissinger had said as much when he had written on the subject years before he became Secretary of State: we *can* survive a nuclear war. Millions would die, but most likely not tens of millions; and civilization would not pass. There were big risks involved here, Rice admitted. But the only way to destroy Communism before it destroyed us, the only way to insure the dominance of the White Race, was to take big risks. Wasn't that true? Wasn't that true? Wasn't it?

McAlister stopped the tape recorder.

The President said, "*Jesus H. Christ!* Did you get the names of those twelve agents in Moscow?"

"Yes."

"The Russians will have to be told about them. Can a Dragonfly be—disarmed?"

"Yes," McAlister said. "If the Russian surgeons know what to look for."

"We can show them." He shook his head. "Rice is so damned naïve."

"And he must be echoing his mentor—A.W. West."

"How could a man like West, a man who has amassed a billion-dollar fortune, be so simple-minded as to think that private citizens can overthrow foreign governments with impunity? How can he believe that he has any moral right to start a war just because he, personally, thinks it's necessary?"

"Lyndon Johnson greatly increased our involvement in Vietnam largely because he, personally, thought it was necessary. Nixon did the same thing in Cambodia, though on a smaller scale."

"At least they were Presidents, elected officials!"

McAlister shrugged.

"How can West be so naïve as to think that he has all the answers to the problems of the world?" The President's face was no longer bloodless; it was mottled by rage.

McAlister had worked it out in his mind, all of it, over and over again; and he was tired of the subject. He just wanted to go somewhere and lie down and sleep for sixteen hours. From the moment he had entered the Oval Office, however, he had been carefully leading the President in one direction, toward one particular decision; and now that they were halfway to that decision, McAlister couldn't allow his weariness to distract him. "We allowed ITT and a couple of private companies to get away with overthrowing, or helping to overthrow, the Chilean government a few years back. That was a dangerous precedent."

"But didn't they learn *anything* from that fiasco? Look what happened to Chile after the coup d'état. The military dictatorship was inefficient, inept, incompetent! Chile's inflation rate the first year after the coup was seven hundred percent! Because they interfered with the free market, unemployment eventually rose to *fifty* percent. There were riots in the streets!"

"I know all of that," McAlister said. "And I'm sure that Rice and West know it too. But these people are what David Canning likes to call 'masturbating adolescents.' They live partly in a fantasy world. To them, there are never any crossroads in life, just forks in the road, never more than two choices, never more than two ways to see a thing: yes or no, good or bad, stop or go, buy or sell, do or don't, us or them."

Frowning, the President said, "A lot of very nice people look at life that way."

"Of course," McAlister said. "But the difference between the nice people and the men like West and Rice is that the nice people, the decent people, aren't consumed by a lust for power."

"Masturbating adolescents."

"That's how Canning sees them. But that doesn't mean that they're harmless. Far from it. You read in the newspapers about wholesome teenage boys who murder their parents in the dead of night. A fool can be amusing—and be a killer at the same time." He ran the tape ahead for a few seconds, stopped it, checked the numbers in the counter, and punched the *Start* button:

MCALISTER: Unless I'm mistaken, the Russian and Chinese operations are only two parts of a three-part plan.

RICE: That's correct.

MCALISTER: The third part is for The Committee to take control of the U.S. government.

RICE: That's right. That's the core of it.

MCALISTER: How would you accomplish that?

RICE: Assassinate the President, Vice-President, and the Speaker of the House, all within an hour of each other.

MCALISTER: But how would that give you control of the government?

RICE: The President pro tem of the Senate is next in the line of succession. He would move straight into the White House.

MCALISTER: Let me be sure I understand you. You're saying that the President pro tem of the Senate is a Committeeman?
RICE: Yes.
MCALISTER: That would be Senator Konlick of New York?
RICE: Yes. Raymond W. Konlick.
(Excited background conversation)
MCALISTER: But isn't it going to be rather obvious—everyone above Konlick getting killed, and him moving smoothly into power?
RICE: An attempt will be made on his life too. He'll be wounded. Shot in the shoulder or arm. But the assassination will fail, and he'll take on the duties of the Presidency.
MCALISTER: When is this to happen?
RICE: Between two and four days after we trigger Dragonfly in Peking.

McAlister stopped the tape recorder again.

Unable to speak, the President got up and went to the Georgian window behind his desk. He stared out at Pennsylvania Avenue for a long moment. Then he suddenly jerked involuntarily, as if he had realized what a good target he was making of himself, and he came back to his desk. He sat down, looked at the tape recorder, looked at McAlister. "With what Rice has told you, will you have any real trouble getting hard evidence against A.W. West?"

"If you appointed me special prosecutor and gave me a topnotch team of young lawyers and investigators, no one could stop the truth from coming out. We know where to look now. We could nail West and every other man, big and small, who Rice knows is connected with The Committee."

The President sighed and slumped down in his chair. "This country is just beginning to calm down after a decade and a half of turmoil . . . And now we're about to hit it with more sensational news stories, investigations, trials. The rest of my first term's going to be totally wasted. I'll have to spend most of my time defending your investigations against charges of political harassment. I'll be on network television every other week trying to reassure the public. Left-wing extremists are going to get very moralistic and start bombing buildings and killing people in protest of the cruelty of capitalism. And you can be damned sure there won't be a second term for me. Bearers of bad tidings aren't rewarded."

Letting a moment pass in silence, McAlister then said, "And when the dust finally settles, the problem will still be unsolved."

The President looked at him quizzically. "Explain that."

This was the penultimate moment, the point toward which McAlister had been heading ever since he entered the Oval Office. "Well, sir, Rice won't know everyone behind The Committee movement."

"West will know."

"Perhaps. But we'd never get away with using the drug on him that we used on Rice. There will be some men who have extremely tenuous connections with The Committee, men who have protected themselves so damned well that we'll never nail them and might not even suspect them. Once the furor has passed, they'll quietly set about rebuilding The Committee—and this time they'll be much more careful about it."

Sighing resignedly, the President nodded: Yes, you're right, that's the way it will be.

McAlister leaned forward in his chair. "There have always been madmen like these, I suppose. But our modern technology has given them the means to destroy more things and more people more rapidly than ever before in history. West can wage bacteriological warfare against a foreign power. And once that's known, the SLA will get in the act to wage a little of it here at home. The knowledge is available; they just have to think about using it. When the West case is in all the papers, they'll think about growing some germs." He paused for effect. Then: "But there's a way to deal with these kind of people."

"I'd like to hear about it," the President said.

"There's a way we can defuse The Committee and yet avoid all of the investigations, trials, and public agony. There's a way we can keep the lid on the assassinations and all the rest of it—and still punish the guilty."

The chief executive's eyes narrowed. "What you're going to suggest is . . . unorthodox, isn't it?"

"Yes, sir."

The President looked at the tape recorder for several minutes. He said nothing; he did not move. Then: "Maybe I'm ready for the unorthodox. Let's hear it."

"I want to play some more of the tape first," McAlister said. "I want you to be even readier than you are now." He switched on the machine:

MCALISTER: Then Chai Po-han is Dragonfly?
RICE: Yes.
MCALISTER: If he was back in China way last March, why haven't you triggered him by now?
RICE: In order to cover his absence from his room that night in Washington, we made it look like he'd been out carousing. We put him back to bed, soaked him in cheap whiskey, and put a pair of—a pair of lacy women's—panties in his hands . . .
MCALISTER: Oh, for God's sake!
RICE: Because his roommate, Chou P'eng-fei, was more lightly sedated than Chai, we knew he would wake up first in the morning, smell the whiskey, see the lace panties. We didn't foresee, *couldn't* foresee, how these crazy damned Chinks would react. When they got back to China, Chai was sent straight to a farm commune instead of to Peking. He was punished for what they called "counterrevolutionary" behavior.
MCALISTER: The People's Republic is an extraordinarily puritanical society.
RICE: It's crazy.
MCALISTER: Most developing countries are puritanical. We were like that for a couple of hundred years, although not quite so fiercely as China today.
RICE: We wouldn't send an American boy to a slave-labor camp just because he got drunk and took up with a hooker. It's crazy, I tell you.
MCALISTER: They didn't see it as just "taking up with a hooker." To them it was a political statement.
RICE: Craziness. Crazy Chinks.
MCALISTER: Chai wasn't an American. Didn't you see, didn't you even suspect, that American standards might not apply? Christ, you fouled up the project at the very beginning! You screwed up on such a simple bit of business—yet you think you know how to run the world!
RICE: It was an oversight. Anybody could have made the same mistake.
MCALISTER: You're dangerous as hell, but you're a real buffoon.

RICE: (Silence)

MCALISTER: Chai is still on this commune?

RICE: No. He was released. He arrived in Peking at five o'clock this morning, our time.

MCALISTER: When will he be triggered?

RICE: As soon as possible, within the next twelve hours.

MCALISTER: Who is the trigger man in Peking?

RICE: General Lin Shen-yang.

MCALISTER: What? General Lin?

(A flurry of indistinct conversation)

MCALISTER: Is General Lin a part of The Committee?

RICE: No.

MCALISTER: Does he know he's the trigger?

RICE: No.

MCALISTER: He's been used, just like Chai?

RICE: That's right.

MCALISTER: How was it done?

RICE: General Lin keeps a mistress in Seoul. We went to her, threatened her, and got her cooperation. When he visited her last March, we drugged his wine, planted a series of subliminal commands deep in his subconscious mind. When he woke, he had no knowledge of what had been done to him. When he is told to do so, he will seek out Chai Po-han and trigger him.

MCALISTER: When he's *told* to do so?

RICE: Yes.

MCALISTER: Then you've established a sort of double trigger. Is that right?

RICE: Yes.

MCALISTER: Why so complex a mechanism?

RICE: The sophisticated surgical facilities we needed to implant the spansule of bacteria existed only here in the States. We couldn't haul it all off to Korea and turn General Lin into Dragonfly. We had to operate on someone who was visiting the Washington area. Then we had a problem setting up a trigger man. We couldn't use any of the three deep-cover agents the CIA has in China, because they're not Committeemen. So we had to rely on a Westerner who was one of us. Now, Chai Po-han doesn't have much contact with Westerners in Peking. Our man would have a difficult time getting to him without causing a spectacle. General

Lin, on the other hand, has a great deal of contact with Westerners and with his countrymen alike. Our man, we realized, could trigger General Lin; the general could then trigger Dragonfly.

MCALISTER: I understand. But who is your first trigger man, the one who gives the word to Lin?

RICE: Alexander Webster.

MCALISTER: Our ambassador to China?

RICE: Yes.

(A babble of voices)

MCALISTER: Are you saying our embassy in Peking is a nest of Committeemen?

RICE: No. Just Webster.

MCALISTER: You're positive of that?

RICE: Yes.

(Ten seconds of silence)

MCALISTER: What disease is Chai Po-han carrying?

RICE: A mutated strain of the bubonic plague.

MCALISTER: In what way is it mutated?

RICE: First of all, it's transmitted differently from every other kind of plague. Most strains are carried by fleas, ticks, or lice. Wilson's plague is totally airborne.

MCALISTER: It's transmitted through the air? Through the lungs?

RICE: Yes. You're contaminated simply by breathing.

MCALISTER: What are the other mutations?

RICE: It's extremely short-lived and has a very low level of fertility. In three days it will be dead and gone.

MCALISTER: So the Nationalist Chinese can move in then?

RICE: Yes.

MCALISTER: What other mutations?

RICE: The bug needs just nine to twelve hours after it hits your lungs to kill you.

MCALISTER: Is there a vaccine?

RICE: Yes. But Wilson didn't produce much of it. You don't need much if the plague's one hundred percent abated by the time you send in troops.

MCALISTER: How much vaccine is there?

RICE: One vial. Webster has it.

MCALISTER: What about the other Americans at the embassy?

RICE: They will be sacrificed.

MCALISTER: How noble of you.

RICE: It was necessary. They aren't in sympathy with The Committee. They couldn't have been trusted.

MCALISTER: How many people will die if Dragonfly is triggered?

RICE: We have computer projections on that. Somewhere between two million and two and a quarter million deaths in the Peking area.

MCALISTER: God help us.

When McAlister switched off the tape recorder, the President said, "You sounded badly shaken on the tape, but now you're so damned calm. And it isn't over!"

"I've sent my message to Canning," McAlister said. "I have faith in him."

"Let's hope it's well founded, or we're all finished."

"In any event," McAlister said, "there's nothing more that you or I can do. Let's talk about that unorthodox plan of mine."

PEKING: SUNDAY, 1:30 A.M. UNTIL DAWN

The CIA's third deep-cover agent in Peking was very much like the first two deep-cover agents in Peking. He was in his sixties, just as Yuan and Ku had been. His name was Ch'en Tu-hsiu. Like Yuan and Ku, he had lost his family and money when the Maoists assumed power. Like Yuan and Ku, he had fled to Taiwan, but had returned soon enough as a dedicated CIA operative who would live under the Maoists for the rest of his life and pass out what information he could obtain. He had worked hard to prove what a loyal Maoist he was. As a result, and because he was an intelligent man to begin with (as were Yuan and Ku), he was promoted and promoted until he became Vice-Secretary of the Party in the Province of Hopeh, which included the capital city of Peking. And finally, just like Yuan and Ku, he was judged a truthful man by the computerized polygraph.

Canning could not understand it. He examined the machine, found it to be functioning properly, and asked Lee Ann to go through the list of questions once more. Ch'en answered precisely as he had the first time; the machine said he was not a liar; and Canning was baffled.

Lee Ann said, "If neither Yuan nor Ku is the trigger, then it *has* to be Ch'en, doesn't it? I'll ask the questions a third time."

She did that.

The purple line didn't move through any of Ch'en's answers.

After having been misled with Sung Ch'ung-chen, General Lin was very suspicious. He stood stiff and straight, not bothering to work off the excess energy that always filled him, letting it build up toward an explosion. "You mean to say that *none* of your deep-cover agents knows about Dragonfly?"

"I don't understand it," Canning said.

Lin's face was twisted, blush-red beneath his olive complexion. "What sort of trick is this?"

"It's no trick," Canning said.

"This entire affair has been some sort of hoax."

"I don't think so."

"You don't *think* so?" the general raged.

"If it was a hoax," Canning said, "then I was a victim of it too. I don't know why the CIA would want to hoax you or me."

The general moved closer to him, glared up at him. "I want to know why you've come all the way around the world to waste my time here in Peking. What have you *really* been doing in China?"

"Exactly what I've told you I've been doing," Canning said, exasperated. But he could understand the general's anger.

"Sooner or later you will tell me what the trick is."

"There *is* no trick."

"I'm afraid you will not be permitted to leave China until I am given a full explanation," General Lin said. "Perhaps the rules of diplomacy forbid me to drag you out of your embassy and beat the truth from you. But I can see that you remain here, grow old, and die here if you will not explain your real purpose in Peking." He turned away from them and started toward the drawing-room door.

Webster came out of his armchair as if propelled by a bad spring in the cushion. He hurried after Lin and caught up with him in the downstairs hall. "General, please wait a moment. Give me a moment to explain. I can explain this entire affair. Just come up to my office for five minutes, and I'll put your mind at rest, sir."

"Then there has been some trick?" General Lin asked.

"Let's not discuss it here," Webster said. "Upstairs. In my office. That's the proper atmosphere."

When they had gone up the steps, Lee Ann said, "What could Webster know that we don't?"

"Nothing," Canning said. "He's in the dark too. But he can't let Lin go away *that* angry. He has to play the diplomat for a while."

Pushing a lock of her black hair from her face, Lee Ann said, "My opinion is that if the general goes all the way upstairs just to hear a bunch of diplomatic goo, he's going to be twice as angry as he is now. Just my opinion, of course."

"Then he's Webster's problem, not ours."

"What about Dragonfly?"

"Maybe there is no such thing."

"How could that be?" Her eyes were huge.

"Maybe McAlister was using us."

"For what?"

He said, "God knows. But it happens in this business."

"I think Bob was sincere," she said.

"Then he might be misinformed."

"He's not the kind to make a move unless he's positive of what he's doing."

Canning agreed with her. He felt uneasy. He felt as though he had missed something vital.

"What happens now?" she asked.

"That's what I'm trying to figure." He looked down at Ch'en, who smiled at him and nodded. To Lee Ann he said, "We'll see that our friend here is put in a room on the third floor with Yuan and Ku. Then we'll go down to the communications room and get off a wire to McAlister, asking for his instructions."

In his office, Ambassador Webster went directly to the bar in the corner and put ice cubes in two squat glasses. "Is bourbon all right, General?"

Lin Shen-yang stood by the desk, barely able to control his temper. "I do not want a drink. I want an explanation."

"This is fine bourbon," Webster said. "And I've got good branch water to mix with it. They fly my branch water all the way in from Louisiana. Only way to drink bourbon."

"No, thank you," the general said stiffly.

Smiling, the ambassador said, "Very well." He poured bourbon and branch water into his own glass. "You won't mind if I indulge?"

The general glared at him.

Webster took his drink to one of the two overstuffed armchairs that stood in front of his desk. He sat down and indicated that the general should sit opposite him.

"Mr. Webster—" Lin began.

"Please, let's be amiable," the ambassador said. "Sit down and relax. I will explain everything."

Reluctantly, General Lin sat in the other armchair. He perched on the edge of it; he refused to be comfortable.

Taking a long, cool swallow of his drink, the ambassador said, "Do you know what branch water is? It comes from certain streams, river *branches,* in Louisiana. It's pure, perfectly tasteless. It is the only way to mix a whiskey. In Louisiana we know how—"

"I am not interested in Louisiana or in your branch water," the general said curtly. "I want that explanation."

Webster sighed. "I was just savoring the moment. But if you insist . . ." He put down his drink on a small round side table. He smiled at the general and said the key phrase: "Yin-hsi is as lovely as a swan in the lilies."

General Lin's eyes glazed. His mouth sagged open, and he leaned back in the armchair.

"Can you hear me?" Webster asked.

"Yes," Lin said faintly. He stared *through* the ambassador.

"Do you know how to find the home of Chai Chen-tse?"

"Yes."

"Chai Po-han is there now. Do you understand me?"

"Yes."

"You will go to him and say that phrase which you have been taught. Do you understand me?"

"Yes."

"When you have spoken those words to him, and to no one else but him, and in privacy with him, you will return to your house and go to bed. Do you understand me?"

"Yes."

Webster picked up his drink and sipped it. He enjoyed seeing the general sitting there, mouth open and eyes blank as the eyes of a moron. "When you wake in the morning, you will not remember this conversation we are having. You will not remember your visit to Chai Po-han. You will not remember having said anything to Chai Po-han. In the morning you will go about your business as you ordinarily would. Do you understand me?"

The general hesitated.

"Do you understand me?"

"Yes."

"Once more. Do you understand me?"

"Yes."

"Go to Chai now."

The general closed his mouth. His eyes refocused, but they still did not look quite normal. He got up and left the ambassador's office, closing the door behind him.

Webster picked up his drink and took it back to his desk. He sat down in his high-backed posturmatic chair. From the bookshelves behind him, he withdrew a copy of *The Wind in the Willows*. He opened the book and removed a flimsy sheet of paper that had been pressed in the front.

The paper was a copy of the order for Chai Po-han's transfer from the Ssunan Commune to Peking. A clerk in the Office of Revolutionary Education had taken it from the files the very day that the transfer had been approved and had passed it to an old gentleman who pedaled one of the few remaining bicycle rickshaws that still operated in Peking. The clerk had received a handsome sum, all in good Chinese yuan, without knowing why anyone would so desperately need to know when Chai was coming home. Like all of his kind, the rickshaw operator was extremely independent; after all, he conducted business in defiance of a Party order outlawing rickshaws, and he had done so for many years now. The Party had decided to let the rickshaw operators die off gradually, while issuing no new licenses. Therefore, the officials ignored the rickshaw men—and the rickshaw men, independent as they were, made good conduits for certain kinds of information. This particular old gentleman had passed the transfer notice to Webster when Webster had taken a rickshaw ride around Wan Shou Shan's lake—as he managed to do once or twice a month. In his turn, the old gentleman had received another substantial sum in yuan. Back at the embassy, after spending hours translating the ideograms into English, Webster saw that Chai was coming home, and he wired the news to Rice.

Now, if the train had been on time—and Chinese trains were always on time—Chai Po-han was at home, and the Dragonfly project could be launched at last. In twenty minutes, or half an hour at most, General Lin would trigger him. Chai would puncture the spansule within a few minutes of the general's visit, as soon as he was alone and could find a sharp instrument. The plague virus would spread rapidly through Chai's system, reproducing in his bloodstream. Within two hours millions of deadly microorganisms would be passing *out* through the alveolae in his lungs. Then he would begin contaminating the very air that Peking breathed, and the flight of the Dragonfly would have begun.

Webster smiled and drank some bourbon and branch water.

Chai Po-han had written a long letter to his parents, explaining his decision to leave them like a coward in the middle of the night and seek political asylum at the United States Embassy. It had been a most difficult letter to compose, and he had wept freely as his pen had drawn the characters which spelled out his future. But now it was done, folded and sealed in a red-lined envelope. He put the envelope on the center of his bed and turned away from it before he lost his courage and tore it to shreds.

Taking only one bag of mementos and remembrances, he slipped out of his room and went along the dark hall to the rear door of the house. Outside, he strapped the leather bag to the handlebars of his brother's bicycle.

The United States Embassy was less than two miles away. Even if he took the long way around, used only the back streets and lanes, he would be there in ten or fifteen minutes. He would need another fifteen minutes to slip into the compound without being seen and stopped by a Chinese patrol. In half an hour he would be talking with the United States ambassador, and he would have taken the last irrevocable step into a new life.

The embassy's communications room was in the basement. It was a rather uninviting, thirty-foot-square, concrete-wall chamber with no carpet and no windows. It contained a telecommunications computer as large as four refrigerators arranged side by side. There was also a radio-controlled Telex printer, a Telex sender, a traditional wireless machine, a desk, two chairs, a filing cabinet, and a pornographic Chinese calendar made in Hong Kong: semi-abstract but altogether recognizable human figures engaged in coitus, a different position for each month.

The night-duty communications officer was a man named Pover. He smiled and apologized to Lee Ann for the calendar and asked if he could be of assistance.

"I want to send a message to Robert McAlister care of the White House communications center. Can do?" Canning asked.

"Oh, sure," Pover said. "What's the message?"

Canning handed him a sheet of paper on which he had written:

> Three deep-cover agents negative.
> Repeat negative. No trigger man.
> Send instructions soonest.

"I'll have it out in a minute," Pover said.

"How long do we have to wait for a reply?" Lee Ann asked.

"Not long these days," Pover said. "The wireless is really a laser. It sends the message out on light pulses that are bounced through a telecommunications satellite. The message will be at the White House in maybe two minutes. How long will it take them to get it to this McAlister?"

"No more than half an hour," Canning said.

"Then your reply should be here no more than an hour from now, depending on how fast they are at the other end. You want this put into code?"

"No," Canning said. "As is. It'll save time."

Lee Ann said, "Can we wait here for our answer?"

"Oh, sure," Pover said. He went across the room and took down the pornographic calendar before he sent the message.

Chai Chen-tse watched as General Lin picked up the sealed envelope from Chai Po-han's bed. In answer to the question that the general had just asked, he said, "Yes, open it. By all means."

Lin Shen-yang used his thumbnail to break open the flap. He

withdrew several sheets of paper from the envelope and began to read them. Halfway across the second page, he dropped everything, turned, and left the room.

Following him into the hall, Chai Chen-tse said, "What is wrong?"

General Lin was already at the front door.

"What is it? Where is my son? What has he done?" the elder Chai asked plaintively.

But the general didn't stop to answer him.

The night air was cool.

The streets were for the most part dark and silent.

Chai Po-han abandoned his brother's bicycle in the park across the street from the back of the diplomatic compound. The gate to the embassies was out on the north side, always opened but always watched. He hid for a few minutes behind a sculptured hedge, cloaked in darkness, until the motorized patrol had passed. Then he got up and dashed across the wide street to the seven-foot-high wall. He threw his satchel over to the other side. Then he jumped, managed to catch the top of the wall with his fingers, pulled himself up, found toeholds between the bricks, and climbed.

At three o'clock in the morning, bells rang in the embassy's communications room. The Telex began to chatter and the wireless set clicked and the computer's print-out screens lit up in a soft shade of green. White letters began to roll up on the computer screens' green background: two identical sets of letters on two screens:

XXXXXXXXXX
WASHINGTON
URGENT URGENT
FROM—R MCALISTER
TO—D CANNING

"Hey," Pover said, "there hasn't been time for them to reply already. We just sent your message out." He ran over to the Telex and glanced at the lines of print that were clattering out of that machine. "It double-checks," he said. "This must be something they sent almost simultaneously with our transmission."

Canning and Lee Ann went over to stand in front of the computer screens.

The screens cleared and more white words rolled up on the electric green background:

```
          SECONDARY TRIGGER MAN
          GENERAL LIN SHEN YANG
          : : : : : : : : : : : : : : : : : :
          : : : : :PRIMARY TRIGGER
          MAN AMBASSADOR WEBSTER
          : : : : : : : : : : : : : : : : : :
          REPEAT PRIMARY TRIGGER
          MAN AMBASSADOR WEBSTER
```

"Can this be true?" Lee Ann asked.

Canning stood there for three more minutes, reading the rest of the message, then he turned and ran from the communications room.

Lee Ann ran after him.

When he reached the steps he caught sight of her out of the corner of his eye. "You stay here."

"Like hell!"

Canning took the steps two at a time all the way up to the fourth floor.

Chai Po-han tore his trousers and skinned his knee coming off the wall. He spat on his hand and rubbed the spit into the wound.

This is not the most auspicious way to begin a new life, he thought.

He picked up his satchel and limped past the first four pink-brick houses until he came to that one which displayed the flag of the United States of America. He went to the front door, hesitated only an instant, and rang the bell.

Alexander Webster had the most infuriating smile that David Canning had ever seen. He shook his head and kept smiling and said, "I'm afraid you're too late."

"Where's the general?"

"Doing what he's been programmed to do," Webster said happily.

Canning stood in front of the desk, impotent, his hands fisted at his sides. He wanted to reach out and grab Webster by the lapels of his dressing gown and shake the hell out of him. But that was pointless.

Holding up his glass, Webster said, "Would either of you like a drink?"

Lee Ann came over from the doorway and stood beside Canning. "You'll die in the plague just like the rest of us."

"Oh, no, Miss Tanaka. I've been vaccinated."

"It doesn't matter," she said. "You'll end up in prison."

"By the time I go home," Webster said, "my people will be in charge of the country—and the prisons." He gave them another infuriating smile.

Canning said, "What do you—"

The telephone rang, startling them.

Webster looked at it for a moment, waited until it rang again, and picked it up. "Yes?" He listened for a moment, and tension came into his broad face. His brows beetled. He glanced up at Canning, licked his lips, looked quickly down at the blotter. "No. Don't send him up. Well, I don't care what—"

Sensing the sudden panic in the ambassador's voice, Canning leaned forward and jerked the receiver out of his hand. He said, "Who is this?"

"James Obin," the voice at the other end of the line said. "Who are you?"

"Canning. You brought me in from the airport this afternoon. What's the matter? Why did you call Webster?"

"Well," Obin said, "a young Chinese man just came to the door asking for political asylum. It's never happened before. I haven't the slightest idea what to do about it. And he seems to be somewhat important, not just your ordinary citizen."

"Important?" Canning asked. He kept one eye on Webster and saw that the man looked confused and nervous.

On the phone Obin said: "He speaks passable English. Tells me his father is in charge of the Central Office of Publications here in Peking. Father's name is something like . . . wait . . . I have it all written down here . . . have trouble pronouncing these names, so this might not be exactly right . . . Chai Chen-tse."

Astounded, Canning said, "You mean you've got Chai Po-han down there with you?"

It was Obin's turn to be astounded. "You know him?"

Canning said, "Put him on the line."

A moment later a somewhat shy male voice said, "Yes?"

"Chai Po-han?"

"Yes, sir."

"Your father is Chai Chen-tse?"

"That is correct."

"Mr. Chai, do you know a man named Lin Shen-yang? General Lin Shen-yang?"

"He is well known. A hero of the Republic."

"Have you seen him this evening?"

"General Lin?" Chai asked, perplexed.

"Yes."

"No. I have not seen him."

Canning shivered with relief. "You wait right there, Mr. Chai. A young lady will be down to meet you and bring you upstairs."

"Yes, sir."

Canning hung up and turned to Lee Ann. "Dragonfly is downstairs right this minute. He's here to ask for political asylum. He doesn't seem to know what he is, and I don't think he's been triggered."

Without a word she left the room and ran down the fourth-floor hall toward the stairs.

Behind the desk, Alexander Webster seemed to have aged twenty years in two minutes. His muscular body had shrunk in on itself. He said, "I guess you'll call this a miracle when you look back on it years from now."

"No," Canning said. "I don't believe in miracles. I don't even believe in coincidence. Somehow, his coming here tonight is tied directly to what you people did to him. I can't guess how, but I'd bet on it."

Shortly, Lee Ann returned with Chai. He was a slender, wiry, rather good-looking young man. He smiled at everyone.

The night bell rang only in James Obin's bedroom. It shrilled again just as he was sliding between the sheets.

"What in the hell is going on here?" he grumbled. He pushed back the covers, got up, stepped into his slippers, and picked up his robe.

The night bell rang again.

"Coming, coming, for God's sake."

When he was at the head of the stairs, he heard the bell ring again, behind him in his room.

"Must be a night for mass defections," Obin mumbled to himself. The heels of his slippers slapped noisily on the steps. "Twenty million Chinese have suddenly decided to move to Chicago." When he reached the first-floor hall he heard pounding at the front door. "You're really not going to like Chicago," he told the defectors on the other side of the door. "Wait until you learn about smog and traffic jams." He twisted the lock and opened the door and said, "Oh. General Lin."

Without being invited, the general stepped inside, squeezing past Obin. He said, "A young man named Chai Po-han has come here seeking political asylum."

"As a matter of fact, yes," Obin said. "But—"

"I must see him."

Obin realized that there was something odd about the general. The man was too stiff, too tense—and yet, had that look about the eyes of someone who had been smoking grass or popping pills.

"I must see Chai," General Lin repeated.

"I'm afraid that might not be possible. He *has* asked for political asylum. In any event, you'll have to go through Ambassador Webster."

"Where is Chai?" the general demanded.

"He's upstairs in Mr. Webster's office. And—"

The general turned away from him and went toward the stairs.

Running after him and grabbing him by the arm, Obin said, "You can't just barge—"

During his programming in Seoul, the general had been told to get to Chai Po-han at any cost once Webster had triggered him. He could perform, now, in none but a brutal fashion. He struck Obin across the face and knocked him backward into the first-floor hall. Then he turned and ran up the steps.

One moment was peace, the next chaos.

They were all listening to Chai Po-han as he explained about the Ssunan Commune. Webster was still behind his desk. Chai was in one of the armchairs, and Lee Ann was in the other. Fortunately, Canning was on his feet, standing beside Lee Ann, facing Chai, the open office door on his left.

Suddenly, heavy running footsteps echoed in the corridor, interrupting Chai's story. An instant later General Lin Shen-yang burst into the room. His face was a reflection of his tortured mind: wild-eyed, loose-lipped, nostrils flared. He saw Chai and lunged toward him. As he moved he said, "Dragonfly must spread his wings."

Canning brought out his silenced pistol—and was knocked off his feet as a bullet tore through his right shoulder.

Lee Ann screamed.

Rolling, Canning came up onto his knees and saw that Webster had taken a gun from the center desk drawer. The ambassador seemed surprised that Canning was still alive. Before he could get over his surprise, Canning shot him in the face.

An unsilenced gunshot boomed behind him.

He twisted around in time to see Lee Ann fall in a heap, and he felt something snap inside of him. He raised his eyes and saw the general staring stupidly at the smoking revolver in his own hand. The man did not appear to remember that he had drawn and fired it. Indeed, he had probably been following his program and nothing more—an automaton, victim of drugs and subliminal suggestions and modern technology. Nevertheless, Canning put one bullet in his stomach and one in his chest and one in his throat.

The general fell backward, knocking over a floor lamp as he went, landing with a crash.

Chai Po-han, Canning thought.

Dragonfly.

Lin had triggered him.

Where was he now?

Biting his lip hard enough to take his mind off the pain in his shoulder, Canning struggled to his feet and looked around the room.

Chai was standing in a corner by the bookshelves. He had torn open the front of his shirt and was gently pricking his left shoulder with the point of a letter opener that Canning had earlier noticed on Webster's desk. A thin trickle of blood was running down his chest. He stabbed himself again, lightly, gently, then dropped the instrument.

The spansule was broken.

Chai was infected.

For a moment Canning almost buckled under the knowledge of his defeat. Then an energizing thought hit him like a hammer striking a sheet of white-hot steel: the plague virus required a human host, a culture in which it could survive and multiply, living flesh on which it could feed; no virus grew in a dead man; Chai could not infect anyone if he could no longer breathe . . .

As if he had just awakened from a trance, Chai said, "What is happening here?"

"Too much," Canning said. He staggered close enough to put his last two bullets dead-center in Chai Po-han's head.

The boy fell into the bookcases and slid to the floor, dead beyond question.

Dropping his pistol, Canning went back to Lee Ann and knelt at her side. She was lying face-down on the floor. She had been shot in the back, low down, just left of the spine, and she had bled quite a lot. He touched her and began to cry and was still crying when James Obin and the others came up from downstairs.

EPILOGUE

NEW YORK CITY: OCTOBER 25

A.W. West was scheduled to have drinks at five-thirty at the Plaza Hotel, where his Swiss attorney was staying during a one-week visit to New York. Prior to that engagement, however, he stopped in at Mark Cross to personally select and purchase a fine matched set of hand-tooled leather luggage that was to be a wedding gift for his favorite nephew.

When he and his bodyguard came out of the Mark Cross store, West decided to walk the short distance to the Plaza. The day was seasonably warm. There was a fresh breeze moving down Fifth Avenue, gently rustling women's skirts. West waved away his limousine, which was waiting at the curb, and set off toward Fifty-eighth Street, where he would cross to the far side of the avenue.

West's bodyguard walked a pace or two behind and to the right of him, studying everyone who approached and passed by them. But he was not particularly worried. He knew that hit men worked around a target's routine, picking a hit point they knew he would cross at a certain time. But this walk was unplanned, unpredictable. There was little chance of any trouble growing out of it.

West wasn't worrying about security precautions. He was just enjoying the walk, the breeze, and the lovely women one could always find on this part of Fifth Avenue.

A Cadillac limousine, not quite so elegant as West's own Rolls-Royce, pulled to the curb a hundred feet ahead, and a well-dressed man climbed out of it. He walked back in the direction of Mark Cross, toward West.

There were so many people on the street who bore watching that West's bodyguard paid scant attention to this one. After all, the man didn't appear to be a thug; he was chauffeur-driven, London-suited, respectable.

As the man from the Cadillac approached West, he smiled broadly and held out his hand.

West frowned. This man was a stranger. Nevertheless, West reflexively raised his own hand to let it be shaken.

"What a surprise!" the stranger said. Shaking with his right hand, he raised his left hand and showed West the miniature spray can that he held.

"What—"

It was very fast, very clean, and probably invisible to anyone nearby. He sprayed West in the face. The spray can went *pssss.* It was a short burst.

Don't breathe! West thought. But he had gasped in surprise, and the thought was too late to save him. Although the gas was colorless and odorless, West felt suddenly as if he were smothering. Then there was an explosion of pain in his chest, and he fell.

The stranger went down on one knee beside him.

The bodyguard pushed through the ring of people that had formed already. "What the hell?"

"Heart attack," the gray-eyed man said. "I'm a doctor. I've seen it before. Call an ambulance." He tore open West's shirt and began to forcefully massage his chest, directly over his heart. He glanced up after a moment, saw the bodyguard, and said, "For God's sake, get an ambulance!"

The bodyguard got up and ran toward the corner of Fifty-eighth and Fifth Avenue in search of a policeman.

After another half-minute the stranger stopped working on West, and said, "He's gone. I'm afraid he's gone." He stood up, adjusted his tie, shook his head sadly, and melted away into the crowd a full minute before West's bodyguard returned.

NEW YORK CITY: NOVEMBER 5

Prescott Hennings stopped at the water fountain in the lobby of his office building. He took a long, cool drink. When he raised his head he found that a rangy man with eyes the color of sheet metal had moved in extremely close to him. "Excuse me," Hennings said.

"Mr. Hennings?"

"Yes?"

"Prescott Hennings?"

"Yes."

The stranger brought a small aerosol can from his jacket pocket and held it up. The can was so small that the stranger's hand concealed it from everyone but Hennings. "Do you know what this is?" he asked pleasantly.

"I don't know you. If you're some sort of salesman or inventor, I don't want to know you," Hennings said, beginning to get irritated.

"No, no," the stranger said, smiling. "I didn't invent it. It was invented by some very clever men at Fort Detrick a few years back. If I spray your face, the chemical will give you a fatal heart attack that'll pass any autopsy. That's what happened to Mr. West, you know."

Alarm flushed into Hennings' face.

Canning sprayed him.

Hennings wheezed and staggered back against the fountain. He clutched at his throat, gagged, and fell down.

"Here!" Canning shouted to the other people in the lobby. "Get a doctor! An ambulance! This man's having a heart attack!" He knelt down beside Hennings and examined him. When several other people crowded around, Canning said, "I'm afraid it's too late. Poor fellow."

By six o'clock that evening he was back at the new house just outside of Washington. When he got there, Lee Ann was practicing walking between the parallel bars that were set up for her in the recreation room. The private nurse who worked with her every day was not there.

"Where's Tillie?" he asked.

"I sent her home. I promised I'd just sit in my wheelchair and read until you got here."

"This is a hell of a trick."

She struggled to the end of the bars and collapsed into his arms. "Walking? Not much of a trick. Billions of people do it every day. I used to do it all the time—and I will again."

"You know what I mean," he said, holding her close, holding her on her feet. "What if you'd fallen when there wasn't anyone here to pick you up?"

"I'd have taken a nap on the floor." She cast an impish grin up at him.

He couldn't stay angry with her. He lifted her and carried her around to her wheelchair at the other end of the parallel bars.

"How'd it go?" she asked.

"Just like West."

"Marvelous. You're a good man at your trade."

"Is it starting to bother you—what I'm doing?"

"No," she said. "It would bother me if you *weren't* doing it. If you weren't getting rid of them, I'd wonder if *anyone* was—and I wouldn't sleep nights."

He knew exactly what she meant.

THE WHITE HOUSE: NOVEMBER 21

Andrew Rice was on time for the meeting in the Oval Office, but the President and Bob McAlister were already there. He shook hands with McAlister and said good morning to the President. As he sat down, the chair squeaked under him.

"Cold as the devil out there," McAlister said.

Rice said, "Damned early in the season for snow flurries in Washington."

Boring in his left ear with an index finger, the President said, "Shall we get on with it?"

McAlister turned to Rice and said, "Andy, you're as fat as a house."

Andrew Rice's eyes glazed over; he stared through McAlister. His mouth sagged. He waited.

Clearing his throat, the President said, "Andy, when Senator Konlick died in that automobile accident the week before last-well, that took care of the list of Committee leaders you provided us with a couple of months ago. Now, we feel certain that there are men in this thing that you didn't know about back then, men whose connections to it were all but invisible so long as West, Hennings, Konlick, and the others were there to run the show. Now, with The Committee's leadership gap, one of these silent partners must have come forth."

"Yes," Rice said dully. "I was contacted by Cabot Addingdon."

"The real-estate millionaire from Massachusetts who ran for the governorship a few years back."

"That's right," Rice said.

For the next half-hour McAlister and the President pumped him for information. Then McAlister brought him out of the trance, and they sat around talking about trade agreements so that Rice would not suspect the real nature of the meeting.

Later, when Rice had gone to perform a series of make-work tasks for the President, McAlister said, "I'll pass on Addingdon's name to David Canning."

The President wiped a speck of ear wax from his fingertip onto his suit jacket. "Bob, I believe you're looking worse by the day."

"I was going to ask for three weeks off in December."

"By all means."

"I'll fly down to the Caribbean and just relax. That's all I need. Just some rest in the sun."

That was *not* all he needed. He also needed to regain some of his self-respect, although he knew that he would never regain all of it. He had beaten The Committee by adopting its methods; he had sacrificed morality for expediency. How could he live with that? Even if it *was* the only thing he could have done, how could he live with it? He needed to find a way to carry the burden of his guilt without collapsing under it. He needed to come to terms with the man he had become and didn't want to be.

"Are you still having trouble sleeping?" the President asked.

"Yes. And you?"

"I'm using sleeping tablets. I'll have the White House physician prescribe some for you."

"Thank you, sir." McAlister hesitated. Then: "I have this recurring nightmare."

"Oh?"

"I keep dreaming that The Committee *knows* that we've made a zombie out of Rice. I keep dreaming that they've implanted a second set of subliminal keys in him, deeper than ours—and at any time they are going to use him against us."

The President sat up straight in his chair. "God, that *is* something to think about."

"I've been thinking about a lot of things, too many things," McAlister said wearily. "That's why I can't sleep well."

"The Caribbean will put your mind at ease."

"I'm sure it will," McAlister said, forcing a smile.

But as he had considered the necessity of adopting The Committee's methods in order to destroy it, he had recalled something that William Pitt had said in the House of Commons in 1783, a quote which McAlister had often used in speeches: *Necessity is the argument of tyrants; it is the creed of slaves.* He knew he was no tyrant, and he was fairly sure he could say as much for the President. But they had established a dangerous precedent here. What of the men who came into office after them? Would they be decent men? Or would they be tyrants who, if they discovered this precedent, would point to it and declare themselves driven by necessity and institute a wider policy of government violence in order to stifle all disagreement with their policies? It was something to lie awake and think about at night. It scared the hell out of him.

ABOUT THE AUTHOR

K.R. DWYER (a pen name) was born in 1945 in Everett, Pennsylvania, and grew up in nearby Bedford. He is a graduate of Shippensburg State College and worked for a time as a tutor for underprivileged children with the Appalachian Poverty Program. His books (under his own name and pen names) have been published in more than a dozen languages and have sold over four million copies.